BRIARDARK

WARHAMMER™ HORROR

WARHAMMER™
HORROR

BRIARDARK

TALES OF MHURGHAST

C L WERNER

WARHAMMER HORROR
A BLACK LIBRARY IMPRINT

First published in Great Britain in 2022 by
Black Library, Games Workshop Ltd., Willow Road,
Nottingham, NG7 2WS, UK.

Represented by: Games Workshop Limited – Irish branch,
Unit 3, Lower Liffey Street, Dublin 1,
D01 K199, Ireland.

10 9 8 7 6 5 4 3 2 1

Produced by Games Workshop in Nottingham.
Cover illustration by Svetlana Kostina.

See Warhammer Horror on the internet at

blacklibrary.com

Find out more about Games Workshop
and the worlds of Warhammer at

games-workshop.com

Printed and bound by CPI Group (UK) Ltd, Croydon, CR0 4YY

To Nicole, for somehow sticking to my brother.

WARHAMMER™
HORROR

A dark bell tolls in the abyss.

It echoes across cold and unforgiving worlds, mourning
the fate of humanity. Terror has been unleashed, and
every foul creature of the night haunts the shadows.
There is naught but evil here. Alien monstrosities drift
in tomblike vessels. Watching. Waiting. Ravenous.
Baleful magicks whisper in gloom-shrouded forests,
spectres scuttle across disquiet minds. From the depths
of the void to the blood-soaked earth, diabolic horrors
stalk the endless night to feast upon unworthy souls.

Abandon hope. Do not trust to faith. Sacrifices burn
on pyres of madness, rotting corpses stir in unquiet
graves. Daemonic abominations leer with rictus
grins and stare into the eyes of the accursed. And the
Ruinous Gods, with indifference, look on.

This is a time of reckoning, where every mortal soul
is at the mercy of the things that lurk in the dark.
This is the night eternal, the province of monsters
and daemons. This is Warhammer Horror. None shall
escape damnation.

And so, the bell tolls on.

CHAPTER ONE

Fog seeped into the fur cloak, chilling the man within. The heavy pelt of a barrow-bear was ordinarily enough to fend off the cold, but when the mist drifted in from the Sea of Sorrows and Lhunaghast was on the rise, someone might sit right beside a roaring bonfire and never feel warm. At such times, the chill wasn't a thing of the flesh but of the spirit. A draft from the underworlds of Shyish.

Such days as this, gloomy and forbidding, were ones when most folk kept close to home and huddled together around the hearth. A steaming mug of spiced flip and a bowl of warmed nuts to turn back the cold, witchbloom hung at all the windows and a bone effigy over the door to ward off restless gheists. The image of his wife tempering her drink with a toddyrod flashed through the man's mind, the sound of his children giggling as foam boiled up from the mug and spilled on the floor. Emelda, no matter how many times she made flip, was always surprised by the eruption of foam, and her disgruntlement was always a source of amusement to Cicely and Marden, no matter how big they'd grown.

Samuel Helmgaart felt cheated that he'd had to forsake that tranquil scene. There were few such indulgences for the people of Felstein. Life in the frontier community was relentlessly grim, so what pleasures presented themselves had to be enjoyed when they arose. There was a bitter corner of his heart that resented Hochmueller for taking him away from the hearth. Certainly, one of the man's cattle had been killed, but the animal would be just as dead tomorrow as it was today. Samuel was annoyed with himself that worrying about the townmaster's reaction could intimidate him so much that he'd gone out to follow whatever signs he could make out and try to track the predator, even when he knew it would be a fruitless chore in such conditions. He knew from the start that the trail would lead back to Briardark, and once there, he'd never be able to follow the tracks in the fog.

Briardark. Instinctively, he brushed his fingers down his right arm. It wasn't a thing of flesh and blood but an instrument of gears and pistons, a bronze-plated replacement for the one he'd lost years ago to a skullsnapper that had decided to make its lair in the forest. The ghoulish beast, as much wight as it was bear, had torn the arm out by its roots with its jaws. By some miracle, Samuel was able to crawl back to Felstein. An even greater miracle had been the arrival of duardin traders months later. It was the clever forgemaster among their group who'd crafted his new arm for him, demanding only the skullsnapper's carcass for payment.

A month after getting accustomed to the mechanical arm, Samuel returned to Briardark. When next the duardin came, he had the forgemaster's payment waiting for him.

'You're the beasthunter of Felstein and it's your job to hunt these things,' Samuel muttered to himself, annoyed that with all the monsters he'd killed he should be stymied by a mere wolf. The gears in his arm grumbled as he shifted his grip on the barbed boar spear he carried, the tines of its vicious cross-piece dripping with condensation. He glanced back at the dark forest with its labyrinth of thorny undergrowth. He was better than anyone in Felstein when it came to following a trail. Mama Ouspenskaya claimed it was because the spirits of Shyish hovered about him and gave him guidance even if he was unaware of their presence. Samuel preferred to believe it was his own talent and skill that made him so capable.

'Spirits or no, you've failed this day,' the beasthunter scolded himself. As he tightened the bronze hand about the boar spear a low, lonely howl rang out from deep in the forest. There was a mocking quality to the animal's cry. Letting him know without question that it was somewhere in Briardark and he'd failed to find it. Barrow-foxes sometimes showed that kind of mischievous-ness, but Samuel had never seen a wolf display such a jeering attitude. Then, it held true that wolves were pack animals, and a lone wolf, such as the beast that had raided Hochmueller's pas-ture, became strange and capricious in its ways.

'Keep laughing, old dog,' Samuel grumbled. 'We'll play this game again, you and I. You think you're clever, but you're not clever enough to stay away. When your belly's empty, you'll come back, and next time I'll not lose your trail.' He firmed his oath by reaching under his tunic and drawing out the little bone disc he wore around his throat. The skeletal visage of Nagash, Emperor of the Underworlds, leered back at him. Samuel spat on his fingers and rubbed the spittle onto the carved skull, sealing his vow to run the wolf to ground. He felt a new chill rush through his veins, as though his own blood curdled at the promise he'd made to the grim god of Shyish.

'Tomorrow,' Samuel sighed, turning his back on the forest. 'For today there's nothing more to be done.' He smiled as he let the bone charm fall back against his chest. It wasn't quite true.

There was the long walk home and then the waiting hearth and a mug of spiced flip, the smiles of his children and the arms of his wife. No, there were still things to be done, but not such things as concerned wolves or his vow to Nagash.

The tall meadows of stalk-grass beyond the borders of Briardark gradually faded into the cultivated surroundings of Felstein. The insane grins of scarecrows greeted him as he approached the fields, their ragged clothes festooned with bits of glass and shiny metal to entice birds to them. The wooden frames were coated in a gluey resin to trap the crows and provide some meat to go along with the farmers' harvest. Here and there a columnar haystack reared up above the ploughed rows, each surmounted by a carved pumpkin to frighten grots and make the greenskinned thieves think the settlement was surrounded by gargants. Samuel thought only the stupidest greenskin would be deceived by such a crude trick, but if it eased the worries of his neighbours, there was no harm done.

Past the fields, the barns of Felstein rose. Each was painted a vivid red, and on their sides were drawn complex hex signs to repulse the attentions of wandering nighthaunts and malevolent spirits. Samuel was even more dubious of the efficacy of the hex signs than he was of the pumpkins. Certainly, they hadn't kept a glaivewraith from preying on Felstein when he was a child. Twelve people had died before an exorcist from Gothghul Hollow arrived to dispose of the murdering phantom.

The town itself appeared beyond the barns and stables of the outlying farms, a few lanes of tamped earth that wound their way between several dozen shops and houses. The market square was at the centre of the settlement, with the sprawling town hall stretching across one side and the sombre temple of Nagash squatting in one corner like a great stone spider. Warehouses, workshops and the Skintaker's Swallow, Felstein's only inn, formed the other borders of the square. The ghoulish bulk of the witches' tree loomed at its centre. A massive black gallows-oak, it had been struck dead in the days of Samuel's grandfather when the depraved sorceress Natalia Kolb cursed it before she was hanged from its branches. Even dead, the tree persisted as a place of execution, and the skulls of four witches were nailed to its trunk with spikes of iron – a warning to any others who would treat with the Ruinous Powers.

Samuel nodded to those he passed in the square as he made his way to the far side of town. It was a smart thing to keep on friendly terms with his neighbours, especially when the post of beasthunter was keenly desired by so many. Results weren't enough to retain the position – there was a fair amount of politicking to take into account as well. Samuel was grateful not to run into Hochmueller, however. No amount of politicking was going to offset his failure to catch the wolf, especially if the beast started ranging into more pastures. Felstein's townmaster, Thayer Greimhalt, would like an excuse to dismiss Samuel and appoint one of his cronies as the new beasthunter. It irked Thayer to have a man in that role who wasn't a subservient lickspittle.

It was with a sigh of relief that Samuel started up the path to home. The half-timbered house had a small plot of land attached to it, just enough to grow a kitchen garden and keep several dozen chickens. An old gryph-hound was curled up in a nest just inside the gate. Its plumage was dull and a few bald spots showed where its feathers had fallen out. The creature raised its head at the sound of Samuel's approach and opened its beak to chirp an excited greeting.

'There, boy, I've come back safe again,' Samuel said, scratching the gryph-hound's neck. He could feel Saint's disappointment as it detected the smell of Briardark on his clothes. The creature had loved roving with him in the forest, helping him on his hunts. Now the animal was too infirm for such activity, all but blind and without the stamina to trot across Felstein, much less prowl the forest. He'd been chided several times by friends and relatives for keeping such a useless animal, but Samuel felt otherwise. Saint had accompanied him on many a hunt in its prime, and he wasn't about to desert a loyal companion in its old age.

'I was looking for a wolf,' the hunter told Saint, 'but the dog was too crafty for me.' The gryph-hound uttered a mournful clack deep in its throat. Samuel often suspected that it understood far more of what was being said to it than people thought. He patted the top of the feathered head. 'Maybe if you'd been with me, things would have been different.'

Saint stretched its lean body, its clawed paws displaying their talons. They were still sharp and deadly, but the gryph-hound wasn't fast enough to use them effectively. A neighbour's cat liked to tease Saint every morning, jumping down in the yard and slinking just out of reach of those claws. Saint tried to catch the intruder every day, but the cat was always two steps ahead. A contest between the old gryph-hound and a more substantial predator would end far worse.

Samuel shook his head, and in doing so he noticed Saint's food bowl close to the nest. A few scraps of meat remained at the bottom of the dish. 'You've had your supper, I see,' Samuel stated, stepping away from the gryph-hound. 'Well, I must see about getting my own. Since breakfast I've only had some dried sausage to keep me going.' The gryph-hound settled back into its nest but watched him until he'd reached the door. In everything, Saint remained protective of its master and his family.

After the damp chill of the forest, the warmth inside Samuel's home was almost intoxicating. He had to stop just over the threshold and let himself adjust to the difference. The smell of roast mutton greeted his nose, and he could see that settings were still in place around the long table that dominated the common room. The flicker of rushlights burning from sconces on the beams and pillars created an inviting glow, while the fire in the hearth crackled and sparked. Samuel swung the door shut and savoured the tranquillity.

Leaning against one wall, he could see the shaft of the spear Marden had been carving and polishing for a fortnight. His son idolised Samuel and had no greater dream than to become Felstein's beasthunter after his father. The boy was well on his way, too. His eyes were sharp, his ears were keen, and he had an almost instinctive knack for woodcraft. Samuel thought his only advantage over Marden was that of experience, but that would come in time. When he was ready, Marden was going to be a better beasthunter than Samuel ever was.

The handiwork of his other child was draped across a chair. Samuel shook his head. He had to stop thinking of Cicely as a child. She was old enough to be married – indeed, some of the gossip-mongers complained that he hadn't married her off several years ago. There was certainly no dearth of suitors for such a pretty daughter. Some people thought it was miserliness on Samuel's part, his reluctance to part with a dowry. The truth was that some of Cicely's admirers had hinted they'd expect no dowry at all, but still they'd been turned away. When his daughter wed, Samuel wanted it to be a matter entirely of her own choice. She was too bright and inventive to be smothered by a loveless marriage.

Samuel took a few steps towards the chair and studied his daughter's work. Unlike Marden, Cicely was following their mother's example, learning the trade of seamstress and weaver. Aside from helping Emelda with the mending and tailoring that came their way, Cicely had decided to embark on a project of her own. She was weaving a tapestry, one that when finished would depict their entire family, from immediate siblings to distant cousins. The hunter was careful not to touch the rich burgundy cloth with his rough hands – he'd been scolded before for inadvertently undoing some loose threads – but instead let his eyes

range across the woven figures. There were only rough outlines
for now, but he enjoyed trying to decipher who each one would
be when she was finished. So far, the only image he was certain of was his own, and only because there was a second figure
crouched at his feet that had the unmistakable shape of a weary
old gryph-hound.

'We raised good children,' Samuel whispered to himself. That
was Emelda's testament, the home all around him. It wasn't the
crude efforts of a beasthunter that made the house a fit place to
inhabit, much less bring up children.

'I thought I heard you come in.'

Samuel was so lost in his thoughts that he spun around in surprise when he heard the voice. Emelda stood at the door leading
into the larder, a platter of turnips in her hands. There was a
smile on her face, but there was worry in her eyes and an edge
of doubt in her tone.

'I'm sorry I left it off so late,' Samuel said. He rested his boar
spear beside the weapon Marden was carving. His metal fingers
clung to the haft for a moment, forcing him to concentrate harder
on making them let go. When a bit of damp got into the duardin
mechanism, the arm sometimes became sluggish about obeying
him. 'The track wasn't so easy to follow as I thought it would
be.' He shook his head and sat down at the table. 'If I'd been
better equipped, I'd have stayed out tonight. Try to catch it when
it comes out again.'

Emelda set the platter down. 'I hate it when you stay in the
forest. I worry all night when you do. I pray to Nagash when you
aren't home.' She closed her hand over Samuel's, the one that
was truly his own, and her eyes were bright with emotion. 'I tell
him if he wants to take somebody, he should take me, not you.'

Samuel stroked his wife's cheek and presented what he hoped
was a reassuring smile. 'When Nagash decides to harvest someone,
no prayers will stay his hand. And the King of Death doesn't swap,

so don't waste your breath trying to make deals.' He eased his hand from Emelda's grip and began carving slivers of meat from the leg of mutton on the table. 'Is all of this for me, or haven't any of you eaten?' he asked. He glanced at the other plates. 'I've said before you shouldn't wait on me.'

'Marden insisted,' Emelda said. She turned towards the hall leading to the other rooms. 'He wanted to celebrate your killing the wolf.'

'That's why we have mutton instead of soup.' Samuel shook his head. 'The boy's still too much the dreamer. Hope's a good thing to have, but you should never depend on it.' He tugged at his ear, annoyed by this reminder of the worshipful confidence Marden had in him and ashamed that he'd failed to meet his son's expectations.

'They've been waiting. I'll just call them now.' Emelda started into the hall, but Samuel motioned for her to stay.

'Just call them to supper,' the hunter said. 'Let me be the one to tell Marden I didn't catch the wolf.'

Emelda gave a start when she turned to find Marden just behind her in the hall. Samuel frowned, wondering how much his son had overheard. That question was soon put to rest.

'You don't need to,' Marden said. 'One look at your spear tells me it hasn't been cleaned.' A touch of frustrated pain edged into his voice. 'Nor do I see it stained with wolf's blood.'

Cicely couldn't remember a more miserable meal, not even when a herd of pestigors had laid waste to the region and Felstein was stricken by famine. Watery soup flavoured with chicken bones was preferable to slices of mutton when there was such an air of tension in the house.

Across from her sat the primary culprit. Marden was junior to her by five years, at that age where he was no longer just a boy but neither had he grown into a man. He was a strapping lad with muscles conditioned by hard work and robust training. He had the squared jaw and hawkish nose of their father, even if his hair was the same coppery hue as their mother's. But where Samuel's visage had a cautious, even studious bearing, in Marden's face there was yet that stamp of childish naivety. Certainly, it was immaturity that had caused him to be so obstinate and petulant, treating their father's failure to catch the wolf as a kind of personal affront. Or was there something else in play? Whenever she met his eyes, she thought she saw anxiety there, some worry he was trying to hide from their parents but which he couldn't conceal from his sister.

Samuel was at his place at the head of the table, still arrayed in his hunter's cloak. Normally he'd have changed before sitting down, but when he came back so late at night he was too hungry to observe the usual niceties. This time, however, he merely picked at his food. Cicely could see that Marden's disappointment had deeply hurt their father. His efforts to speak to her brother were alternately awkward or brusque, either conciliatory apologies or harsh reprimands about Marden's attitude.

Cicely sympathised with Samuel. In many ways they were alike. She not only shared her father's black hair, but she'd developed many of his traits as well. She could understand the great pride that burned in his heart, for it was in hers too, a pride that had been cut to the quick by Marden's ugly words. Samuel would rather lose his other arm than the respect of his son. That pain ran deep, and he didn't know how to make it go away. So instead he returned Marden's distemper with his own.

Emelda sat beside her husband, trying to act the peacemaker. It was a role she didn't care for but which she'd had to take on before when mediating disputes between relatives and neighbours. She'd never been thrust into an argument on this scale in her own home before, and that difference made her situation even more uncomfortable. She kept twirling a coil of her coppery hair around her finger as she fumbled for something – anything – that might interrupt the strife between father and son. In her efforts at turning the conversation down a different path, she instead forced the issue.

'Cousin Anya visited today,' Emelda said as she put a turnip on her plate. 'It sounds as though Thayer won't relent. He wants what is due on the house or he'll evict them.'

'Rukh should never have taken that loan,' Samuel grumbled. 'Once Thayer gets someone under his thumb, he makes sure to keep them there.' He took a sip from his mug of flip and wiped his lips with his sleeve. 'I still say the man was elected only because half the town owes him favours.'

'Rukh and Anya certainly regret it now,' Emelda agreed, 'but what's done is done. She thinks his crop will be better next year, and if Thayer would only wait...'

'Thayer won't wait,' Samuel said, scowling. 'The man enjoys making other people miserable. You're right, Rukh probably will have a good harvest next year. That's why Thayer will evict them now. Probably give the farm to Alastair...'

Cicely's lip curled at the name. 'Alastair's a worse bully than his father. At least Thayer had to work for what he has. Alastair just expects everything to be handed to him.' She stabbed her knife into the mutton, imagining for a moment that it was Alastair's face. 'A viper suckled by a hyena.'

'Enough of that kind of talk,' Emelda scolded her. 'It is sufficient to say you dislike someone and leave it at that.'

'But *he* doesn't leave it at that,' Cicely protested. 'Three times he's come swaggering over here to ask – no, to *tell* – me to marry him.' She ticked off each instance on her fingers. 'It's been two months, so we should be hearing from him again. Unless he's too busy moving into Cousin Anya's house.'

Samuel pounded his fist against the table. 'If I'd only caught Hochmueller's wolf! The pelt and the bounty money would have been enough to help Anya's family.'

'Then why didn't you catch it?' Marden's words were stinging, but Cicely thought they weren't so much angered as afraid. She gave her brother a wary look, trying to decipher the reason for his emotions.

Samuel locked eyes with his son, pain and rage in his gaze. Cicely had never seen such a look before. 'Grow up, boy,' he snapped. 'You think it's all some kind of game.' He lifted his mechanical arm, letting the light gleam across its bronze coating. 'Well it isn't. Each hunt is as serious as the grave. I match my skills against the beast's cunning. Tomorrow might be different, but today the wolf won. Sometimes that's how it plays out. You have to bide your time until the beast makes a mistake.'

'And how much time do you think you have?' Marden said. 'I heard Alastair boasting that Felstein would have a new beast-hunter. Thayer's wanted you gone for years, and not catching Hochmueller's wolf is just what he's been waiting for!'

Cicely gasped. There it was. Out in the open. This was the reason Marden was upset. Not some childish notion of their father's infallibility but the very real fear that their entire world was going to be upended by Thayer.

'There's been bad blood between myself and Thayer for years,' Samuel said before swallowing a mouthful of flip. He tried to sound dismissive of Marden's concern, but Cicely could tell he was worried.

'It's true that Thayer doesn't like your father,' Emelda interjected, 'but he knows there isn't a better man in Felstein to be our beasthunter.'

Marden shook his head and grunted with exasperation. 'Mother, what does Thayer care if beasts raid the pastures? He's townmaster – he doesn't own herds, he owns the people who own the herds. His only concern is putting people obligated to him into every important position in town.' He shifted his gaze to Samuel. 'Whatever enmity there was before, it's never been expressed publicly before. Not like this. He's using Hochmueller's wolf to turn people against you so he can-'

'Enough!' Samuel growled, his face turning red. 'We'll speak no more about it. Tomorrow I'll get the wolf and that will be the end of it.'

'And what if you don't?' Marden prodded.

'Father said to stop,' Cicely warned her brother. Tempers were rising all around and it was obvious there was no purpose continuing the argument. Obvious to everyone but Marden and Samuel.

'What if the wolf gets away again? What if it kills again? How many days do you think he'll wait before Thayer stirs up the people to take your post away from you?' Marden thrust each question at Samuel as though he were jabbing the hunter with his own spear.

'I'll get the wolf and that will be the end of it!' Samuel spilled his drink as he slammed the mug down on the table. 'I know what you're trying to do. You want me to take you on the hunt. I told you once and I'll tell you again, when you grow up you can come with me.' He shook his finger in Marden's face. 'If you ever do grow up.'

Marden gave no response. He simply rose from his chair and walked away. Cicely had never seen him so pale and grim. It was as if a banshee had called away his spirit and left this husk behind. Every muscle looked tense and his eyes were like glowing embers, such was the burning emotion in them. She started to follow him, but her mother motioned her to stay.

Samuel glanced at the hallway when the sound of Marden's door slamming shut reached the table but otherwise gave no notice to his son's withdrawal. He simply stared down at his plate and listlessly picked at his meal. Cicely could see that he was pensive, turning over the exchange and regretting his angry words. But there was more than that. Marden's worries were justified. Everyone at the table knew that. Allaying those worries was Samuel's burden, and right now he was feeling that onerous weight. He'd failed to catch the wolf today and he didn't know how many more chances he'd get. How many more chances Thayer would permit him.

It was with a sense of relief that Cicely finally finished her food and quit the table. The brooding atmosphere had become unbearable. She wanted to help Samuel, to shoulder some of the responsibility pressing on him, but she knew she couldn't. Even her mother couldn't. A sense of helpless frustration was creeping up on her, threatening to consume her the longer she stayed, so she took up her unfinished tapestry from its chair and headed back to her room. Work would take her mind away from the family's troubles.

Cicely paused in the hallway. She looked to Marden's door and decided to speak with her brother. Perhaps she could make him see their father's perspective, or at least make him understand that Samuel hadn't meant his harsh words.

When she opened the door, however, Cicely found no sign of her brother. He wasn't in his bed or sitting in his chair. A cold breeze wafted in from the open window. An even colder dread closed icy fingers around her heart. She remembered what Samuel had said and knew at once where Marden had gone.

Her brother had gone to hunt the wolf.

Alone.

CHAPTER TWO

The chill of the night wrapped itself about Cicely as she scrambled out the window. She shivered at the abrupt transition from the warmth of her home to the bleak outdoors. Wisps of fog crawled through the kitchen garden. Big grey slugs oozed across lettuce and celery to gnaw at the leaves. A creeping thing, partway between spider and caterpillar, moved around the vegetables, devouring the molluscs as it went.

A stray moonbeam teased its way down through the clouds to illuminate the garden. Cicely froze and turned anxiously back towards the house. She watched the window near the front door, relieved that she didn't see one of her parents peering out at her. Likely her mother was helping Samuel with his augmetic arm. He had to take it off before retiring for the night so that it wouldn't chafe his skin while he slept.

Rushing through the garden, Cicely paused when she saw Saint peering out from its nest. The gryph-hound observed her, its feathers ruffling with excitement. She felt sorry for the old brute, a bit guilty that it thought she'd come outside to play with it. She also felt a twinge of dread. If Saint started making noise, it might draw her parents' attention.

A black shape suddenly appeared on the wall that bounded the yard. Cicely recognised the slinky outline as that of the neighbour's cat. At once, Saint's attention shifted. Its plumage bristled with a different sort of agitation and it sprang from its nest to screech at the trespassing feline.

Cicely changed her route, crossing through the garden and climbing over the wall rather than using the gate. The noise Saint was making was certain to draw her parents. To escape their notice, she had to get away from the gryph-hound's nest. Taking a firm hold on the cold wall, she pulled herself to the top and glanced at the lane beyond. The fog was growing thicker, and she couldn't see the least trace of Marden. If she was going to stop him, she had to intercept him.

She hurried down the path to the lane outside their yard. For a moment she debated which way to go, then considered that Marden would likely have taken the most direct route to the forest. That would take him through the centre of town. Cicely glanced back at the house, the light shining from the window. No, she told herself, she couldn't go back and tell their father. Samuel would be even angrier with Marden if he found out, and she didn't want her brother to get into any more trouble. She'd catch up to him and make him come back. That was the best way.

The streets of Felstein were empty. The town enjoyed some protection from Pater Kosminski – the priest of Nagash regularly prepared periapts that were nailed to lampposts to drive away nighthaunts and other prowling apparitions. The charms became steadily less efficacious as the hours of night lengthened, however, and between midnight and the hour of the jackal, they were so weak that spirits would scratch at windows and knock on doors even in the middle of town. The timid and the prudent retreated behind locked doors long before the periapts weakened, and it was only the brash and the bold who ventured far from their homes after sunset.

Her course through town took Cicely past the one establishment that drew people out after nightfall, tempting them to defy the darkness so that they might commune with spirits of a different kind. The windows that fronted the Skintaker's Swallow blazed with light. Raucous laughter and the wheezing strains of an accordion trickled out across the market square. Cicely saw the door open and the figure of a man stagger out. From his stout build and bald pate she thought it was Otho, the butcher, but couldn't be certain. Whoever he was, he took only a couple of steps before deciding he hadn't had his fill. Gripping the post supporting the tiled overhang that stretched above the inn, he swung himself around and staggered back through the door he'd just closed.

For an instant, Cicely was distracted by the stumbling man. When she turned back around, she was startled to see another figure emerge from the shadow of the inn's overhang. Hope flickered through her veins as she thought it might be Marden. When the shape stepped into the light, she was disillusioned of that hope.

'Awfully late for Cicely Helmgaart to be abroad.' The words were slurred by drink, but there was no mistaking the voice, or the arrogant face. Alastair always had that haughty, disdainful expression, twisting what Cicely would otherwise have conceded was a handsome visage. His clothes were finely tailored, brought in by merchants from distant towns during market days especially for Thayer and his son. He wore a massive gold signet ring on one hand, moulded into the image of a raven, fitting it over his basilisk-skin glove. He had a crimson vest over his black tunic, and a light grey cape rippled from his broad shoulders. His leggings were slashed, black above and crimson below. The tops of his leather boots were dagged, each frayed end tipped with a gold button. From the top of his fair head to the hobnailed soles of his boots, every aspect of Alastair's appearance sneered, 'I'm better than you.'

'I'm busy,' Cicely told Alastair. She tried to step past him, but he simply ducked back and put himself in her way again.

'Got tired of waiting for me to come to you, so you came to me?' Alastair asked. When he spoke, the stink of ale was on his breath. He plucked at his vest, tapping the gold buttons with his signet ring. 'Of course, you wouldn't be the first,' he boasted.

Cicely wondered if that was meant as a jab at Lucilla, her closest friend. She'd made a spectacle of herself last spring, trying to turn Alastair's head. The allusion didn't improve her temper.

'Out of my way.' Again she tried to step past Alastair. 'I've things I have to do,' she said when he stretched his arm and blocked her path again.

'So you say.' Alastair nodded, then smiled down at her. 'I say the lady does protest too much. I know why you've been putting me off. You wanted to be sure of my regard for you. Well, my intentions haven't changed.'

'What about my predecessors you were just mentioning?' Cicely retorted, slapping aside his arm.

Alastair frowned for a moment, then smiled. 'Mere dalliances. Nothing serious, I assure you.' His eyes gleamed in the light shining through the windows. 'Nothing that changes things.'

'I don't have time for this,' Cicely sighed. Every moment Alastair made her waste gave Marden that much more of a lead. He might even now be crossing the fields outside Briardark.

'Really? Don't you think you've put me off long enough?' Alastair stroked a lock of Cicely's hair until she recoiled from his touch. The man scowled and dropped both arms to his sides with a shrug. 'I've done everything I can. I even told your father I wouldn't ask for a dowry. I even told *my* father not to ask for a dowry, and you *know* what it took to get a concession from a miser like him. I don't know what else I can do to convince you I'm sincere.'

Cicely fixed him with a stern look. 'Sincerity isn't the problem,' she said. 'I don't feel anything for you, Alastair. You're simply not the kind of man I could have feelings for.'

'Then tell me what sort of man you expect me to be,' Alastair grumbled, acid in his tone. 'Tell me what I have to do.'

There was no warmth in the smile Cicely turned on him. Tartly she said, 'You can start by getting out of my way.'

Alastair looked at her for a moment, then shambled to one side. Cicely expected him to grab her as she strode past, but pride made her disdain to show that she was worried. She didn't even glance at him as she went by. It was only when she was halfway across the square that she deigned to look back. He hadn't moved from the spot, though she could see that he was still watching her. For just an instant there was something almost pitiable in the way he stood there with his shoulders lowered and his chin against his chest.

Damn the idiot! Cicely turned her back on Alastair and hastened on through Felstein's darkened streets. His interference had done nothing except increase the lead Marden already had. She didn't know if it was possible to catch her brother before he could reach Briardark.

Cicely picked up Marden's trail in Hochmueller's fields. This much, she reflected, was the easy part. They both knew where Samuel had been, so it wasn't any test of skill to find the boy's tracks where she expected to find them. It would be once she had to really search for signs that she'd be in trouble. Unlike her brother, she hadn't any aspirations of becoming Felstein's beasthunter after their father, and she hadn't encouraged those skills in her own life. Now she was regretting staying so close to the hearth and not going along with Samuel when he invited her on some of his more mundane hunts.

The scarecrows grinned at her with their carved faces as she hurried through the fields. The darkness and fog only heightened Cicely's desperation. She knew Marden had come this way, but with her limited vision he might be only twenty yards from her and she wouldn't see him. She thought of calling for him but reconsidered. If Marden heard her then he'd try to deliberately avoid her, knowing she'd try to take him back. She thought of something Emelda had told her often. 'When a man's half a fool, don't be surprised when he goes the rest of the way.'

The tracks, at least, were clear enough. While she had those to follow, Cicely felt a glimmer of hope. She tried to listen for any sound that might betray Marden's presence. All that rewarded her vigilance was the rustle of field rats and the flitter of bats. An owl's hoot from off in the distance was like a peal of thunder to her intent ears, yet of her brother she had no sign.

Dread set upon her when she noted the ground under her feet change. No longer cultivated land, instead it was now broken and uneven. Wiry weeds erupted from the soil in dark clumps, the cobweb crowns of their seedpods swaying in the wind. Cicely knew she'd reached the end of Hochmueller's farm. She was now on the narrow strip of cleared ground that stretched between the feeble outskirts of civilisation and the shadows of Briardark.

Cicely felt her heart hammering inside her chest. Her breath came in short gasps as she decided what she would do. Marden's trail continued. He'd gone past this point. Any notion that he'd be daunted by the mad prospect of entering Briardark at night had to be abandoned. Like Samuel, he was proud and stubborn, but unlike their father, lacked the experience to justify that pride or the hardiness to endure stubbornness. Marden had plunged ahead, a cocksure youth determined to prove himself.

Anger flushed through Cicely's veins. If Marden was foolish, then what was she? Her brother might have delusions about how dangerous the forest was, but she didn't. There was a reason a man like Samuel commanded so much respect in Felstein, and much of that lay in Briardark's grim reputation. Many who entered it were never seen again. Cicely knew this, even if Marden had forgotten, yet still her feet moved forwards across the weeds. Her terror was almost palpable, but it wasn't enough to overcome her own determination. Marden wasn't going to be one of those who vanished in the forest.

She was going to find him and bring him back.

Her first impression of the forest was a black shadow reaching out from the fog. The trees, gnarled and twisted, clawed at the sky with their skeletal branches. The bushes that clustered thick along the ground were jagged with thorns, their odious flowers nestled behind spiked stalks to entice birds and bugs to their doom that the plants might glut themselves on necrotic fluids. Vivid stands of green mushrooms, luminous and bloated, oozed against fallen trees. Tangled sheets of cobweb dripped down from the boughs, spiders as large as Cicely's fist scurrying along the strands to bind trapped bats and jab them with venomous fangs. The rotten stink of death was everywhere, a morbid miasma that clutched at her with choking fingers.

'Marden was brave enough to go this far,' Cicely told herself, trying to whip up her faltering resolve. The argument wasn't convincing. There was a thin margin between bravery and stupidity, and she couldn't put her brother's actions on the more favourable side of that line. 'All right, then I'll be stupid too,' she chided herself. Distinct in the scum of loam nearby was the impression of a boot. A beetle lay crushed in that track, its antennae still twitching. Marden had been this way only a moment before. Foolish or not, she wasn't going to turn back when she was so close. If she did and her brother never returned, that would be something she'd have to live with the rest of her days.

The gloom of the forest pressed in all around her. The fog, in a perverse way, acted to brighten things near at hand, but its veil shrouded anything farther as completely as any darkness. Cicely felt her other senses grow more alert, rallying to support her diminished vision. Her ears picked up the furtive forest sounds, the little creeping things scrambling through the underbrush, the drip of condensation from branches, the crack and groan of the trees themselves. Once she heard the sharp yip of some frightened animal and then the ripping sound of claws in flesh as a predator tore into its prey. She muttered an appeal to Nagash that it wasn't an omen, that Marden hadn't met a similar end in his reckless pursuit of the wolf.

Almost on cue, Cicely lost Marden's trail. Distinct enough for her to follow with her limited facility for tracking, she now found it hard to detect even the least sign. A broken twig, the suggestion of an impression, these were all she had to follow now. None of them were even clear indicators that what she followed was her brother. While his footsteps had been so evident she found she'd taken a strange reassurance from them. They'd been the tracks of a hunter, confident and in control. These faint signs were furtive and wary. Were they even Marden's, or was she now following the track of the beast he'd come here to hunt?

Cicely berated herself for her lack of foresight. She'd been so sure of catching him before he reached Briardark that she hadn't even brought a knife with her. Feeling an apprehensive chill crawling down her back, she stepped over to a nearby tree. It took all her strength, but at last she was able to break off a low-hanging branch and crack it down to size so it would serve as a rude club. The noise of her activity sounded deafening to her. Anything prowling the forest knew where she was now.

Her attention drifted to one of the fungal clumps, the mushrooms glowing like corpse-fire. Her thoughts turned to greenskins and stories she'd heard of monstrous orruks who could tear someone in half with their bare hands. Orruks, though, were just stories, distant travellers' tales. It was their smaller kin, the grots, that made her blood cold. Those had been seen around Felstein in the past and, if anything, were more terrible to her than orruks. The bigger greenskins were brutal but quick in dealing death. Grots were more malicious and delighted in tormenting anything weaker than themselves...

Fingers tightening around her club, Cicely turned away and tried to concentrate on the meagre signs she had to follow. Scuffed moss, a scarred mushroom, these were all the traces she could find, and it took all of her focus to spot them. So intent was she on her task that she couldn't say how long the sounds started before she was consciously aware of them. Once she was, however, her entire world boiled down to that stealthy tread. She listened with an intentness that was painful as something crept through the shadows of Briardark. Cautious and measured, she'd sometimes wait nearly a minute after hearing one step before the next would reach her ears. She tried to remember everything Samuel had tried to teach her, but she'd resisted his instruction too firmly for much of it to come back to her now. She seemed to recall that deer might move in such a way, but if it was a deer, wouldn't it be moving away from her, a potential hunter, rather than drawing closer? And wouldn't a predator use such slow, precise tactics when stalking its prey?

Cicely found a big tree and set her back against it. She remembered when Samuel had been slashed by a carrion-cat on one of his hunts and how the animal had waited until it could come at him from behind before lunging for him. She didn't know if wolves behaved the same way, but she drew some little measure of security feeling the solid timber against her shoulders. Right now, she needed all the reassurance she could find, for she knew her nerves were at the edge of panic.

You're a brave girl, aren't you? Cicely scorned herself. At once her father's words returned to her. He'd told her that bravery wasn't a lack of fear – that was foolishness. Bravery was being afraid but doing what you had to do all the same. That bit of advice rekindled the faltering spark of her resolve. Her club raised, she waited as the sounds came closer.

Through the fog, Cicely now detected a shadowy figure. Her breath froze in her chest. The silhouette was human-shaped but appeared smaller and distorted. Her mind raced with the thought of grots. Grots with their sharp knives and toothy grins, their fiendish laughter and pitiless eyes.

Suddenly the figure rose up and almost doubled in size. It now looked human in its proportions, and Cicely's thoughts turned to deadwalkers and deathrattles, ghouls and vampires and the legions of undead that prowled the lands of Shyish. A more practical side of her brain tried to quiet her fears. The figure had looked small because it was crouched over. Following signs just the way she had been. The idea took root, and it was with a gasp that she realised whoever was there was moving along her own trail.

A moment more and the shape pushed through the fog so that she had a clear image. A sob of relieved laughter spilled from her when she saw that it was Marden. Far from her finding *him*, he had instead found *her*. Cicely noted that her brother had at least armed himself for this venture, carrying his new hunting spear and the foot-long knife Samuel had given him on his last birthday.

Marden gave her a perplexed look. 'Cicely, whatever are you doing out here?'

Cicely stepped away from the tree. All her fear turned to anger now that she'd found her brother. She slapped him across the face, her eyes flickering with fire. 'That's my question to ask,' she snarled. 'What do you think you're doing?'

Marden rubbed his stinging cheek and gave her that hangdog

look that always got under his sister's skin. 'Trying to help father,' he said, his voice more sombre than Cicely had expected it to be. His eyes brightened slightly when he saw some of the intensity leave her expression. He gripped her hand. 'Cicely, I think I *can* help father,' he continued, excitement swelling every word. 'I think I've found the wolf's trail!'

'These tracks are fresh,' Marden told Cicely. There wasn't anything so clear as the smashed beetle to prove that to her. Indeed, without him pointing it out, she wouldn't even have recognised the marks for any kind of a track, much less that of a wolf.

'All the more reason to leave. Now,' Cicely replied. She was irritated that she'd allowed Marden to convince her to linger in Briardark this long, but his arguments had persuaded her to at least hear him out before forcing him to go home. She'd let him lead her a bit deeper into the forest to show her the signs he'd been following.

Marden shook his head. 'We can't do that. Father is depending on us.'

'You've done enough,' Cicely insisted. 'You found the trail. Now we go home and tell father.' It was on the tip of her tongue to explain that Samuel had the skills and experience to carry off the hunt, but she knew that argument would just make Marden dig in his heels even more.

The youth tapped the butt of his spear against the ground beside the faint print. 'These tracks are fresh,' he emphasised. 'If we go back, the trail will go cold and the wolf will get away again.'

Cicely shook her head and gave an exasperated sigh. 'Then let it get away.' She laid her hand on Marden's shoulder. 'Can't you see how reckless this is? You've never hunted anything like a wolf before. Something that might turn...'

'And attack me?' Marden finished. He wagged the sharp tip

of the spear in the fog. 'Don't worry. I know what to do when I find the wolf.'

'No, you don't,' Cicely said, acid in her tone. 'You only *think* you know. You've never been in a situation like this. Father has.' She bit back the rest of what she was going to say when she saw the pained look in Marden's eyes. To her surprise, the reason had nothing to do with any slight against her brother's pride.

'It's because of father that I have to do this,' Marden explained. 'That vulture Thayer will get someone else posted as beast-hunter unless the wolf is brought in. Every night it's still on the loose, the more people start listening to him.' His hand tightened around the spear. 'Cicely, our family would lose all standing in Felstein. If we're not beasthunters, then we're nothing. Without that position, without the income from pelts and bounties, father wouldn't be able to keep Thayer from taking everything from us. We'd be left without a home, like Cousin Anya. I have to do this. For father. For all of us.'

Cicely digested her brother's words. She still found everything he'd done to be stupid and reckless, but the motivation had more maturity about it than she'd expected. She'd been so certain of how she would handle Marden and bring him back when she found him, but now she found herself on the wrong foot. She didn't know what to do.

'Father's taught me how to do this,' Marden assured her. 'You're right, I don't have the experience, but I do have the skill.' He nodded at the faint prints. 'I found the tracks, didn't I?'

Reluctantly, Cicely had to concede that point. And with that one concession, she found herself being borne along by Marden's other arguments. She felt like she was caught in a river, unable to resist the current. The threat to their entire family was more immediate than even Marden suspected. Alastair had made that clear enough. He wouldn't stop until they were wed, whatever hardship he had to inflict to break her defiance.

Still, Cicely wasn't going to let Marden have everything his own way. 'Okay,' she said, 'but I'm staying with you. You're not hunting the wolf alone.' Her brother frowned, but she wouldn't compromise. 'That's my condition. Besides, if I'm here then I'm not running home to fetch father so he can pin your hide to the barn.' She waved her hand at the wolf tracks. 'I might not be able to read signs like you, but I've picked up enough from father that I know how not to give us away and spoil a hunt.'

Marden nodded slowly. He removed the big knife from his belt and handed it to her. 'Here, you'll need something better than that old stick.' His expression was grave as he added, 'Just in case.'

The knife felt strange in Cicely's hand. Marden had always been fanatically protective of it, cherishing it as his prized possession. It wasn't until that moment that she really appreciated the bond between them. 'Let's get going,' she said. 'The Helmgaart brood against Briardark.'

Marden smiled and led the way. Cicely was impressed by the silence with which he moved, and surprised that she was able to match his stealth.

The fog maintained its ghostly luminance, throwing into stark relief their immediate surroundings while leaving everything else invisible. Cicely listened for the least sound, recalling her own distraction following Marden's trail. Maybe she couldn't find the wolf's tracks, but she could try to keep vigil while her brother did. The role appealed to her, the familiar aspect of the older sibling protecting the younger. She realised she'd never stopped doing that, perhaps provoking Marden to keep trying to prove that he was capable of handling things on his own.

Her brother stopped beside a rocky shelf that stretched along an opening in the trees. Marden gave it a worried look, but appeared to dismiss his concern a moment later when he found another print. Cicely didn't understand at the time, but she soon discovered what had provoked Marden's fear. A hundred yards further on, he gestured for her to stop. He spent longer than usual looking over the ground. Cicely thought it was just because he'd lost the trail.

'Nagash's black bones,' Marden cursed. He stabbed a finger down at a little mark at the edge of the shelf. 'It climbed up on the rocks. It knew it was being hunted.'

Cicely stared at the shelf, then at her brother. 'Can you pick up the trail again?'

'Across that?' Marden grumbled, kicking the edge of the shelf. 'I think that's the trick the wolf must have used to slip away from father.' He lifted his head and stared out into the fog. 'It could be miles away by now.'

Suddenly a low, throaty growl rose from behind them. Cicely felt her stomach lurch as dread seized her. The siblings turned. Standing on the rocky shelf, only a few yards behind them, was the thing they'd been hunting.

The wolf hadn't run away – it had doubled back. Roles had reversed. Now, it was the hunter and they were the prey.

CHAPTER THREE

A heavy stone dropped into the pit of Cicely's stomach. She felt sick with terror at the sight of the fearsome beast. More horrible than she'd imagined, the wolf wasn't a living thing but a decayed creature of death. Its pelt hung from its rotten flesh in mangy tatters, its bones exposed where the skin had sloughed away. Instead of eyes in its denuded skull there were only two pits of ghostly light. Dire wolves, such beasts were called. The hunting hounds of Death.

She took a faltering step back, her eyes locked upon the necrotic wolf. Cicely's lungs burned for fresh air, but she dared not even breathe. The least sound might spur the beast into action. Send it leaping down at them with its snapping fangs and flashing claws.

'Whatever you do, don't run,' Marden hissed at her. She could see him from the corner of her eye. He was trembling and his skin was white as marble. Her brother was every bit as terrified as she was, but the long hours learning their father's trade made him keep his wits. Cicely knew Marden was right, as much as her instincts told her otherwise. Running was a guaranteed way to spur a predator into action. Perhaps the kurnothi who were said to dwell in the most isolated forest glades could outrun a wolf, but she knew no human could muster such speed. Even a decayed, undead thing such as this one would run them down.

Marden turned his head slightly, keeping one eye on the wolf as he whispered to his sister, 'When I say run, we both run.' His lip quivered as he spoke, and his eyes were so wide that they seemed to have doubled in size. 'It can only catch one of us.'

Cicely choked down the sickness that tried to bubble up her throat when she heard those terrible words. She knew what Marden had in mind. She wasn't going to let him do it. 'We both go home, or neither of us does.' Her fingers gripped the knife he'd given her. 'Together, we might scare it off.'

'Don't argue,' Marden snapped. 'Do as I–'

The wolf chose that moment to spring from the shelf. Marden was quicker to react. Cicely found herself violently shoved aside and ended in a sprawl on the ground. She twisted around when she heard Marden scream. In pushing her away, he'd put himself in the beast's path. The wolf's claws had ripped gory furrows down his chest, but it was the sight of the creature's fangs buried in her brother's shoulder that curdled her blood. Crimson gushed from the wound as the predator jerked its head from side to side and worried his flesh. The hand gripping his spear hung limp at his side, immobilised by the wolf. All Marden could do was punch at the creature's decayed body with his other hand. And scream.

Fear pulsed through Cicely as she lunged up from the ground and launched herself at the wolf. She was terrified of this ravening, undead thing, but she was more terrified that it would kill her brother. Almost before she knew what she was doing, she was stabbing the knife into the beast. She could see the mangy pelt and withered flesh part as she drove the steel into it. She could feel bone splinter under her blows. No blood bubbled from the undead body, only a putrid smell of decay.

The wolf released Marden from its grip, leaving him to collapse in a bloody heap. It spun about, trying to snap at Cicely. Instead of recoiling, she pitched forwards and straddled the vicious beast. She plied her knife with crazed fury, causing strips of the pelt to fall away and expose the mouldering skeleton within. The wolf snarled, a dry and hideous noise that bore no resemblance to the howl of a living animal. It circled around, trying to throw her off its back, but Cicely retained her hold. She didn't relent in her attack but kept on stabbing, carving slivers of bone from ribs and spine.

'Look out,' Marden gasped from where he lay, the weakness of his voice chilling Cicely's soul. Before she could react to the warning, the wolf suddenly pitched onto its side and she was thrown to the earth. She ended in a sprawl, the knife skittering free of her grip. The beast was only prone for a moment, flipping back onto its paws and bounding towards her.

Cicely felt the wolf's claws rake down her back, ripping through her clothes to tear her flesh. It snapped at her head, trying to seize her by the neck. For a hideous moment, she thought its fangs were clamped about her throat as it tightened and she found she couldn't breathe. When the creature tugged at her, however, she realised why she was choking. Its fangs had caught the hood of her cloak and were pulling at that rather than her. Even so, she knew it was only a matter of moments before it realised its mistake. The brute might have less mass than it did in life, but the weight pressing down on her was still too great to throw off. She was caught beneath the wolf and unable to free herself.

'Get away from her, you cur!' Marden's shout was accompanied by a squelching sound. Cicely was just able to turn her head enough to see her brother standing over the beast. He had one hand clasped against his bleeding shoulder. The other held the spear he'd rammed into the creature's side, sinking it several inches into its body.

The weight pressing down on Cicely was suddenly gone as the wolf jumped away. She scrambled towards the rocky shelf, keeping it to her back so the beast couldn't get behind her again. She saw the undead creature twisting and snapping at the spear lodged in its body.

'Cicely, get out of here!' Marden shouted. He stood glowering at the wolf, his only weapon now a rock he'd grabbed. His face was pale from blood loss and she could see him trembling with fear.

'I'm not leaving you,' Cicely declared. She glanced around, trying to find something she could use as a weapon. If she could just find the knife again...

'Don't be a fool,' Marden hissed. 'There isn't time.' But even as he spoke the words, time ran out. The wolf, in its crazed efforts, finally managed to pin the end of the spear under one paw and secure it to the ground. Exerting itself, the beast twisted its body and ripped the spear from its flesh. A living animal, even if it had survived such a manoeuvre, would have slunk away to lick its wounds. The dire wolf's undead frame had no sensation of hurt or injury, just the primordial hunger to destroy. It turned about and fixed its glowing eyes upon Marden.

'Run!' Marden yelled at Cicely. The beast was already in motion, bounding for him in a lupine rush. He swung at it with the rock as it sprang at him. Cicely heard the crack of shattered bone as the blow struck the beast's skull. Then Marden was pushed to the ground, the wolf pressing down on his chest with its paws. Its head darted forwards and it clamped its jaws around his neck.

Cicely wanted to cry out, but she bit down on the panic that threatened to overcome her. Instead, she dashed to where the spear lay. She seized it in both hands and charged at the wolf. In her desperation to save her brother, it was only when she thrust at the beast that she noticed the spear was splintered and its head was still lodged inside the brute's body. The broken weapon slammed into the beast's flank but didn't pierce its hide.

The wolf spun around, Marden's blood dripping from its jaws. Cicely could see where the rock had cracked the side of its muzzle, loose bits of skull hanging from its necrotic flesh. The creature fixed her with its malignant stare. Again, she heard that dry, rattling snarl. Slowly it stepped away from Marden. Her brother lay in a puddle of gore, his throat viciously savaged. She heard a faint groan and saw him make a feeble motion with his arm. For the moment, at least, Marden still clung to life. That fact galvanised the fragments of her courage.

'Come and get me, you stupid mongrel,' Cicely snarled back at the wolf as it started to circle her. When it came too close, she swung at it with the spear, using it like a club. The splintered end smacked against the creature's muzzle, dislodging several of its fangs.

The impact infuriated the beast. It drew back only to leap forwards, hurtling towards Cicely like an arrow. She swung at it again, striking it in the side, but without sufficient force to overcome its momentum. She spilled to the ground with such violence that all the air was knocked out of her. As she gasped for breath, the wolf leered down at her. Her brother's blood spattered her face as it loomed over her, ready to sink its fangs into her flesh.

The tableau held for an instant, and then Cicely's vision was blotted out in darkness and pain.

'Yes.' The word drifted through Cicely's awareness. Vaguely, she recognised it as her voice.

'Then we will proceed,' another voice replied, piercing the

oblivion of Cicely's thoughts. She struggled to make sense of the words. They were important, but she didn't know why.

A numb, dull fogginess smothered Cicely's mind. It was a strain for her to even recall who she was. The image of Samuel rippled through her memory, but it took an inordinate effort to attach a name to him, or to realise he was her father. Images flashed through her brain without meaning or context, some slipping away, back into the fog, before she could categorise them. Alarmed by her disorientation, she opened her eyes, hoping what she would see would make more sense to her than her chaotic thoughts.

Chilling horror pulsed through Cicely when she saw the grim, scraggly trees and the rocky shelf. Briardark! The forest's name leapt into her mind, bringing with it a surge of alarming memories. At once she recalled Marden coming here to hunt the wolf and the disaster that had followed. A sob wracked her as she expected to find the beast chewing at her entrails. There was more confusion than relief when she found that she was intact. Gingerly, she raised a hand to her throat. She *knew* the wolf had bitten her, yet the skin wasn't torn. Had it all been some ghastly nightmare then?

Cicely turned her head and flinched. Only a dozen feet away, sprawled on the ground in its monstrous decay, was the dire wolf. Her eyes widened as she stared at it, waiting for it to notice her and resume its attack. Only when she saw that the spectral eyes no longer blazed from the sockets of its skull did she begin to realise that the wolf was no longer undead... It was simply dead.

Her mind whirled, trying to account for how the fearsome beast could have died. Certainly, it was nothing that she'd done. Had Marden managed to rally, throw himself against the wolf in some incredible effort? As these questions assailed her, Cicely noticed for the first time that the ground under her was soft and warm. She looked down, stunned to see that she was lying on a woven blanket. She tilted her head back and saw that a crude lean-to of sticks was partly blocking her view of the sky.

'You are safe.' The words drifted into Cicely's awareness with the vagueness of shadows. In the hazy fug of her mind, she couldn't even say how long the person had been speaking to her. The voice, soothing but firm, just seemed to drift through her senses. Even when she was able to focus on it, it was with a bleary resignation. Her attention was riveted by the brutal observation that the voice wasn't Marden's. The feeble hope that her brother had rallied to save them from the wolf was shattered.

'You can move,' the speaker told her. Cicely turned her head to see a man sitting beside her. He was dressed in a black coat with doubled ranks of bone buttons running down its breast and the folds of a capelet hanging about its shoulders. A wide-rimmed hat with a short, flat-topped crown squatted on his head. His face was lean, the skin tight against the underlying bones, with sunken cheeks and a prominent jaw. His flesh had a grey colouring to it that, while not sickly, didn't suggest a robust vivacity either. His eyes, however, were vibrant, deep pools of aquamarine that glistened with intensity. The hair that peeped out from under his hat had a steely colouring. Cicely judged him to be older than her father, but other than that, she couldn't really estimate his age. He might be sixty or a hundred, for all she could tell.

Cicely propped herself up on her elbows and faced the stranger. There were many things she didn't understand, but at the moment only one seemed important. 'My brother?'

The man closed his eyes and shook his head. 'I'm sorry. It was too late to help him.' He gestured to his left. Cicely shuddered when she saw Marden's body lying a small distance away. Though he'd been arranged in a peaceful pose, there was nothing peaceful about the horrible wound on his shoulder or the viciously gnawed ruin of his throat. Cicely wanted to cry, but her eyes remained stubbornly dry.

'I heard the sound of your fight,' the man explained. 'I rushed to see if I could help. I was too late to save the boy, but not too late to assist you.' He reached down and patted a leather satchel resting beside him on the ground.

'The... the wolf?' Cicely muttered.

'You'd already dealt it considerable damage,' the stranger said, a note of admiration in his tone. 'It only needed a few cracks from my walking stick to finish shattering its skull. The malefic energy that animated it dispersed once that was done.'

Cicely let her gaze drift back to the dead wolf. A shudder swept through her, ending in a sob when she thought of the beast's teeth worrying at her brother's throat.

'You're fortunate to be alive,' the man told her. 'Providence must have favoured you that it was someone like myself who came to your aid.' A brief smile pulled at his lean face. 'Oh, any lout could have cracked the creature's skull, but you'd been badly mauled and only someone of my talents could have helped you then.' He patted the satchel again. 'I had to dig rather deeply into my bag of tricks and work throughout the night... but I was able to rekindle the vital spark before it could flicker away.'

The man's words brought a new horror to Cicely. Her hands flew to her throat, still afraid she'd find the flesh torn by the wolf's fangs. She only half believed that the unmarred skin under her fingers was her own. A dumbfounded look crept over her face.

'An old unguent from Mournhold,' the stranger explained, taking a little box made from polished shell out of the satchel. 'There's cryptkraken ichor in the paste that has regenerative properties of such potency that even a troggoth would benefit from using it.' The flash of levity left his face, and his expression became grave. 'No, you aren't mistaken. The wolf came very close to killing you.' He pointed his finger at her, and Cicely looked down to see her clothes covered in blood.

Amazement at her survival raced through her mind, but almost immediately there was a feeling of intense, torturous guilt. She looked back at Marden. She was alive and her brother wasn't. Shame flared through her.

The stranger seemed to pluck the very thoughts from her mind. 'I could only help one of you,' he said apologetically. 'The boy was in far worse condition than you. I had to focus on who I thought had the best chance to live.' He glanced at Marden. 'Family?'

Cicely managed a feeble nod. 'My brother,' she rasped. She turned her eyes back to the stranger. 'I know you tried... did what you thought best...' She hesitated. 'I don't even know your name.'

'There's no reason why you should,' the man said, 'as I haven't given it.' He straightened his back and held his head high. 'You may call me Verderghast. I was once addressed as "healer", but that was a very long time ago, in places more refined than these.'

Cicely's hand went back to her unmarred throat. 'It can only be the grace of Sigmar that a physician was travelling through Briardark.'

Verderghast frowned. 'I fear you must credit prejudice and paranoia for my being here,' he said. 'It is the bane of humanity that those who shun progress are the prevailing voices.' He rapped one hand against his chest. 'You look on a pariah, an outlaw driven to wander the land. There are those who would condemn me as a heretic and worse, merely because I refuse to accept that there are boundaries beyond which human knowledge must not explore. I have been hounded into exile by those who see any new idea as dangerous.' He tapped a finger against the box of unguent. 'That my theories are borne out by my results makes me doubly dangerous to such people.' There was such contempt in the way he said the last word that Verderghast might have been uttering the name of a Chaos god.

'Forgive me,' Verderghast said. 'I like to think of myself as an altruistic person, but I'm not so noble that a touch of bitterness hasn't crept into my soul. The threat of being burned as a witch because of an unorthodox approach to medicine creates a somewhat jaded perspective.' He bowed his head. 'I beg your indulgence.'

Cicely couldn't bring herself to care overmuch who Verderghast was or what other people thought of him. He'd helped her. That was all that was important right now. That... and dealing with the poor, mangled body of her brother. She felt shame burning through her when she looked at Marden. He was dead and she was alive. That was the terrible reality now.

'Will you help me with Marden?' she asked. 'He's too heavy for me to carry alone.' Cicely saw the hesitance in Verderghast's expression. 'Please, Felstein is just beyond the forest.' She drew herself onto her feet, casting aside the blanket. 'We can't leave him here.' She felt her exasperation rising. The image of scavengers coming to pick at her brother's corpse made her almost frantic.

Verderghast looked up at her. 'I'm sorry, but I can't,' he said. 'I can't run the risk that someone would recognise me. The hunters would be after me again.' A deep sigh shook him. 'I'm weary of wandering. I just want to rest.'

'I won't tell anyone who you are,' Cicely insisted.

'I know you will keep my secret,' Verderghast said, with such a note of certainty in his voice that it made Cicely uncomfortable. 'But, still, someone might recognise me.'

'Marden has to be given a proper burial,' Cicely said, fear edging into her words. Now it was no longer the vision of ghouls picking over her brother's corpse that alarmed her but that of his restless spirit roaming Briardark as a nighthaunt because his body hadn't been buried.

'Of course he does,' Verderghast agreed. He stood and pointed a finger at the sky. 'It will be morning soon,' he said, indicating the faint lessening of the darkness overhead. 'Surely someone will come looking for you?'

Cicely knew her parents would be waking up right about now. Once they realised the children weren't there, Samuel would be on their trail. If her father noted that Marden's spear was missing, he'd know where they'd gone and make straight for Briardark. She looked down at her brother's body. Even that much of a delay felt abominable to her. 'I can go to Felstein and lead them back,' she said. She fixed Verderghast with an imploring gaze. 'Will you watch Marden until we return?'

Verderghast slowly nodded. 'I understand your urgency. I'll stand by the body.' He waved at the surrounding trees. 'I'll be able to hear you coming before you get here. I can slip away before anyone sees me.'

Cicely squeezed Verderghast's hand, unable to find words to express her gratitude. Turning around, she retraced the route she and Marden had taken before. Her every step felt impossibly heavy. Marden was gone, and soon she would have to tell their parents what had happened. That eventuality terrified her more than the wolf's fangs.

Verderghast watched Cicely until she vanished among the trees. She'd be safe enough from the denizens of the forest. The medicine he'd used on her would keep them at bay. Besides, most of the things in Briardark were nocturnal and didn't stir during the day.

That observation spurred the physician to walk over to the dire wolf. His eyes roved across the battered carcass. 'They did quite a lot of damage to you. More than might be expected.' He prodded the body with the toe of his boot.

At once the wolf rolled over and stood up on its decayed paws. The head, partly smashed, leered forwards, its fangs clacking against each other when it snapped its jaws. The eerie glow of its eyes blazed back into spectral vibrancy. The beast glowered at Verderghast, its wasted body tensed for violence.

The physician merely stared back at the undead animal, unperturbed by its menacing pose. Boldly, he stepped forward and, ignoring the bared fangs, reached down to inspect the broken skull. 'Nothing too tragic,' he said. 'A bit of attention will set you right again.' Verderghast patted the beast's head, scratching a maggot out from its mangy pelt.

'You performed admirably.' He looked aside at Marden's body, then stared after the track Cicely had taken. 'Now to see how the girl suits her role.' A grim smile set itself across his face. 'The only question is how long it will take. Yes, that's still the uncertain factor.'

Verderghast stirred from his reverie and gestured to the revived wolf. 'Away to your lair,' he commanded. He watched it lope off through the underbrush opposite where Cicely had gone. 'Rest well, my friend,' he called after the undead.

'There may be more work for you before I am finished here.'

CHAPTER FOUR

Samuel rolled his spoon through the bowl of porridge. In the hour he'd been sitting at the table he'd taken only a few mouthfuls of his dinner. It was cold and gelid now, tugging at his spoon, resisting his vacant motions as though to say to him what Emelda couldn't. *Enough.*

His wife was seated across the table. She'd finished eating some time ago, but she'd made no move from her chair even to clean away the soiled plates. Emelda didn't say anything – she simply sat there. Waiting.

Grief was a selfish thing. The thought stabbed at Samuel. He knew his wife was hurting every bit as much as he was. Marden's loss was devastating to both of them. The father's sorrow didn't surpass that of the mother. One glance at Emelda was enough to show him that. But for the past hour he hadn't seen Emelda. His eyes were fixed on the wall, but even that he didn't see. His gaze was piercing that wall, roving through Felstein's streets and across its fields to the solemn shrine of Nagash and the grim yard that surrounded it. He saw all the old stone markers, weathered by the elements, and he saw the new plinth that rose up from that morbid ground. He watched as the black casket was lowered into the yawning pit while Pater Kosminski recited prayers to the Lord of the Dead that Marden's spirit would find rest and his bones enjoy peace in the grave.

Samuel's pain replayed the scene again and again. He shivered despite the fire blazing in the hearth, for it had been cold there in the Garden of Nagash and memory recalled that chill in all its intensity. He could smell the musty, cloying scent of the cemetery, a distillation of broken hopes and buried dreams.

He knew Emelda wanted to talk, to share the pain with him instead of letting it push them apart. Samuel knew this, but he couldn't let go. He couldn't let her into the darkness he was feeling. His mind stirred from his mournful reflections long enough for a ray of clarity to sizzle through him like one of Sigmar's thunderbolts. His grief was selfish, but in a way far different than he'd realised. Shame was what had raised these barriers between himself and what family he had left.

The hunter's eyes didn't move, but instead of the wall and the scenes beyond it, he now focused on Emelda. He had to tell her, just in case she didn't already know. Of course she didn't know, otherwise she'd have wasted no more time on him, trying to ease his pain.

'It's my fault,' Samuel said, his tone as dead as anything buried in the Garden of Nagash. He let the confession linger, expecting to see hate in Emelda's visage. When the anticipated reaction didn't happen, he tried to make himself understood. 'Marden's dead because of me. He went into Briardark to prove himself to me. It's my fault.'

Emelda's eyes were moist with emotion. She reached across the table towards him, but her hand stopped before touching his. 'You can't blame yourself. Marden' – her voice cracked when she spoke his name – 'chose to go to hunt the wolf. You didn't make him do anything.'

'Didn't I?' Samuel pushed the cold porridge away and stared up at the ceiling. 'Didn't I send him out there? Everything I did sent him into Briardark.' He coughed as the bitterness tightened in his throat. 'It flattered my pride to have Marden emulate me, trying to become a beasthunter. But I never did enough to make him ready. I didn't do enough to teach him his own limitations. To guide him right.' He lowered his head and clapped his hands to his face to hide the tears. 'My pride wouldn't let me show him any other way.'

'Marden wouldn't have chosen differently,' Emelda said. 'He was our son, and it was because you did raise him right that he wanted to be like you. He wanted to make you proud because he was proud of you. Can't you see that?'

Samuel knew her words were meant to soothe, but they only magnified his pain. 'I should have been content to be humble. Satisfied with lesser things. Then our son would still be alive.'

Motion from the side of the table drew Samuel's notice. Even more than Emelda's, in his grief he'd become oblivious to Cicely's presence. Like her mother, she'd remained silent until he was ready to talk about his pain. He could barely look at her now, thinking how he'd nearly lost both of his children. Cicely had told of following Marden's trail and trying to stop him. She'd been too late – thank Sigmar! If she'd been there when the wolf found her brother…

'You aren't to blame,' Cicely said, her face pale and drawn. 'Marden did what he felt he had to do. If you want to blame someone, why not Thayer Greimhalt? It is his greed that has put so much pressure on everyone. His grasping for more and more power.'

The suggestion only deepened the guilt in Samuel's heart. He shook his head. 'Problems with Thayer were no concern of

Marden's. He was just a boy. He shouldn't even have thought twice about the man.'

'How could you keep him from knowing?' Emelda asked. 'Thayer has pushed and pushed until no one could ignore what he's doing. Rukh and Anya are on the cusp of being turned out of their home. Thayer keeps pushing to have you replaced as beast-hunter. Then there is that son of his, always coming around–'

Samuel slapped his bronze hand against the table, denting its surface. Anguish gripped him. 'These weren't troubles to concern Marden. Blood of the Mortarchs, what's more important for me to do than to shield my own children from such worries! A father who can't keep his own family safe is less than nothing. Unfit for even his carcass to pay the bone tithe.'

'Marden didn't want to hide behind you,' Cicely retorted. 'You misjudge him and cheapen his memory if you think he could ever have been content to sit back and not take a hand. We went into Briardark because it was what needed to be done.'

Samuel's head shot up, his eyes latching on to his daughter's, his mind seizing upon the word she'd used. '*We?*' he repeated. 'What do you mean *we* went into the forest? I thought you followed him to stop him!'

For an instant Cicely trembled at the challenge in his tone, but then he saw her resolve stiffen. There was an edge of defiance when she looked back at him. 'That wasn't the whole truth. I found him before he tracked down the wolf. Marden was determined to help you by killing the beast, not to prove himself to you but because he felt you needed his help.' Her show of strength faltered and sorrow settled over her again. She sank back in her chair. 'I followed him to stop him, but I stayed to help him. I was there when he fought the wolf.'

The confession struck Samuel like a physical blow. He reeled in his seat, stunned by the revelation. Dimly he was aware of Emelda's horrified gasp. 'You might have been killed too!' she was saying as she rushed over and hugged her daughter close to her. He could hear the two women sobbing, their emotions breaking free of all restraint.

He tried to keep control of the turmoil roiling inside him. He tried to reason against the fury that blazed up from the core of his being. Samuel attempted to keep hold of his love for Cicely, but the harder he tried, the more it fled from his mind. All he could see was Marden's torn body as they'd found it in Briardark. All he could think of was his son lying buried in the dirt, consigned to the keeping of Nagash.

Samuel's eyes were as cold as the plinth in the Garden of Nagash when he looked at his daughter. 'You're telling me that you are responsible,' he said, each word dripping off his tongue like poison. 'You're telling me you could have stopped Marden... and didn't.'

Emelda was shocked by his speech, but he could see from Cicely's face that his accusation had struck true. He took no satisfaction from being right. Instead, he felt hollow inside. A compounding of the loss he'd already suffered.

Cicely made no reply. She stepped away from the table and headed to the door. Emelda started after her, but Samuel held her back. 'Let her go,' he said. Then a knot of anger welled up inside him. 'She's done enough already.'

The door slammed shut as Cicely left their house. Emelda pulled free of Samuel's grip but only got as far as the door before she stopped.

'She's hurting just as much as we are,' she told him.

Samuel walked over and clasped Emelda with his good arm. 'She's hurting more than we are,' he said. 'Because she knows she could have prevented his death and she didn't.'

'Then go after her. Tell her you understand.' Emelda pulled away and gave him a stern look. 'You were hard with her. She couldn't have stopped the wolf, and I don't think she could've stopped Marden either.' Tears rolled down her cheeks and her tone became imploring. 'Go to her. Tell her...'

A groan shuddered through Samuel's chest. 'I can't,' he declared. 'I can't because, Sigmar forgive me, I can't forgive her.' He felt the tear that slithered down his cheek, a thing as much of bitterness as sorrow.

'Our son is dead,' Samuel whispered. 'And she could have kept it from happening.'

Cicely hurried through the streets of Felstein, heedless of her path, eager only to put distance between herself and the house. She felt the bite of her father's words with every step she took. If she closed her eyes, she saw him glaring at her.

It was a relief when she saw Lucilla come out of the bakehouse with a basket of bread. She ran to catch up to her friend before she got too far away. 'Lucilla! Wait!'

Lucilla turned. She was a few years older than Cicely, but the heat of working in her family's bakehouse made her look older still. There were already a few wrinkles at the corners of her eyes and her flaxen hair always had a brittle look to it. She had a demure disposition, or at least had come to adopt one after Alastair's cruel rebuff of her affection. After that, she'd tried to be much more private about her thoughts. At least with everyone except Cicely.

'I'm so very sorry about Marden,' Lucilla said. 'I can't even begin to imagine how horrible you must feel.' She jostled the basket she was carrying. 'I was just taking this bread to the tavern. Would you walk with me?'

Cicely smiled and fell into step beside Lucilla. Before they'd gone even a few yards, she was telling her friend her troubles. '...and father felt like he was responsible for Marden going into the forest, so I tried to make him feel better by letting him blame me instead.'

Lucilla's eyes widened with shock. 'But he can't really think you're to blame!'

'I am to blame,' Cicely said. 'If I were in his place, I wouldn't forgive me either.' She clenched her hands until she felt her nails bruise her palms. 'If I'd just forced Marden to leave Briardark, he'd be alive now.' Shame welled up inside her. She averted her face from those they passed in the street and didn't reply to the sympathetic words offered to her by neighbours.

'You can't let yourself believe that,' Lucilla insisted. 'The wolf killed Marden, not you.'

Cicely shook her head and fixed tired eyes on Lucilla. 'I feel unclean,' she said. 'My skin crawls with the stain of what I've done.' She drew back her sleeve and held her arm out to her friend. 'I can't believe no one else can see it.'

'That's nonsense,' Lucilla snapped. 'There's nothing wrong with you. You're just upset. Who wouldn't be!' Her eyes glistened with sympathy. 'You shouldn't have told them what really happened. You could have let your parents still think you weren't there when the wolf attacked.' She shivered at the idea. 'I'd have fainted at the wolf's feet if I'd been there. You're lucky Marden killed it before it could get you.'

Cicely frowned. She dearly wanted to tell Lucilla the entire truth, but Verderghast had insisted on no mention of his involvement and she saw no way to relate the entire story without mentioning him. It was easier to give Marden full credit for destroying the wolf.

'But the wolf's carcass was gone when we went back for Marden,' Cicely muttered. It was a point that deeply troubled her.

Lucilla shivered again. 'It must have only been stunned. Think of it, if it had recovered while you were there...'

'Father says it rallied after I left and slunk away to some dark corner of Briardark to lick its wounds.' Cicely wasn't cheered by Samuel's explanation. She was concerned that Verderghast had been attacked when the beast recovered. Only the lack of any signs of struggle at the scene gave her any comfort. Even if the wolf had killed Verderghast with a single bite, there would have been evidence of it dragging away his body. Instead there were only the wolf tracks leading back into the trees. The physician had been careful to erase his own footprints. She worried that Verderghast didn't know the wolf's horrid vitality had returned and that it might hunt him when it was recovered. Still, she'd kept true to his wishes and not revealed his presence to anyone.

The bustle of activity drew Cicely from her brooding. She looked up to find that her route had taken her into the town square. A crowd was gathered around the gallowsoak where the witch Natalia Kolb had been executed. A table had been moved to the base of the tree, and on it stood Thayer Greimhalt. The townmaster was arrayed in the opulence he could afford, but even the ermine-trimmed coat with its collar of gryphon feathers couldn't hide that rich living had set its stamp on the man.

'It's hard to imagine, but my mother says Thayer looked like Alastair when he was young,' Lucilla said, a strange mix of wistfulness and pain in her tone.

Cicely scowled at the elder Greimhalt. Now he was bald and flabby, his sharp features dragged down by heavy jowls and droopy eyes. 'He's more like some human spider. Only he uses his voice to spin his webs.'

The anger in Cicely's words surprised Lucilla. 'I… have to get the bread to the tavern,' she said hastily as she scurried across the square.

Cicely returned her attention to the townmaster's oratory.

'It is not that I don't empathise with Herr Helmgaart,' Thayer was telling the crowd gathered in the square. 'Indeed, it is because I do sympathise with his loss that I say we *must* take action ourselves.' He turned and pointed in the direction of Briardark. 'The vicious beast that killed Samuel's boy is still out there. Who can say when it will strike again?' He waved aside an objection someone in the crowd raised. 'Yes, I know there are some who think the wolf has crawled off to some hole to die, but are you willing to take that chance? Are any of you?' His eyes glittered as he looked across the townspeople. Uneasiness flashed on his face when he noticed Cicely at the edge of the square. Perhaps her presence tempered the rhetoric that followed.

'I am not saying we replace Helmgaart,' Thayer insisted. From the confused murmurs Cicely heard, she guessed that Thayer's speech had been trending towards that conclusion until that point. 'His service to this community has been exemplary until now, and that is a debt Felstein cannot ignore. That is why I say that now, when Samuel has suffered such a loss, it is left to the rest of us to act. An interim beasthunter must be appointed to go out and hunt this murdering wolf before it can strike again. Not a replacement, merely a substitute until Samuel...'

Cicely glared at the pontificating townmaster. Thayer wasn't going to let the earth over Marden's grave settle before exploiting the tragedy. She didn't have to consult Mama Ouspenskaya's cards to know that once Thayer had his *temporary* beasthunter appointed, her father would be edged out completely and his stooge would retain the post. It sickened her to think that by attempting to help their father, Marden had forced the very crisis he'd been trying to avert.

She didn't linger to hear any more of Thayer's speech but turned and hurried across the square. A familiar figure called to her from the Skintaker's Swallow as she passed the tavern. A moment later, she heard Alastair jogging up to her.

'Father's long-winded,' he said as he fell into step beside her. 'I don't blame you for leaving.' He still held a stein in his hand and gave it a flourish that sent foam spilling over its brim. 'I always need some fortifying when he starts on one of his harangues.'

Cicely gave Alastair a dark look. The scene was so much like the one on the night Marden had gone to the forest. Alastair intruding on her business, commanding her attention. Delaying her while her brother went onwards to his doom. If not for Alastair, she might have caught Marden in the fields before he found any sign of the wolf. She would have turned him back then, she was convinced of that. Whatever role she'd played in Marden's death, it was because Alastair had interfered.

Alastair frowned when he noted the hate in Cicely's gaze, but he failed to guess its cause. 'Don't worry about what my father is saying. It's a bunch of hot air. No one is going to replace Samuel.' His expression grew sombre, and a bit of the customary swagger left his posture. 'I'm sorry about what happened to your brother.'

'Why? Because now there's one less person to throw out when your father finds a way to steal my father's house?' Cicely's face pulled back in a contemptuous scowl. 'You don't fool me, Alastair Greimhalt. The only person you care about is yourself, and if you're sorry about Marden's death, it's only because even slime like you knows not to press his suit while my family is mourning.'

Alastair took a step back. He had a strange look that Cicely had never seen before. 'Do you really think so little of me?'

'You've no idea,' Cicely told him. 'You treated Lucilla poorly, but there's more than that.' She jabbed her finger against his chest. 'You delayed me when I was trying to find Marden. But for you I would have caught up to him before he followed the wolf's trail.'

Alastair grabbed her hand. 'Cicely, if I'd known...' His voice trailed off into a surprised squawk. He released her fingers as though he'd been burned. 'Your hand... it is so cold.'

Cicely drew away from him. 'Not half as cold as my heart is when it comes to you,' she stated. 'What did you think? You'd offer to intercede with Thayer if I agreed to your proposal?'

'If that is what it would take,' Alastair said. His visage was stern when he stared at her. 'You know you're the only woman in Felstein for me. You'll be my wife.'

'Soulblight take your blood,' she cursed him. 'Keep away from me.'

Alastair took a swallow from his stein and smiled at her. 'You're too emotional right now. I understand how your grief has twisted your mind.'

Cicely bristled at the condescension in his tone. 'Grief hasn't changed anything,' she said.

'It has,' Alastair nodded at her. 'You should look at yourself, Cicely. You're sick with grief. Just a shadow of who you are.'

Cicely marched past Alastair. She hated to admit it, but he had provoked her. The anger that had driven her from the house had found a new source of ire. Right now, she just wanted to get home before she said anything that would bring more trouble to her family. Even with that intention, she could not keep from throwing a last remark at Alastair as she walked away.

'You can tell *your* father that I'll tell *my* father about his little speech. I'm sure he'll be happy to hear about it. *That* should really make you popular with *all* the Helmgaarts.' She didn't glance back to see the effects of her words. She preferred to think she'd worried Alastair and didn't want to be disillusioned by seeing one of his loutish smirks grinning back at her.

Cicely felt drained by the time she reached the house. She thought it must have been Thayer's intrigues and the subsequent altercation with Alastair that had so exhausted her. Certainly, added to the anguish of Marden's loss, the stress caused by the Greimhalts hadn't done her any favours. Her eyes stung as though she'd spent too long looking up at the moon, and each step taxed her body that little bit more than the one that preceded it. She fumbled at the gate and had to catch her breath before swinging it shut behind her.

She could see a light glowing behind the shutters of her parents' room. That at least brought some relief to her. Weary as she'd become, she dreaded a confrontation with her father. She knew one was inevitable, but she wanted it later rather than sooner. After she'd got some rest and recuperated a bit.

There was a rushlight in the front room when she walked inside the house. Cicely smiled. Her mother would have left that burning for her so she could pick her way down the hall to her own room. Whatever had happened, she was reassured by this loving gesture. At least she still had her mother's affection. How dearly she wished she could be certain her father would eventually forgive her.

Fatigue dragged at Cicely as she moved through the house. She strained to keep as quiet as possible, wincing at every creak that rose from the floorboards and the faint scraping when she brushed against the walls. She didn't want any stray noise to bring Samuel out. She just didn't have the energy to face her father. It was an anxious moment when she crept past her parents' room. Her senses were keyed to the least sound, but she didn't hear anyone stir.

Cicely hesitated when she came to Marden's room. Impulsively, she opened the door and stepped inside. The room was unchanged from the night they'd gone into Briardark. She saw the blanket laid out on his bed, the pillow pushed up against the wall so that her brother could look out the window while he tried to fall asleep. How many times she'd seen him lying there, just looking out at the night, his eyes focused on tomorrow.

She walked about the room, stirring memories of him with each step. The little table where he liked to whittle animals from bits of driftwood. His knife was there right now, beside it a half-carved mammoth, its trunk curled up and back across its forehead. She could smell the fresh-cut wood as though he'd been there only a moment before and had merely stepped out of the room.

The impression was too bitter to sustain. Cicely turned to the wardrobe, her eyes lighting on an old, threadbare cloak draped across the door. How many times had their mother tried to mend that shabby thing, and how many times had Marden stubbornly hidden it from her? He'd got it from a knight who'd visited Felstein many years ago. Likely the warrior was just happy to be rid of the mangy thing, but for Marden it had been an exotic treasure.

All the reminders and mementos of her brother's life, everywhere she turned. Looking on them, Cicely felt a bittersweet sensation, the warmth of her love striving against the misery of loss. But there was something more as well. There was guilt, and the longer she lingered, the louder its voice grew.

When she could entertain the guilt no longer, Cicely turned to leave. As she did, her eyes fell upon the table. She thought the knife wasn't where it had been, that there were more wood chips on the table. What was undeniable was the carving. It was still unfinished, but the animal emerging from the wood was no longer a mammoth.

It was a wolf.

Cicely put her hand to her mouth to stifle a sob of horror. As she bit down, her horror was magnified.

She knew her hand was in her mouth, knew her teeth were pressing her flesh. She knew these things, but she couldn't feel them. Whipping her hand away, she brought the rushlight down. In the flickering glow she could see the marks of her teeth, but she couldn't feel them. She brushed the knuckles of her other hand against the marred skin but still felt nothing. Then she brought the rushlight close. Despite the nearness of the flame, she had no sensation of heat until it was several inches nearer to her elbow than her wrist.

The observation sent terror pulsing through her. Alastair's talk about her hand being cold and her looking sickly took on a new importance. Cicely wasn't so careful about being quiet as she dashed into her room. She used the rushlight to fire the wick of a candle, then hurried to the chest where she kept her mirror. Throwing aside the other contents, she drew the mirror into the light.

It was only a square of polished silver a few inches wide, something Samuel had found in Briardark on one of his hunts and brought back as a gift for her. She'd worked over it for several months to restore it and had taken pride in being the only girl her age in Felstein with such a fine mirror.

Now she looked at it not with pride but with fear. She rubbed at her face as though she might be able to change the reflection somehow. The image stubbornly stayed. Pale and drawn, ghastly in the candlelight. Whatever strain she'd been under, whatever guilt had wracked her mind, she was stunned to see such a grim toll these things had taken on her. Small surprise Alastair had called her sickly.

Sickly? Cicely's mind strove against the weird exhaustion that dragged at her. Surely that wasn't normal, not the way such profound weariness had suddenly fallen upon her. Then there was that awful numbness, that deadening of her senses. She could move her hand, twitch her fingers, but the flesh around them was devoid of sensation. As she poked and prodded at the afflicted hand, her fingers strayed up her arm. The numb area was higher now, almost to the elbow.

Cicely staggered to her bed and fell against the blankets. Desperately she tried to convince herself that these things were imagination, tricks of her own mind. Then she remembered that Alastair had been the first to notice the change.

By Nagash's crown, what was happening to her?

A revolting probability whispered through her consciousness. The wolf! The beast had mauled her with fang and claw. She would have died like Marden if not for Verderghast's ministrations. As miraculous as the physician's treatment had been, however, maybe he'd missed something. Maybe there'd been some awful disease carried by the wolf's claws. Maybe that was why she'd *imagined* the carving changing into a wolf.

Oh, if only she'd imagined *that!* She leapt from the bed and started across the room. Her intention was to check and see if the carving had really changed or if she'd just... but what would she do if it had changed?

Terrified of what she might find, Cicely instead crept back to where she'd dropped the mirror and stared down at her image. The night slowly strengthened its hold over Felstein while she studied her reflection and tried to reason out what was happening to her.

And what she could do to stop it.

CHAPTER FIVE

'We have nowhere else to turn.' Anya held the hand of her youngest son while she spoke. Her other two children stood behind her, their faces filled with a piteous display of confusion and anxiety. They didn't understand what was happening, but they knew it was serious.

Emelda opened the door wide and gestured for the family to come inside. Samuel watched from his chair by the hearth as they entered his home. He tried to keep his expression neutral, to avoid any visible sign of worry. Five more mouths to feed and just when his position as Felstein's beasthunter was more precarious than it had ever been. When Emelda glanced his way, he saw she was just as worried.

Rukh followed behind his family. Every inch of the man was redolent of the guilt he felt. There wasn't any need for Samuel to upbraid him about taking the loan that had given the grasping Thayer a hold over them. Rukh was fully aware of his mistake and felt bad enough already.

'I know it's an imposition,' Rukh said, his hat in his hands and his eyes turned to the floor. 'But it would only be until...'

Samuel looked over at Emelda. He tried to wear a smile that had more assurance in it than his heart did. 'Stay as long as you need to,' he told his cousin.

The embers of Rukh's dignity were whipped up by Samuel's charity. He stopped fiddling with his hat and looked directly at the hunter. 'I just need you to take care of Anya and the children,' he said. 'I'll leave in the morning. There's a miller in Darkhaven Hill who I've heard lost his apprentice. I'll go there, and once I've established myself in the town, I'll arrange for my family to join me.'

It was an unlikely prospect, Samuel thought to himself. Rukh could work himself down to a skeleton and not earn enough as an apprentice miller to relocate his family. He didn't want to broach that subject, however. Not when he saw the desperate hope Rukh's words lit in his wife's eyes. He was also afraid to hear what might be the real story. The work waiting for Rukh in Darkhaven might be far less wholesome than grinding grain. It was said that resurrectionists had been raiding the community's extensive cemetery to provide bodies for sepulchrists in Blightmoor, up near the hill country. He'd sleep better not knowing for certain that a member of his family was involved in the profane corpse trade.

Instead of prying into Rukh's story, Samuel simply offered him his hand. 'I know you'll do your best,' he found himself saying, though his thoughts were far different. He nodded to Anya. 'We can set you up in...' Samuel choked when he found Marden's name on his tongue. 'The first room. I'll get the wood room cleared out for the children. A few furs tacked on the walls should keep it warm for them.'

The youngest child tightened his grip on his mother's hand and fairly cringed against her leg. Anya tussled his head and smiled at Samuel. 'Enoch has been especially frightened by everything. It'll be best if I keep him with me.'

Emelda walked over to her. 'Of course,' she assured Anya. 'I'll help you get your things situated, and Samuel and Rukh can get the wood room ready for Barnabus and Amelia.'

Rukh turned back to bring in the few possessions they'd been able to take when Thayer dispossessed them. As Samuel started to help him, he noticed Cicely sitting off to one side. She had a vacant look and was tightly focused on the thread she was working. Irritation flashed through him. 'Put that down and help your mother,' he told her. He had to repeat himself before she reacted. Cicely had a weary cast in her eyes when she turned to him. It seemed like it took her a moment to make sense of what he'd said, but she eventually set down the thread and followed after Emelda and Anya.

She's making herself sick from guilt over Marden, Samuel thought. The observation brought a sense of satisfaction with it. If she'd acted differently, his son would be alive. The hunter brooded on that notion while he watched Cicely shuffle down the hall and into her brother's room. *I wish it had been her instead of him.*

Horror churned in Samuel's gut. Icy numbness crackled down his living arm. He was disgusted by the thought that had slithered into his mind, revolted that any part of him could feel that way. For an instant he had an urge to go after Cicely and apologise. Then bitterness welled up inside him again. He didn't wish her dead, but she was still responsible for Marden. He couldn't get past that. Not right now.

'Which way is the room?' Rukh's question intruded on Samuel's musing. The farmer's hands were filled with the bundles his family had brought with them.

'This way,' Samuel said, his voice strained from emotion. He didn't so much as glance at Marden's room as he led his cousin past the door on their way through the house.

* * *

Dinner was a tumultuous affair that evening. There wasn't enough room at the table for everyone, or enough stew in the pot. Samuel had to butcher a second chicken and Emelda had to cook a second meal, by which time the children were hungry again and licking their chops as they watched the Helmgaarts fill their bowls. Anya had taught them enough manners not to beg, but Cicely could see what they wanted just the same. She rose from the stool she'd taken in the corner of the room and distributed her supper to Barnabus and Amelia.

'I'm not very hungry anyway,' she told her mother when Emelda gave her a concerned look. From the sternness on Samuel's face, she felt her father didn't care much what she did. She quickly turned away and scrambled back to her seat. Any time she caught Samuel's gaze, she could feel the accusation. *You killed Marden.*

Cicely sat with her face turned away. It was more than just the accusing glances from her father or the unspoken appeals from her cousins. The heat from so many people in the room at once created a stifling atmosphere. She felt as if the very air was trying to choke her. The noises from the children were becoming a vexation, refusing to relent for even a moment. The awkward chatter of the adults, half-conversations that no one was actually interested in. Her parents were thinking only of their grief, Rukh and Anya only of their indebtedness to the Helmgaarts and the humiliation that had brought them so low.

The room felt as though it were closing in around her, filling up with the heat and the noise. Almost she would prefer Marden's room. She dreaded the moment when Anya would take up occupancy there. Would her cousin find a wolf or a mammoth on the table? Cicely had been unable to work up the courage to look for herself. If it was a mammoth, then her nerves had been overwrought and she'd imagined things, but if it was a wolf, then it meant something uncanny was at work.

She felt her hand. Even in this sweltering room, it still felt cold to her touch. *That* wasn't imagination. Or was it? She remembered Klausner, the hermit of Briardark, and how the recluse had gone insane. Samuel had run him down and brought him back to town so he could be shipped off to Gothghul Hollow. Klausner had been convinced he was a dragon and boasted of his thick scales and mighty wings. To the madman they were real, even if they existed only in his mind.

Cicely tried to reassert control over herself, as if by force of will she might fight down her delusions. For a moment, she strove to enjoy the companionship of the crowded room. As the minutes stretched away, she found it hard to be in their presence. Not mere guilt, but a physical affliction bore down on her. There was a stinging in her eyes when she looked at someone, an awful burning glow, like an aura that exuded from each of them. It was the most painful around the children. Like looking directly into a roaring fire. Her parents and older cousins weren't as bad by comparison, at least as far as stinging her eyes went. Instead, there was a different effect, something that maybe she'd notice if she could bear to hold her gaze on the children long enough. It was something she was utterly unable to account for. It seemed like she could see through them in a fashion. She could see red lines curving through their bodies and a great crimson mass where she knew their hearts to be. Horrible as it was, she knew that what she was seeing was the blood in their veins.

'You don't look well,' Emelda said, staring at her daughter across the table. 'Are you feeling ill?'

The question sent a shiver through Cicely's flesh. If her mother saw it, then it wasn't just in her mind. She'd applied powder to her hands to disguise the pallor that had crept into them, yet her mother still noticed a change. Her skin really was growing paler. It was more than morbid fancy.

'I'm just tired,' Cicely replied. She had no desire to burden Emelda with the idea that she was sick. Besides, for some reason she felt ashamed of her weakness. Marden had given his life for her. It cheapened his sacrifice if she'd been infected by the wolf.

'Are you sure you're okay?' Anya asked.

Cicely shook her head. 'I'm just not hungry, cousin,' she said. Quickly, she left the stool and hurried back down the hall to her room. She could hear the others talking about her. Emelda was reminding their guests about the great grief the family had suffered and that Cicely had been very close to her brother. She heard Anya and Rukh mutter sympathetic apologies. Cicely waited a moment, hoping to hear Samuel say something, but her father's voice didn't manifest. Perturbed, she slipped into her room and closed the door behind her.

The moment the door was shut, Cicely felt a sense of relief. Only when she was away from them did she really appreciate the strain being in such a small space with so many people put upon her. More than just that stinging glow she either felt or imagined, it was the sounds they made, the chatter of their voices, the susurrus of their breath. The dull, thumping pulsations that exuded from them, incessantly pounding against her mind.

She sank down into the chair where she'd left the tapestry she'd been working on. It would be a portrait of her whole family when she was finished. *If* she could ever finish, she corrected herself with a feeling of disgust. The joy she'd once felt working on it was gone; only a sense of obligation, the loathing of a thing left undone, kept her picking away at it with needle and thread. Cicely stared at her incomplete work, trying to make sense of the unfinished figures. Herself, her parents, they all seemed even less distinct than they had been. Dull and faded, like apparitions glimpsed through a dirty glass. Only Marden's image was clear to her. Distinct in every way, every bit of his personality captured in the tapestry. She felt tears shaping in her eyes when she looked at him, all of her guilt and grief rising to the fore.

But the tears wouldn't come. No matter how they stung her

eyes, Cicely never felt them sliding down her cheeks. Finally, she brushed them away with her cuff, the inability to cry only further darkening her mood. She tore her gaze away from the tapestry and glanced about her room.

Everything seemed dull and faded now. There was only one small spot that stood out with any kind of vibrancy. It was something that she shouldn't ordinarily have noticed from across the room, but now the contrast it made against the lustreless surroundings made it stand out like a bonfire.

It was a spiderweb stretching across the corner of her window, and within its cords was the withered husk of a fly. The dead insect was what alerted her attention, her awareness fixating upon it with that same inexplicable attraction that made Marden's image so defined while the rest of the tapestry seemed murky.

Was this only morbid imagining? Cicely held her head in her hands as her shudders intensified. Was she going insane? Or was it what she'd feared? Was everything she experienced real, some horrible affliction caused by the dire wolf's attack? Something Verderghast had failed to remedy when he'd saved her life?

Cicely didn't know. She scarcely had the courage to even ask the questions. She roughly rubbed her arm until the concealing powder was brushed away. Her skin was in such a state that she could see the bones beneath her transparent flesh.

Cicely fell back into her chair. She didn't cry out. She just sat there and trembled in the growing dark.

What was happening to her?

The next day, Rukh left the Helmgaart house to make the journey to Darkhaven, but that evening Samuel had visitors of a very different sort. A small delegation of Felstein's farmers led by old Hochmueller. The subject of their visit was easy enough to guess. Samuel had Emelda and Anya lead the children outside while he discussed what would doubtless prove to be a grim topic. Briefly, he debated fetching Cicely from her room, but decided it was unlikely his daughter would overhear anything from where she was. She'd been shunning the company of others ever since they'd taken in their cousins. Emelda fretted it was a symptom of illness, but the bitterness in Samuel's heart gave him the opinion that if anything was making Cicely sick, it was being responsible for her brother's death.

Once Emelda hurried little Barnabus into the yard and closed the door, Samuel turned to his guests. 'It doesn't take a turn of the spirit cards to guess what you're here for,' he stated.

A grizzled swineherd named Roderick was the first to reply. He scratched his bushy black beard with one hand while readjusting his belt with the other. 'Aye, we're here about the wolf. The one that got your boy.' The last remark brought some stern looks from the other farmers. As if there could be any confusion about which wolf anyone in Felstein would be talking about.

'Samuel's girl said it was killed by Marden,' old Hochmueller reminded them, his voice a mere crackle. In his youth he'd been lured away from town by the wail of a banshee and had narrowly escaped being strangled by the murderous nighthaunt. He wore a muffler to hide his neck, but those who'd seen him without it said the skin was grey and wrinkled where the spectre had grabbed him.

'We didn't find no carcass when we searched Briardark.' That was the rejoinder offered by Balthas, who had cornfields to either side of the town. The only man in Felstein covetous enough to plough the tract adjacent to the cemetery. Even Thayer wasn't that grasping in his greed. Unfortunately for Balthas, his avarice was paired with a brain a drunk ogor could outwit.

'We went to where Marden was attacked and looked around,' said Lugos, whose farm, like Hochmueller's, went right up to the forest's edge. 'I'd hardly call that a search.' He nodded to Samuel. 'You think the wolf was in such a bad shape it crawled off to some hole to finish dying?'

Samuel's eyes were hard as steel when he answered. 'If I didn't believe that was true, do you – do any of you – think I'd be here?' He waved his arm in the direction of Briardark. 'If I thought there was any chance that beast wasn't dead, I'd be out there tracking it down, and not the shadow of Nagash himself would keep me from finding the butchering cur!'

Hochmueller gave the others a solemn look. 'There you have it. Who better to tell you than a father who's lost his son. I've told you. Lugos has told you. There's been not a sign of this beast since the boy died. We've neither of us lost any more animals to it. Nobody on our farms has heard its howls. The beast must be dead – or gone from these parts, which is just as good.'

'There's them who says different,' Balthas said. His attempt at a wise nod had more comedy about it than sagacity. A few of the other farmers had to stifle laughs.

'Thayer Greimhalt has wanted to make someone loyal to him beasthunter for years now,' Samuel declared. 'Surely all of you can see that.'

Nicklas, a young farmer with a small plot to the west, stepped forwards. 'Of course we see that, otherwise we wouldn't be here. Thayer's using this situation to his own ends – none of us, at least, are credulous enough to doubt that. But it doesn't mean there isn't a real threat.' He paused for a moment, trying to find words to express his concern. When he spoke again, Samuel caught a note of accusation in his tone. 'You say the wolf's dead, but how can we be certain? And if it isn't gone, can we take that chance? You've lost one child, and there isn't one of us who doesn't sympathise, but I've four of my own to think about. Roderick has two. Lugos has five. Even Balthas has managed to sire half a dozen of his own.' Samuel could see the dullard flicking his fingers as he counted to verify the children attributed to him by Nicklas.

'None of us wants to risk it,' Roderick said. 'Understand what we're afraid of. The pain you're going through right now... none of us wants it to happen to him.'

Lugos sighed and shook his head. 'That's what makes even those of us who know better listen to Thayer's promises.' He looked directly at Samuel. 'We're afraid. Afraid of the very thing our beasthunter is tasked with keeping away from our fields and our homes.'

Samuel clenched his hands at his sides. 'I tell you, the wolf is dead,' he growled.

'And if it isn't, do you think anyone Thayer appointed could do a better job of keeping us safe?' Hochmueller asked the others.

'I tell you, the wolf is dead,' Samuel repeated, irked as much by Hochmueller's comment as he was from direct confrontation.

'All we're asking is that you make sure,' Roderick told him. 'If the wolf's dead, as you say, then a man like you can surely find its carcass and bring it back for all of us to see.'

'That would knock Thayer's arguments right out from under him,' Lugos said. 'Louse wouldn't know to piss or go blind if you did that. Not after all the talk he's been doing.'

Samuel nodded. He had little affection for Thayer, and even less after he'd dispossessed his cousins, but at the same time he resented being forced into action in this way. 'It won't be so easy as you suppose,' he told Roderick. 'A dead animal doesn't leave fresh tracks to follow. Finding an old trail isn't as easy as finding a fresh one.'

'Then ya should have followed 'em when they was fresh,' Balthas interjected. Even the less supportive farmers like Nicklas and Roderick gave him a black look.

'I had to bury Marden,' Samuel stated, pushing each word through clenched teeth. His tone was clear enough that even Balthas understood he'd overstepped decency.

Hochmueller sputtered an apology as the atmosphere in the

room became tainted with hostility. 'We don't think Thayer's quite ready to force the issue. We just wanted to hear from you what you thought. What you might do.'

'If there's any chance of bringing the body into town...' Lugos started.

Samuel turned and opened the door. 'I'll let you know what I decide.' He motioned for the delegation to leave. He knew he wasn't making an impression on them that would bolster their confidence in him. He also didn't care. When they were gone, he dropped into his chair and closed his eyes.

Marden was dead, and all anyone seemed to care about was the thing that killed him. Samuel felt contempt for them all in that moment. More concerned about the murderer than the victim. To send him off into the wilds of Briardark looking for a carcass before the earth over his son's grave had even settled.

Samuel was tempted to let Felstein appoint one of his stooges beasthunter. The town didn't deserve better.

He looked down the hall towards the bedrooms, his gaze fixing on the door to Cicely's. 'Why didn't you stop him?' he groaned. 'Why didn't you make him come back before it was too late?'

The peculiar agitation of her senses confounded Cicely at every turn. Things that should be clear became distorted while some that should be vague became magnified to hideous prominence. Sitting alone in her room, trying to work on her tapestry, she'd barely been able to hear her cousins playing in the other room or her mother and Anya working in the kitchen. When the farmers came in, she could only make out fragments of their conversation. But those fragments came to her ears as if she sat in the same room listening to them. The snatches of talk all had to do with Marden and the wolf.

After Samuel grew angry and made the men leave, she heard her father speaking to himself. No, not speaking – he was whispering, though his words came to her with such distinction he might have been at her very ear. Why didn't she stop Marden? She felt her father would never cease to ask that question. She knew she would never stop asking it herself.

Cicely thought about what she'd overheard. The townspeople wanted Samuel to go back to Briardark and find the wolf's body. It was a dreadful thing to imagine, her father alone, picking through the grim forest for the beast's carcass. And what if it wasn't as dead as it should be? Cicely had increasingly come to believe that Verderghast had taken the body, but what if she was wrong? What if the dire wolf had revived and crept away on its own? If the undead monster was still active, it might lie in wait for her father and take him by surprise.

A grim determination welled up inside her. She dreaded going back to Briardark, more than ever before, after the tragedy that had come upon her family there. A tragedy she'd played her part in allowing to happen. But now she had a chance to avert another tragedy. She could go back and find out if the wolf was dead or not. She could warn her father if the beast yet lived.

She had to return to Briardark and find Verderghast. The physician could tell her what had happened to the wolf and maybe even save her father the trouble of looking for its body.

Cicely set aside her stitching and fetched a shawl before slipping out the window and heading for the forest. As she did, her eyes fastened on the ghastly condition of her forearm. The part where she'd rubbed away the powder was almost invisible, only the bone and veins beneath the skin looking to have any substance about them. Even the areas where she'd applied powder were taking on a waxy appearance, as though her flesh was becoming mouldy.

Yes, she had to find Verderghast, and not just to learn what had happened to the wolf. She had to learn what had happened to her as well.

She had to know what horrible affliction she was suffering from, and what she could do to stop it.

CHAPTER SIX

The hour was late when Cicely slipped through Hochmueller's fields and entered the forest. The risk of being spotted and someone telling her father was too great to chance going by day. However he might feel about his daughter, she was certain that Samuel would go after her and try to stop her. She couldn't let that happen. Her dread of Briardark wasn't half so great as her terror of the eerie changes happening to her. She *had* to find Verderghast. Alone she might do it, but she knew that if her father was around the reclusive physician would never show himself.

There was another reason for making the journey by night. Cicely's eyes had been changed by her affliction. Daylight caused her vision to become cloudy, like she was trying to look at things through a strip of thin gauze. She suffered no such hindrance at night. Indeed, the deeper the shadow, the more clearly she could discern what lay within. It was a horrible reversal of the natural order, and she had no better example of its weirdness than she did now.

Cicely would never forget that tragic venture with Marden. Every impression made upon her that night was as fresh in her mind as when it had happened, right until the wolf had finally borne her down. She remembered Briardark as a labyrinth of darkness with unseen creatures crawling through the brambles and deep patches of impenetrable shadow that exuded an aura of mystery and menace. Now it had all changed. There wasn't a blotch of shadow she couldn't see through, exposing old stumps and moss-covered boulders. Any of the furtive rustles in the undergrowth were quickly traced to a creeping toad or a skittering mouse. She could even see the owls and bats as they flittered through the forest in search of prey, the blackness of the sky offering them no concealment to her gaze.

Verderghast had to know what was happening to her. Cicely didn't dare tell anyone else about the ghastly affliction. With Thayer stirring up sentiment against Samuel, it would take little proof to convince Felstein that his daughter had become some kind of monster. She could almost hear them marching through the streets in a mob, shouting that the wolf's bite had poisoned her. That she was becoming a vargulf or some other fiend of the night. The worst thing for her was that they might be right.

Cicely was easily able to pick her way through the forest with her nocturnal sight, but Briardark's very vastness daunted her. There wasn't any way to be certain Verderghast was even still in this part of the forest. Given his inclination to keep away from people, it was foolish to think he'd linger so close to the town as when he'd saved her from the wolf. Indeed, he'd have even more reason to withdraw to the interior after sending her back to Felstein.

'Verderghast!' Cicely yelled. 'It's me, Cicely Helmgaart! The woman you saved! I need your help!' Her cries echoed through the desolate forest, seeming to take on macabre differences of inflection and tone as they raced through the shadows.

She hesitated while she listened to the echoes. It felt as though her voice was carrying across the whole forest. Focused on finding Verderghast, she hadn't given due consideration to what else might be out there listening to her. The vision of the dire wolf roused from its hidden lair sent a shudder through her. If the beast wasn't dead, then it would surely hear her and come hunting her. Intent on claiming the prey it had been cheated of.

Cicely looked back in the direction of Felstein. No, there wasn't any relief for her there. Whatever was happening to her was getting worse. If the wolf was still out there, at least it would be a quick end. Firming her resolve, she called out once again, 'Verderghast!'

She was never sure how long she roamed through the forest calling the physician's name. It felt like hours, but it might only have been minutes. All she knew was that the end of her search came as an abrupt shock.

'You called to me?' As if conjured up by a spell, Verderghast was suddenly there, leaning against a half-dead tree. He looked just as Cicely remembered him. It took her a moment to appreciate why that fact made her afraid. Unlike her father, or her cousins, or Alastair, there was no unnatural distortion when she looked at Verderghast. He was... unchanged.

Cicely couldn't hide her shock at the physician's abrupt appearance. She stared at him, unable to speak. Verderghast smiled and pushed himself away from the tree. He took a few steps towards her, then his expression slipped to one of gravity. 'You look a fright,' he muttered as he regarded her.

Cicely held her arm out to him and drew back her sleeve, wrenching the cloth until it was up past her elbow. Skin that hadn't been dusted with powder or slathered with cream stood exposed. Or would have had there been anything to see. Instead, there was that horrible translucence and the visible bone within her flesh.

'Help me,' Cicely gasped. It was all she could manage to keep standing as her body convulsed with horror at the sight of her own arm.

Verderghast drew back for a moment, a grim look in his eyes. He withdrew a crooked stick from his belt, and when he came near to Cicely, he employed the instrument to examine her in lieu of touching her with his own fingers. 'My poor child,' he tutted as he prodded her arm with the stick, moving it up and down and from side to side. She could feel the contact only as a dim tingle against numbed flesh. She could see that there was still substance there for the stick to touch, however transparent it might have become.

'What is happening to me?' Cicely sobbed.

The physician shook his head apologetically. 'I had hoped this wouldn't happen,' he said. 'I'd hoped I was able to cleanse your wounds so thoroughly that this wouldn't occur.' His arms dropped to his sides in a helpless gesture. 'The creatures of Nagash carry with them the blight of the grave and can transmit that corruption to those upon whom they do injury. The dire wolf's fangs...' His voice trailed away into a solemn whisper.

Cicely felt choked by fear. Everyone in Felstein had heard the tales of those who escaped from the undead only to become undead themselves. A scratch from a ghoul's claw or the bite of a vampire's tooth and the survivor found there was no survival after all.

Her head felt as if it were spinning. She reeled to one side and slipped down to rest against an old tree stump. Mirthless laughter welled up from deep inside her. 'I thought you saved my life,' she cackled cynically.

Verderghast tapped the examination stick against the palm of his hand. 'So did I. I thought I had conquered any side effects, that I'd defeated the necromantic poison.'

Cicely wanted to cry, but the tears wouldn't come. She just

looked up at the physician. 'What is happening to me? What *will* happen to me?'

'I brought you back from the very cusp of death,' Verderghast said. 'Now death is trying to reclaim you.' He turned his face up towards the black sky. 'Your energies are being drained off. Bit by bit, speck by speck, every hour there is less of you. You'll continue to lose substance until everything is gone.'

'Nagash have mercy,' Cicely groaned. Her heart went cold at the picture Verderghast proposed. To gradually have her body fade away, evaporating around her. The transition from living woman to ethereal wraith. She pleaded with Verderghast to save her from such a doom. 'Please, there must be something you can do. Some way to cure me of this!'

Verderghast grimaced. 'I refuse to admit there is no hope,' he declared, snapping the examination stick in two and hurling it to the ground. He stared intently at Cicely. 'You mustn't resign yourself to death. There's a way to save you.' His eyes beamed with excitement. 'Your energies are being drained away, but if you were to replenish them, then you could restore yourself!'

His excitement infected Cicely with a cautious hope. 'Replenish my energies,' she said. 'Is there a way to do that?'

'If you are brave,' Verderghast said. 'If your will is strong enough to do what must be done.' He stepped closer, and this time didn't balk from touching her but instead took her hand in his. His hand felt like ice under her fingers, and Cicely tried to pull free, but he held her fast. 'Your will to live must be strong enough to do what you must do. You must want to live more than anything else. Do you want to live, Cicely?'

She gave an emphatic nod. The intensity in his tone had emboldened the faltering hope of a moment before. She believed now that there really was a chance she could be saved. 'I'll do anything,' Cicely said.

Verderghast released her hand. He reached beneath his coat

and removed a small fold of cloth. It had a strange, uncanny air about it. Cicely knew without being told that it was incredibly old. So ancient it had no right being in the world.

'What is that?' she asked, drawing away.

'Salvation,' Verderghast told her. He turned the folds outward and exposed a curious object.

'A needle?' Cicely was dumbfounded. Yet that was what seemed to be resting inside the ancient cloth. A needle fashioned from some dark, shiny material that gleamed like glass and seemed to suck into itself what little light there was in the forest. Faintly she thought she could discern some sort of markings, weird glyphs both beautiful and hideous in their graceful ranks.

'You were delirious after the wolf attack,' Verderghast said. 'You muttered many things in your delirium. That was how I learned you are a seamstress.'

Cicely almost laughed. It was absurd. Here she was, her body evaporating into a wraith, and Verderghast was talking about sewing!

Instead of laughing, however, she just nodded again.

'There is a chance, then.' Verderghast pressed the cloth and the needle into her hand. They felt so cold that they burned her skin. It was an effort not to fling them away into the dark, but she could sense there was an awful power within the needle. A force too great to simply throw away.

'Take this,' the physician said. 'Use the needle to sew the images of others. The magic bound into it will transfer the energy of whoever the image belongs to into yourself.'

Cicely stared down at the onyx needle with incredulity. 'This is too incredible to be real,' she protested. The obscene aura that exuded from the object frightened her. As much as part of her wanted to believe in its power, another part of her prayed it was nothing but a charlatan's trick.

'Incredible or not, it is a chance for you to live.' Verderghast closed her hand over the cloth. 'Take it. Use it. Anyone whose image you create will have their life force drained off in substitution of your own.'

As though in a daze, Cicely rose to her feet. She pondered the import of what Verderghast was telling her to do. 'It could be any image, not just a person's.' She gave the physician a frantic look. Suddenly she was even more afraid of this thing he'd given her. Not because it wouldn't work, but because it would.

'It doesn't have to be a person,' Cicely emphasised. Verderghast said nothing. His silence sent her fleeing from him as though he were a venomous serpent.

'It doesn't have to be a person,' Cicely swore as she left Briardark. She kept telling herself all the way through Felstein. By the time she'd reached her home, she'd almost convinced herself it was true.

Cicely sat on the corner of her bed for some time, just staring at the strange packet Verderghast had given her. The cloth still had that horrible sense of antiquity about it. She wondered if it was something woven by the aelves, for certainly no other sort of material could be as ancient as she felt this to be. Her revulsion for the thing had softened into a morbid attraction she couldn't account for. Yet another symptom of the affliction that assailed her?

The onyx needle, by contrast, felt fresh and new. She couldn't explain the impression. Perhaps it was simply that anything would seem new when set against that hoary old cloth.

She picked up the needle and wondered what kind of magic it held. Cicely had little experience of physicians, but she understood them to avoid the arcane. Their practice involved herbs and poultices, remedies that were much more mundane than the spells of witches and wizards. What sort of doctor was Verderghast that he'd studied magic enough to employ it in his cures?

She wondered if perhaps his exile from civilisation wasn't as innocent as he'd made it out to be.

Looking at the needle, she couldn't help but see the fading skin around the fingers that held it. As her condition deteriorated, how long would she even be able to hide what was happening to her? How long before she was discovered?

Elsewhere in the house, she could hear someone stirring. Probably Emelda, rising to get breakfast ready. It wouldn't be too long before her mother came to Cicely's door and called her to eat. Cicely might be excused, but she knew that was only a delaying tactic that wouldn't work long. Whether today or tomorrow, the reckoning would come.

Her attention shifted to the unfinished tapestry. Not for the first time since she'd returned home. Cicely wasn't sure why she hadn't already experimented with Verderghast's needle. Was it because she feared it wouldn't work, that the physician had lied to her simply to ease his own conscience? Or was it because she was afraid it would work? What would it mean, to siphon energy from something and draw it into herself? Would the subject grow tired or sick? Worse than that? And how much energy would it take to replenish her own and be cured of her affliction?

'Only now do you think of these questions,' Cicely berated herself. If she'd been half as smart as she thought she was, she'd have asked Verderghast when he gave her the needle.

The sounds of activity in the house finally decided her. Cicely walked over to the big oak rocking chair and picked up the tapestry. She plucked the old copper needle from the fabric. Bending down to the box of materials on the floor, she fastened a string to the onyx one and set the tapestry across her lap. The images of her family smiled back at her. Samuel and Emelda and Marden, each in varying stages of completeness. She shifted the heavy fabric around, finding for herself an empty space. Her fingers hesitated, the new needle just touching the surface.

'It doesn't have to be a person,' she whispered before thrusting the needle into the tapestry. Her gaze drifted to the window and fastened on a big yellow flower growing in her mother's garden. She determined to use the flower as her subject. Once that choice was made, her fingers flew about their work. Never had she laboured at such a feverish pace. The needle darted in and out like a firebrand. She fixed different-coloured threads to its eye with a speed that surpassed conscious thought.

Almost before she realised, the work was done. At the far corner of her tapestry there was now a flower. Only it wasn't the flower in her mother's garden. The image that met her gaze wasn't full and vibrant. It was wilted and sagged on its stem, its petals falling away. This wasn't the picture she'd woven. At least, it wasn't the image she'd started to create.

Cicely shifted the tapestry around so that she could get a better look at it. When she did, she noticed her hands. They were normal again! The skin was solid with no hint of that terrible translucence. She couldn't see the blood and bone beneath her flesh. Amazed, she spun around and looked about the room. Everything was as it should be. The shadows were dark, the light was bright. She saw her cousins' cat stroll past her bedstead and there was no strangeness about its appearance, no stinging glow or horrible sense of the blood flowing through its body.

'Praise Sigmar,' Cicely said, weeping. This time she could feel tears against her cheeks. It had worked. Everything would be all right now. The relief she felt was so profound that it shook her to the core. She rushed to the mirror and just stared at herself. She smiled and laughed, clapping her hands to her face.

The sound brought a stern rap against her door. 'Breakfast,' her father's gruff voice sounded from the other side. Cicely could hear him stomp off down the hall. Her cheer vanished as quickly as it had come. She hoped Samuel hadn't heard her laughing, not when they were all grieving Marden. She hoped, but she knew it was a vain wish. He'd heard, and if possible, it had made him even more disgusted with his daughter.

Cicely stared back at the mirror, chiding herself for being so insensitive. She didn't want to hurt anyone. Certainly not her family. That she didn't mean to wasn't an excuse.

Gazing at her visage, Cicely gradually noticed the change. At first she tried to tell herself it was a delusion spurred by her guilty feelings, then tried to deny it as a caprice of the morning light. Finally, she had to accept it. Yes, her complexion, robust and healthy a moment before, was growing waxy and pale.

She turned to the window. Out in the garden she could see the flower, wilted and dead. Not as she'd intended to weave it into the tapestry but as she'd in truth added it into the picture. By whatever arcane process, she knew the needle had drained away its life essence and transferred it into herself. She'd been revitalised by the flower, but it wasn't enough.

'Breakfast, Cousin Cicely,' Amelia called timidly from the hall-way. She could hear the child shifting her feet against the floor.

'I'm not feeling well,' Cicely replied. 'Tell my mother I'll be out later.'

Amelia lingered in the hallway. 'Cousin Cicely, have you seen Octavia? I can't find her.'

Cicely's eyes turned to the cat, which was still pacing around her room. A cold knot formed in her throat. She could barely force herself to speak. 'No, I haven't seen Octavia,' she said as she stared at the animal. 'Maybe she's outside. If I feel better, I'll help you look for her later.'

With her cousin's promise, Amelia hurried off down the hall. Cicely felt unclean when she took up the tapestry and stabbed the needle into the cloth. Her eyes were riveted on Octavia, drinking in every detail of the cat's sleek shape. She didn't look at what her fingers were doing as they worked the thread, just remained focused on the animal whose image she was copying. The victim whose essence she was going to steal.

It wasn't of her own volition that her hands finally fell still. Cicely watched Octavia, terrified to see the cat wither like the flower. After a few minutes, however, nothing had happened. The cat continued to prowl about the room, sniffing and purring as she investigated her unfamiliar surroundings.

Then Octavia brushed against the leg of Cicely's chair. She rose quickly, drawing up the tapestry with an instinctive defensiveness lest the cat rip it with her claws. The sudden motion somehow upset the chair. Octavia yowled once as she tried to dart away to safety, but the animal misjudged the direction in which she'd find it. She put herself directly in the path of the falling rocker. The heavy back slammed down on the creature, crushing her beneath it.

Cicely threw aside the tapestry and hurried to raise the chair. Even before she looked, she knew the cat was dead. Her hands weren't pale any more but had instead reverted to a healthy complexion. When she pulled back the chair, she saw that Octavia's skull had been shattered. Blood flowed from the cat's head and formed a pool around the body.

Dreading what she would see, Cicely took up the tapestry again. What she'd sewn wasn't Octavia the way she'd seen the cat, but the animal as she was now. Lying dead with blood gushing from the crushed head. Horrified, she threw the tapestry onto her bed. She stared at her hands again, at their robust colour. The flower had sustained her for only minutes. How long would the cat's essence stave off her affliction? Would it be enough to cure her completely?

As much as she wanted it to be that way, she knew it was too much to wish for. The effect might last days or only hours, but at some point she'd have to use the needle again and add another image to the tapestry.

She turned back to Octavia's smashed little body. Gently, Cicely lifted it from the floor. She couldn't bear the thought of Amelia continuing to search for the animal when it was dead. She'd tell her family there'd been an accident, that she hadn't known the cat had got into her room. Only a part of the truth, but enough to mitigate the shame she felt.

Cicely drew back the bolt on her door. It was best to hurry while her appearance was revitalised. After the example of the flower, she didn't know how long Octavia's essence was going to last.

Before heading down the hall, she cast a lingering look at the tapestry. Whatever it had been before, it was now a gruesome thing. It was also the only thing that might save her.

'It doesn't have to be a person,' Cicely whispered as she closed the door and went to tell her family about the cat.

'It doesn't have to be a person.'

CHAPTER SEVEN

Barnabus and Amelia whimpered while they sat on the floor next to their mother. They were still upset over the death of their cat early that morning. Anya had tried to keep them quiet, but it was difficult to make children so young understand things like decorum. Here they were grieving for a pet while their hosts were grieving for a son. Samuel tried not to display any sign of annoyance. He knew being forced from their home and having their father go away was already tough enough on them. The cat's accident was another hardship heaped on top of the pile.

Samuel lit the candle and set it beside the skull-faced icon that rested in the little niche opposite the hearth. The flicker from the fireplace sent weird shadows spinning across the effigy, lending the crude representation of Nagash a grisly semblance of motion. The hunter curled his fingers together, careful not to exert too much pressure with the metal ones. He managed to fold them into the sign of Nagash and bowed to the representation of the Lord of Death.

'From gheists and ghouls, and all the horrors of the unquiet grave, Lord Nagash please spare this house,' Samuel prayed to the icon. 'Look kindly upon our guests and extend to them the protection that graces this household.'

'Give thanks that he has withdrawn his hand from our daughter,' Emelda whispered to Samuel. He glanced aside to where Cicely sat and studied her for a moment. What Emelda said was true. Cicely *was* looking much better today. Until just now, he hadn't considered the pale, wasted condition his daughter had been in. He'd been too wrapped up in his own grief, too bent on blaming Cicely for Marden's death, to notice her. To really notice her.

He was ashamed of that. The contrast between how she looked now and the day after Marden's death was undeniable and spoke to the depth of her grief. It went far deeper than he'd been willing to believe. In his anger at the abrupt and senseless death of his son, he'd taken a cruel satisfaction in thinking she was tortured by guilt. Only now, seeing the change back to something resembling her old self, did he understand how terribly she'd been affected. He was revolted that he'd drawn any measure of comfort, however small, from Cicely's distress.

Samuel quickly finished the family prayers and walked over to his daughter. Emelda gave him a worried look, but he made a placating wave of his good hand that he could see reassured her. He wasn't going to add to Cicely's trouble. If possible, he wanted to make things right. That was, if his cold attitude hadn't already soured the love between them.

'You really do look better,' Samuel said. Cicely looked up at him, a mix of concern and surprise in her eyes. He forced a laugh, and a wistful note crept into his voice. 'I remember when you were playing in the yard with Marden. He must have been barely seven. He'd made a little sling out of an old piece of doeskin.' The hunter shook his head. 'He hit you with a rock and knocked you down. Even before he told anyone else, he rushed in here and lit a candle so he could ask Nagash not to take you away.' He looked back at the niche with its skull-faced icon.

Cicely gave the slightest smile in return. She too was remembering. Her gaze turned automatically to Marden's chair. Only now it was Barnabus who climbed into it, sniffling over the dead cat. She quickly turned her head and looked back at her father.

Samuel cleared his throat. He didn't know how to say what needed saying. All he could do was express what he felt and hope it made sense. Hope it would make things right. 'I'm sorry,' he began. He crouched down so that he wasn't looming over her. 'I'm sorry I haven't been there for you. It's just... Marden's death... I was angry. I wanted someone to blame.'

'I know,' Cicely said, only briefly looking at him before glancing down at the floor.

'You don't know,' Samuel corrected her, placing his living hand on her shoulder. 'It was wrong for me to think that way. Wrong to blame you. It's a hard thing to accept, but there's no one to blame. Marden made his choice. It was his decision to go into Briardark looking for the wolf.'

'But I could have stopped him,' Cicely whispered, still keeping her face averted.

Samuel glanced over at Emelda. He saw encouragement there. He knew she'd help him if he asked, but the responsibility was his. He had to do this by himself. He had to undo the harm he'd done. 'Why stop there?' he posed. 'The fault could be mine for teaching Marden to hunt. Also my fault that I didn't find the wolf and kill it. Maybe it is Hochmueller's fault for grazing his herd so close to the forest and drawing predators to Felstein. Why stop there? Why not blame the gods? Couldn't Sigmar have sent a lightning bolt to kill the wolf before it attacked? Once you start trying to place blame, where do you stop?'

'But I was there...' Cicely said.

'And I praise the gods that you weren't taken from me too,'

Samuel said. He drew Cicely up from the floor and hugged her close. 'I'm grateful that you weren't killed.'

Cicely stared at her father, guilt creeping back into her features. 'But… wouldn't you rather it had been me instead of Marden?'

The question was itself abominable, and Samuel was disgusted at himself that Cicely thought she needed to ask it. 'No,' he assured her, kissing her forehead. 'Never. Never think such a thing. If you obey only one thing I've ever told you to do, make it that. Don't ever feel like that. I miss Marden, but don't ever think I'd lose you to bring him back.'

Samuel felt his daughter's arms return his embrace. He could hear her soft sobs as they held on to one another. He found tears in his own eyes. He'd been selfish, trying to lock Cicely out from his grief when, at a time of tragedy, the strength of family was in coming together.

'We both love you very much,' Emelda said as she walked over. 'Nothing will change that.' Cicely released her father and embraced her mother. Emelda stroked her hair while she held her.

Across the room, Anya kept her children quiet, not wishing to trespass on the Helmgaarts' reconciliation. Samuel appreciated his cousin's discretion. He gave her a respectful nod, then turned back to his remaining family. When he did, a twinge of alarm worried at him, and his sense of guilt returned. He'd hoped that he could ease Cicely's mind by repenting of the cold treatment he'd shown her. Instead, he saw that the colour had drained from her again. She looked as sickly as she had before. Somehow *diminished* in a way he couldn't quite define.

'Are you all right?' he asked, echoing his wife's question from earlier. 'Are you feeling ill?'

Emelda drew back from their embrace, and her eyes went wide with concern when she looked at Cicely.

Cicely pulled away. She stared down at her hand. For just a moment, Samuel swore he saw a look of absolute horror on his daughter's face. 'I'm just tired,' she explained, the words flowing rapidly, as though she couldn't say them quickly enough. She hurried down the hall to her room, hastily shutting the door behind her.

Anya and her children watched Cicely's withdrawal in befuddlement. The look Emelda shared with Samuel was equally confused.

'I thought I'd made things okay,' Samuel said.

'She just needs time,' Emelda assured him, darting a concerned glance down the hall. 'I am worried that she's getting sick. I wish she'd take some food. It isn't good, starving herself.'

'She'll come around,' Samuel assured her. He made an effort to put confidence in his tone. He didn't want Emelda to worry more than she already was, but whatever was happening with their daughter, he didn't think it would resolve on its own.

What was wrong and how to fix it were problems he'd have dearly liked the answers to.

Once she was inside her room, Cicely collapsed on her bed. Beyond getting away from her family, she didn't know what to do. Her only ambition in that moment was to keep them from seeing the change coming over her again.

She shivered as she thought of the flower. Its energies had sustained her for only minutes, then the bloom of health had started to fade again. Octavia's energies had lasted longer, but now they too must be exhausted. Cicely dreaded to look in the mirror and confirm her fear. She didn't want it to be true. Yet try as she might, it was inevitable that she'd have to see what was happening to her.

When Cicely finally stared at her reflection, she turned away in despair. Her skin wasn't simply pale, it was taking on that horrible transparency that it had before. Her hair had a scraggly, somehow desiccated look, like weeds dried out by the sun. She was changing, only this time the transition was occurring much more rapidly.

Along with the visible changes, there were the other manifestations of her affliction. Her vision was pained by the rushlight burning by her bedstead but exceedingly keen when she glanced into shadows. Her flesh felt cold, but in an abstract way that distressed her because she was aware of the unnatural chill rather than any physical discomfort.

'The needle,' Cicely gasped. She hesitated before making any move, however, horrified by the desperation in her voice. The onyx needle was her only hope, and she clung to it like a drowning sailor to floating debris.

The tapestry was stretched across her lap. She grimaced when she saw the images of the flower and Octavia. Neither had offered her enough essence to sustain her. She needed something bigger and more substantial.

A screeching cry from the yard turned Cicely towards the window. She recognised Saint's angry intonation. The neighbour's cat, again. The sound of the gryph-hound lunging across the yard in pursuit of the trespasser ended when Samuel went outside to call Saint away from the fruitless chase.

Cicely smiled as she set the needle to the tapestry. She felt guilty over what had happened to Octavia, but the neighbour's cat, with its capricious torment of Saint, was another matter. She'd put an end to the feline's taunting.

Yet before she made the first stitch, Cicely's intention waned. Of what good would it be? The cat would only yield her a few hours of recovery and then she'd have to find something else to replenish her energies. She almost tossed the tapestry on the floor in her frustration.

Samuel's voice drifted back to her from the yard. 'I'm sorry, old fellow,' he was telling Saint. 'You might have caught that cat once, but you're just too old now.' There was a piteous sorrow in her father's tone as he talked to the gryph-hound. Cicely could remember when Saint had trotted alongside him on his hunts, sleek and powerful with bright plumage and sharp talons. That was many years ago.

The gryph-hound remembered those days too. Every time Samuel went out on a hunt, Saint tried to go with him. It couldn't understand the decrepitude that had stolen its vigour. She thought of the stiff, painful way it would emerge from its nest every morning. Perhaps the most merciful thing would be to put an end to its suffering.

Cicely set the needle back to the tapestry. Now she had a different subject for her work. She didn't need to have Saint before her to use as a model. The gryph-hound's image was distinct in her mind. She could copy perfectly from memory. A strange thrill crackled through her as she played the needle across the fabric. A larger subject, much greater than the flower or the cat, something far more precise and complete in her mind. There was an eerie energy in her hands as she fixated on the design. She felt at once both elated and revolted by the power held in her very fingertips.

She heard Samuel go back inside while she worked. While she still played the thread into the tapestry, she heard Saint screech again. The cat had returned for a second bout of teasing. She scowled at the distraction, trying to focus on her work. The sounds from the yard had unsettled her enough that her hand had slipped. It was only later that she spotted the mistake, and by then the picture of Saint was almost done. She'd made the gryph-hound's neck turn at a weird angle. Something she doubted anyone but herself would spot, but knowing it was there vexed her. She'd wanted to depict Saint peacefully sleeping, but her slip with the needle lent the image a ghastly quality.

A pained yowl rose from the yard. Cicely was stunned to hear the sound of something scrambling across the roof. She could hear tiles being knocked away and crashing to the ground. Then there came a horrible noise. Part squawk and part yelp, she knew at once that it was Saint.

Throwing back the bolt, Cicely rushed down the hall and out into the yard. The rest of the family was already out there, forming a circle around Samuel. Her father held Saint in his arms. The gryph-hound's head lolled brokenly across her father's knee. Nearby was a shattered tile from the roof.

'By Nagash, what happened?' Emelda gasped.

Samuel glanced around and shook his head. He nodded at a tuft of black fur in Saint's beak. 'He must have caught the cat by the tail,' Samuel declared. 'The cat got away and jumped onto the roof in its panic.' A wave at the tiles lying on the ground explained the rest. 'The cat knocked these tiles loose and one of them broke Saint's neck.'

Cicely could only stare in numbed shock. This wasn't what she'd wanted to happen. She'd wanted Saint to die peacefully in its sleep. 'I'm sorry,' she told her father.

Samuel stood up, Saint's body cradled in his arms. 'It was an accident,' he said, his voice catching slightly. He studied her for a moment. 'If you're feeling better, you can help me lay him under the larch. He always liked to sit out there and feel the breeze.'

Cicely glanced down at her hands. The colour had returned. The needle had done its work. Saint's essence had replenished her own. 'I'll get mattock and shovel,' she told her father, heading for the tool-shed. Emelda ushered their cousins back into the house, leaving her husband and daughter to their sombre task.

The little grave behind the house was soon dug. Cicely walked beside her father as they turned back home. She was ashamed that her deed had brought him added grief. Until they'd buried Saint, she hadn't fully appreciated how attached he'd been to the gryph-hound. Still, she rationalised, how much deeper would

his hurt be if it was her he was burying? That was, if the affliction would even leave enough of her to bury.

She'd been compelled to act as she had, reinvigorating herself with Saint's energy. The gryph-hound was much bigger than
a flower or a cat. She was certain its essence would sustain
her much longer. Perhaps it would even be enough to cure her
completely.

'He saved my life more times than I'm comfortable remembering,' Samuel said when they were walking through the yard. He
glanced over at the nest, which already seemed to have taken
on an abandoned quality. 'There was the time we'd been tracking a fell bat and the thing swooped down on me from the trees
and knocked me to the ground. Saint didn't hesitate but pounced
on its back before it could take wing again.'

'I'm sorry,' was all Cicely found herself able to say.

Samuel kicked one of the broken tiles lying on the ground,
breaking it into smaller fragments. 'The fickleness of misfortune,'
he grumbled. He tried to smile away his agitation as he turned
towards Cicely, but the effort vanished instantly. Instead, there
was concern in his face.

'What is it?' Cicely managed to ask, fear flashing through her.

Samuel bowed his head. 'It was stupid of me to take you with
me,' he said. 'I didn't realise how much helping dig the hole
would exhaust you.'

The fear concentrated itself in the pit of her stomach. 'I feel
fine,' she said, unable to keep a hint of uncertainty from her voice.

'You've been sick, and I just made things worse,' Samuel said.
'It was thoughtless. I should have been cautious. It is just that
you looked better...'

Cicely barely heard the rest. She had to keep from lifting her
hand. If she saw what she thought she would, then all restraint
would be lost. She might go mad if she found that horrible pallor
already creeping back.

Cicely made hurried apologies to her parents the moment she was home. She didn't tarry to listen to Samuel explain things to her mother but raced down to her room. She saw her bewildered cousins Barnabus and Amelia staring at her from the wood room before she slipped inside and closed the door behind her.

For many minutes she just stood there with her back against the door. Cicely prayed it was merely imagination suggested by her father's worry, but it seemed to her that her senses were already starting to revert. The shadows were vibrant while the light was painful. The awareness of a chill she couldn't feel was asserting itself again.

'No,' she protested. 'Even if it won't last, it can't be gone so soon.' Cicely clenched her hands in frustration, digging her nails into her palms. Finally, as she knew she must, she went to the mirror. She bit her lip to keep from screaming at what she saw. Far from sustaining her longer than Octavia's, Saint's essence had already been exhausted.

Cicely sat down and started to cry. All too soon her eyes became incapable of tears. The realisation snapped her back to reality. She tamped down on her emotions and tried to think. There had to be a reason the gryph-hound hadn't revitalised her for longer.

'Saint was old,' Cicely muttered. 'Octavia was young.' Given the natural course of things, how much life could have been left to Saint? Months, perhaps. Octavia might have had a decade more if left alone. Yes, that had to be it. She thought of what Pater Kosminski said about each life being measured by gravesands that trickled through the Glass of Nagash. When life grew short, the sands were few. When there were many years ahead, there was an abundance.

That had to be it! Saint had sustained her for such a short while because it had so little life left. The same with the flower. To keep herself going, she had to be more judicious about what images she sewed with Verderghast's needle. She had to pick young subjects with an abundance of life.

Cicely revolted at the thought and buried her face in the pillows. What was she? Some vampire sucking the life from those around her? No, she wouldn't become such a loathly thing!

The alternative was equally unthinkable. Cicely wracked her brain trying to devise a solution. Then a realisation came to her. She'd been careless before. She hadn't noticed the way she'd depicted Octavia, and perhaps that was why the cat had died. She'd made a mistake in her picture of Saint, giving it a broken neck. But if she was careful, if she was exacting with every twist of the needle...

It probably wasn't even necessary to kill. She could just draw off a little bit of essence. Just a small part to keep herself alive. Cicely was frightened by the idea, terrified that she was wrong. But the more she thought it over, the more she persuaded herself that she was right. She had to take the chance.

Timidly at first, she sat down and began to work on the tapestry. Once more she drew an image from memory. This time it was her cousin Barnabus. She was precise in his depiction, ensuring there was nothing that might portend sudden death. When she was certain there was no mark or mistake, she used red thread to add the smallest cut to the boy's hand. Certain that so slight a thing couldn't possibly deal him any serious hurt, she sat back and sighed. Gradually, she began to feel her energy returning to her.

When the soft groaning and snuffling had started, Cicely couldn't say. She became aware of it only when she heard Anya run down to the wood room. The cry that followed bordered on a scream. Instantly, she heard her parents dash from their room and hurry to the source of the sound.

'He cut himself on one of the broken tiles,' Anya was telling her parents. 'It started hurting him a little while ago.'

Cicely didn't dare open her door but pressed her ear against it. She dreaded to listen but couldn't do otherwise. She had to know.

Her mother's gasp of horror reached Cicely even through the panel. Samuel's voice was grim. 'It looks infected,' he said. 'Bones of Nagash, but it looks gangrenous!'

'He only cut himself a little while ago,' Anya objected, her tone pleading. 'It's such a small cut!'

'Small or not, this is serious,' Samuel insisted. 'Wrap a warm blanket around him. We'll take him to the healer. Pray it is more innocent than it looks.'

Cicely continued to listen while Samuel and Anya hurried away with Barnabus. For her father to decide it wouldn't wait until morning, that they needed to chance the streets of Felstein at night, she knew the gravity of the situation. She sickened at heart with the knowledge, because she knew Barnabus was going to die.

Just as she knew the child's essence was replenishing her own. Just as she knew the needle's magic would accept no half-measures. There wasn't any compromise. When it drew upon something's life force, it took everything that was left.

'It doesn't have to be a person,' Cicely groaned, weeping, as she crumpled to the floor. She pounded her fists against the boards. 'It doesn't have to be a person.'

But tonight, it had been a person, and nothing she could ever do would change that.

CHAPTER EIGHT

The gloom of Briardark had taken on a still more sinister aspect for Samuel. Many dark deeds had occurred in the forest, but none cast such a pall over his soul as Marden's death. That was a mark that would stay with him until he finally entered Nagash's keeping.

'If only I'd searched harder for the wolf,' Samuel chided himself as he prowled among the trees. He'd kept off returning to the forest longer than he'd intended. The disruption to his family demanded his attention at home, but at the last he'd gone back to Briardark. Even if Thayer weren't making noises about replacing him, he'd have come back. He wanted the wolf more than anyone in Felstein. If it was dead, he needed to see its carcass. If it was alive – or undead – he needed to see it destroyed.

Samuel followed a game trail used by deer and wild goats. If the wolf was still around, it was certain to seek prey. Even those undead with no need for sustenance often reverted to the habits they'd possessed in life, emptily pursuing old passions. The dire wolf would be no different. Not unless some greater will had imposed itself over the creature and commanded it to desist.

Samuel felt triumph swell inside him when he spotted a tuft of grey fur caught in some brambles beside the trail. When he examined it, however, he cursed his optimism. The fur was that of some hare, probably seeking shelter in the briars from a bat or an owl. He should have realised it was too close to the ground for what he was hunting. His eagerness was making him see what he wanted to see, not what was in fact there. It was a dangerous thing for any hunter to allow.

'Maybe I missed some sign that day because I was tired and wanted to go home,' Samuel said. He stopped and leaned against his boar spear. He had to tamp down on this self-recrimination. Now that he wasn't indulging in blaming Cicely for her brother's death, he'd come back to blaming himself. He knew it was mental poison, as venomous as a manticore's sting. If he didn't stop, he'd never have a moment's rest. His judgement would be too jaded to trust and he'd never accomplish anything.

'If the wolf is still out there,' Samuel mused, 'then it's become too wary to make old mistakes.' The theory wasn't a pleasant one to consider, but he knew it fit all the evidence. The predator hadn't made any raids on Felstein's flocks and herds as it had before. Now it was exhibiting restraint and caution. The animal had been hard enough to track when its habits included a savage arrogance. Samuel was intimidated by the idea that the wolf would be even harder to find now.

'If it is still out there.' The beasthunter pounded his metal fist against a tree trunk in his frustration. Frightened fools in the village insisted the wolf was still around, people whipped up into terrified idiocy by Thayer's manipulation. No one had actually seen the beast since it had killed Marden. There wasn't even anyone who could reliably claim to have heard its howls. Not so much as a single paw print had been found to show that the wolf was still stalking the area.

Samuel had to pry the bronze fingers free from the trunk with his other hand. As he did so, he gashed his palm on a splinter. He scolded himself for losing his temper and licked blood from the cut, wincing at the sting of his tongue against the split skin. Surrendering to his anger was a bit of his own stupidity. He'd have to give up now and go back, abandon his plan to stay out overnight. The smell of fresh blood would call out to too many things in the forest. If it was just the wolf that might be drawn to his scent, he'd have relished their meeting, but there were too many other creatures in Briardark that would now show interest in him. Blood-bats, for one. No match for a man by themselves, they'd form up in an overpowering flock once they caught the smell of blood in the air. Then there were the shrouded martens, rapacious animals as long as a man's leg that went into an utter frenzy once they caught the scent of wounded prey.

To die in combat with Marden's killer was a prospect that Samuel wouldn't shy away from, but he'd no intention of letting himself be brought down by Briardark's other denizens. Especially in pursuit of an adversary that was probably already dead.

'Back home,' Samuel said with a sigh, binding a rag around his hand. It wouldn't help with the sanguinary scent, but at least he could avoid spattering the ground with drops of blood that would encourage anything taking an interest in him to follow his trail into Felstein. That had happened once, when a hungry barrow-bear had tracked him as far as the square before being driven off by the townsfolk.

The journey back to Felstein passed without incident. At least until the beasthunter was in the town itself. There, Samuel found people watching him from windows and doorways. His neighbours regarded him with severe, sullen expressions, and none offered him greeting when he passed them by. It was Thayer's handiwork. The townmaster had whipped up their fears to a pitch. Without the wolf's carcass draped across his shoulders, Samuel's return only played into Thayer's rhetoric.

The walk through town felt as though it would never end. The brooding atmosphere within Briardark hadn't felt half so hostile as what Samuel now experienced. Angry eyes were set upon him from every direction, watching his every move. If he stood at the centre of a spectrestorm with malicious spirits wailing all around him, Samuel doubted he would feel any more exposed than he did now. When Thayer inevitably appointed another beasthunter, Samuel wondered if there would be any place for his family at all in Felstein or if they would be driven out of the town as pariahs. He was too old to do like Rukh and try to start over somewhere else.

As he approached his home, Samuel found a visitor waiting for him outside the gate. Even from a distance he recognised Alastair Greimhalt. He stopped in his tracks and braced himself for the discussion he knew was coming. He tried to mentally prepare himself for a subject that should have been settled long ago but for Alastair's dogged persistence.

'Herr Helmgaart, a few words with you, if I may,' Alastair said when Samuel drew near.

Samuel started to walk past him and reached for the gate. 'You'll forgive me, but it has been a long day. I'm weary, and at the moment the only thing I want to do is go to bed.'

Alastair followed Samuel into the yard. 'While you still have a bed to sleep in,' he commented. 'I know your search for the wolf was fruitless. There isn't anyone in Felstein who isn't talking about it.'

Samuel spun around and fixed Alastair with a cold stare. 'Let them go out into Briardark and see if they can do any better,' he growled.

'I quite agree with you,' Alastair said. 'Safe in town, few of them have any idea of the hazards you endure out in the wilderness. It is easy to sit back in the Skintaker's Swallow and theorise about how different things would be if you were beasthunter. A far different thing to be the beasthunter and have to perform the feats you claim are so simple.'

'You might try having this talk with your father,' Samuel stated. He turned to go into his house, but Alastair laid a restraining hand on his shoulder.

'I might,' he agreed. 'I might very well do just that. If I had the proper incentive to do so.'

Here it is, Samuel thought. He let impatience show on his face as he waited for Alastair to continue. He took some small consolation that his visitor was uncomfortable broaching the subject on his own and made a few fumbling efforts before finally settling on the track he wanted to follow.

'My father has ambitions to appoint his own man as beasthunter,' Alastair declared. 'That is why he's been putting so much pressure on you. He thinks that by doing so he'll strengthen his own position in Felstein.' Just the trace of a smile crept onto the youth's face. 'But it doesn't have to be that way. I could convince him to change his mind. Stop the pressure.'

'Why would you do that?' Samuel already knew the answer, but the question had to be asked. He wanted to hear it in Alastair's own words.

'I want your daughter,' Alastair said bluntly. 'I want Cicely for my wife.' Abruptly, the confidence and surety evaporated. 'She's the only woman for me. You might not believe this, but I love her.' He shifted uneasily from one foot to the other. 'I've defied my father for her sake more than once. He's tried to arrange any number of more "profitable" marriages for me, but I've remained steadfast. Cicely is who I want.'

'She doesn't want you,' Samuel said with equal bluntness. 'She doesn't love you.'

Alastair scowled at that, a pained look in his eyes. 'She'd learn to,' he said. 'She'd want for nothing with me. My father's the most powerful and prosperous man in Felstein. One day everything he has will be mine, and I'll share it all with Cicely.'

'Maybe she doesn't care about any of that,' Samuel pointed out. He took umbrage at the youth's certainty.

Surprisingly, Alastair conceded the point. 'Yes, maybe she doesn't. She's certainly told me so many times.' A calculating gleam came into his gaze. 'But she does care about you. She cares what happens to her family. She knows what's been happening. She knows there's a threat to your position. I think she'd do anything to help you. All you have to do is ask.'

Samuel had to hold back the anger he felt boiling up inside him. This was extortion of the lowest sort. 'What if I did and she still rejects you?'

'Make her agree.' Alastair shook his head. 'I don't see how you have any other choice. My father won't stop once he's appointed a new beasthunter. You'll lose the house, your property. Then what'll you do? Do you think anyone will take you in as you did your cousins?'

'And you can keep all of that from happening?' Samuel scoffed. 'I think you underestimate Thayer's greed.'

'And you underestimate my father's pride,' Alastair retorted. 'To him it isn't about wealth or power. It's about building a legacy.' He tapped himself on the chest. 'I am that legacy. I am the proof that what he builds will continue on after him. That's what's important. That's why when he learns I will marry there's nothing he won't do if I ask him. He wants to know his legacy is secure, that there'll be grandchildren to carry on. That's my father's dream, Samuel, and against that, he won't scruple over leaving you in your post.' His eyes glittered with anticipation. 'All you need to do is let Cicely be my wife.'

'You'll intercede with your father if I intercede with my daughter?' Samuel put the arrangement in its baldest terms.

'We'll both profit,' Alastair smiled.

Samuel's bronze fist wiped the smile away. Surprised by the sudden attack, Alastair fell to the ground. Before he could rise, the hunter was crouched over him. His metal hand came crashing down again, smacking the youth's face. 'Swine!' he cursed, pummelling him again. 'You dare presume. You think I'd sell my daughter to you?' Each word was punctuated by another blow. Dazed by the flurry of punches, Alastair mounted only a feeble effort to defend himself. Blood streamed from his split lip and broken nose.

'You wretched cur!' Samuel grabbed a fistful of Alastair's hair and pounded his head against the ground. A red haze was before his eyes now. All the anger inside him was rushing out. The tipping point had been reached.

'Samuel!' Only faintly did he hear his name being shouted. When he felt someone grab him from behind and try to pull him off Alastair, he spun about, ready to strike them. His punch froze in mid-swing when he saw it was Emelda. His wife's eyes were bright with horror. 'Stop it, Samuel! You'll kill him!'

The words had the effect of cold water, snapping him out of the red haze that had seized him. Samuel stepped back from Alastair. 'Aye, go slinking back to your father,' he snarled as the youth made a scrambling dash for the gate. He continued to glare after him as he bolted away down the street.

'Oh, Samuel, what will we do now?' Emelda took his hand, wiping his bloodied knuckles with her apron.

Samuel hugged her to him. 'Not what that despicable mongrel wants us to do,' he assured her. 'I'll not pay for our security with Cicely's happiness. That's one thing I'll never do.'

'But what *will* we do?' Emelda persisted.

'I don't know,' Samuel confessed. 'We'll have to find another way.' His voice dropped to a pained growl. 'If I could just catch that damn wolf, everything would change. But if it isn't dead, I'm sure it has left Briardark.'

He pushed away from his wife, holding her at arm's length, and stared into her eyes. 'Don't speak a word of this to Cicely. I don't want her to know what Alastair said.'

Emelda glanced back at the house and the open doorway. 'Too late for that,' she said. 'We could hear you from the front room. Cicely heard every word.'

Samuel shook his head. He'd wanted to spare his daughter from ever knowing about Alastair's extortionate proposal. After the way he'd treated her, letting her make herself sick with guilt over Marden, the very last thing he wanted was something else for her to feel guilty about. The past few days she'd looked much like her old self. She didn't need this to worry over and make herself sick again.

Cicely slipped out unseen and hurried towards Lucilla's house. Her mind was in turmoil. She needed someone to talk to. Someone to confide in.

The bakehouse was closing down for the day. Cicely watched Lucilla's parents sweeping out the shop. She didn't want them to see her, so she slipped around to the back of the building and tapped on Lucilla's window. Her friend opened it a moment later, surprised by the unorthodox visit.

'Can I come in?' Cicely asked. 'Something's happened.'

'Of course.' Lucilla helped her in through the window.

Once she was inside, Cicely told Lucilla what had happened. 'My father just thrashed Alastair. Beat him black and blue. He might've killed him.' She sat down on the edge of Lucilla's bed and gave her friend a frightened look. 'He *would* have killed him if he knew that Alastair kept me from stopping Marden before he went into Briardark.'

Lucilla gasped. 'Oh, Cicely, you mustn't tell him!' she implored. 'For everyone's sake!'

'Is it because you still love Alastair?' Cicely wondered.

The question brought a flush to Lucilla's face. 'I *used* to care about him, but that was long ago,' she said, then hastily added, 'But I'm worried about your father. Thayer would hang him... or worse.'

Cicely felt horror at that idea. 'I thought my father didn't care about me... because of Marden.' She clenched her eyes, wondering why when she felt so distraught, no tears would come. 'He was so cold to me. He blamed me for Marden's death. I thought I'd lost his love.'

Lucilla stood near the window. Cicely could see the pained sympathy in her friend's eyes. 'How awful. How awful.' She, at least, was able to weep.

'But I was wrong, Lucy,' Cicely said, a ray of joy managing to slip into her voice. 'However bitter he seemed, he never stopped caring. That's why my father beat up Alastair.'

'I don't understand,' Lucilla admitted.

Cicely rose and took Lucilla's hand. She felt her friend try to pull away and wondered how cold her grip might feel to someone else. 'Alastair tried to coerce my father into forcing me to marry him. I didn't think even a Greimhalt could sink so low. He threatened my family, Lucy. Thought my father would hand me off like a bit of goods to be bartered.'

'Alastair?' Lucilla dumbly repeated the name, stunned by what she was hearing. Emotion shone in her eyes, defiance stiffening her lip. 'Alastair doesn't love you,' she declared.

'Oh, he made that quite clear,' Cicely agreed. 'He's obsessed, but he isn't in love. He's simply determined to possess someone he can't have.' The smile she turned to Lucilla was sorrowful. 'I'm sorry, but that's the kind of man he is.'

Lucilla leaned back against the wall. 'I know he is,' she said. Suddenly she came bolt upright. 'Cicely! Your father. If he beat Alastair like you say, *he's* sure to tell *his* father. Thayer will put Samuel in irons, or worse. What will you do?'

Cicely paced the room. Dark thoughts swirled through her mind. 'I need to think, Lucy. Can you let me stay here for a little while?'

'Surely you don't even need to ask,' Lucilla assured her.

'Thank you.' Cicely sat down in the wicker chair in one corner of her friend's room. She brooded over the threat Alastair posed to her family. It was in her power to make him go away. She furtively looked up at Lucilla, pained to see the anguish in her eyes. Alastair was no good, just hurting everyone around him.

'I should be going,' Cicely suddenly said. She made her way to the window.

'But Cicely, what will you do about Alastair?' Lucilla asked.

Her friend didn't see the coldness in Cicely's eyes when she replied, 'What I have to do.'

Cicely went straight to her room when she returned home. She took up the tapestry and stared at the half-finished portraits of her family. She looked across the figures of Barnabus and the animals. They'd each been a sacrifice, an offering made to sustain her own life. She had to accept that now. They'd died by her hand. Died to keep her alive.

She hadn't meant to kill her cousin and he certainly hadn't warranted death, but the needle's magic wouldn't accept anything less. The life energy that had been conveyed into her by the child's death had been great enough to sustain her for days. Far longer than that taken from Octavia or Saint.

Perhaps that was the key, Cicely mused. The needle's magic wanted a human life, not that of an animal. That sick feeling she'd had when Verderghast gave her the object was more intuition than imagining. Despite her efforts to tell herself otherwise, it did have to be a person.

So be it. Now that she knew the price the magic demanded, she could show discretion. It was her choice whose image was sewn into the tapestry.

A shudder passed through her as she walked to her chair. What she contemplated was horrible, yet she saw no other way. If she had to kill people to sustain herself, then she would take the essence of villains. Draw off the lives of bad people who brought only cruelty and misery to those around them. Her grim thoughts focused upon Alastair. If he wasn't already the petty tyrant Thayer was, then it was simply because his father still held all the power. The threats he'd made against Samuel... the demands he'd made of her... these were proof of Alastair's true character.

Yes, Cicely decided as she took up the needle. She'd create Alastair's image. Draw off his energies. The conceited rogue was so determined to become part of her life. Now he would, but in a way he'd never have imagined.

Cicely could hear her parents talking in the other room while she worked. Their words were muffled by the intervening doors and walls, but she knew they were talking about Alastair and what to do about his demands. Well, soon that wouldn't be a problem. When she was finished, there'd be no reason for anyone to worry about what trouble Alastair might bring them.

Focused upon her work, Cicely was startled when she heard a firm knock at her door. She stared at the nearly completed image of Alastair. Ordinarily she'd have said that kind of detail would've required days to create, but with the strange onyx needle's spell, she knew it might have only been hours or even minutes. All awareness of time vanished when she tapped into its magic.

Samuel's voice followed the knocking. 'Cicely? May I come in?'

She rose and unbolted the door, stepping back so her father could enter.

Samuel looked around the room, his eyes briefly glancing over the tapestry. Then he focused on her. 'I'm sorry about what happened. Sorry you had to hear any of what occurred between me and Alastair.'

Cicely nodded and gave him a smile. 'I'm not. He needed a good thrashing, and you were the one to give it to him.'

He returned her smile with one of his own. 'You weren't supposed to approve of that. Or at least, you aren't supposed to say so.' He massaged his bruised knuckles. When he noticed her looking at them, he laughed. 'I didn't scrape them on Alastair's face. I was foolish enough to punch a tree while I was in the forest. The tree won.'

Cicely joined in his laughter. The humour broke down the awkwardness of the situation. The tension drained out from the room, but only for a moment. Samuel walked around and his attention returned to the tapestry. He caught it up from where it lay across the chair. Cicely held her breath while he examined it.

'Still working on the family portrait?' Samuel asked. His expression turned sombre when he shifted the cloth around and saw Barnabus and the animals. There was a wistful look a moment later. Cicely could almost read his mind. He was thinking she'd added them as a memento of those they'd lost. He thought she'd sewn them after their deaths, not before.

Samuel shifted the cloth still further and spotted Alastair's nearly completed image. His visage darkened and he set the tapestry down. 'Cicely, you don't have to do anything you don't want to do,' he said.

'What do you mean?' she asked, puzzled by his tone.

'I mean the marriage,' he said, jabbing a finger at the tapestry. 'Adding Alastair to the family portrait.' Samuel scowled, and colour crept into his face. 'He must have been badgering you for some time, trying to make you agree.' Samuel brushed his hand across her cheek. 'You don't have to listen to his threats. Don't think for a moment your mother and I want that.'

Understanding blossomed in Cicely's mind. Her father thought she'd added Alastair to the tapestry because she'd resigned herself to marrying him. Any fear that he might suspect the awful magic she was using vanished from her heart. A sense of relief filled her.

Samuel smiled, misconstruing the cause of her relief. 'We'll find another way,' he promised. Again, he jabbed a finger at the tapestry. 'Get *that* out of your head. We'll leave Felstein before it comes to that.'

Cicely just nodded. 'I'll try, father,' she said. They spoke of other subjects for a time before Emelda called them both to dinner. Cicely barely remembered the meal or anything that was discussed at the table. Her mind was on the tapestry and Alastair's incomplete figure.

When she returned to her room, Cicely had made a decision. While the essence she'd drawn from Barnabus was still sustaining her, she wouldn't finish Alastair's picture. But once she felt the change coming over her again, it would be time to complete the grim task.

Two days elapsed before Emelda made a remark about her daughter looking ill. Peering into her mirror, Cicely saw the ghastly affliction creeping back into her flesh. She took up the needle and quickly finished Alastair's picture. Around his neck she stitched a noose.

A few hours later, Lucilla rushed over to bring Cicely the terrible news. 'Alastair's dead!' she exclaimed, the whole of the Helmgaart household attending her every word as she related the details. 'He was working in his father's barn. Somehow he fell from the loft.' Her voice cracked with emotion. Cicely could see that even now she hadn't quite got over her feelings for Alastair.

'The fall wouldn't have killed him, except as he fell, a rope tangled around his neck,' Lucilla continued, pausing to collect herself after each grisly detail. 'He was all alone in the barn. He might have hung there for hours, slowly strangling.' She brushed away her tears. 'By the time Thayer went to see what was keeping his son, it was too late.'

Emelda embraced Lucilla as she began to cry. Anya and the children appeared to be infected by the display of sorrow. Samuel's expression was stony. He couldn't muster much sympathy for the dead man.

'A terrible accident,' was all the beasthunter would say.

Cicely had no such illusions. Octavia had been an experiment. Saint's death had been intended as mercy. Barnabus had truly been an accident. Alastair, however, required a more deliberate word. An ugly word that sent a chill through Cicely's revitalised body.

Murder.

CHAPTER NINE

'The whole town is abuzz with Alastair Greimhalt's death.' Lugos punctuated the statement by taking a sip of the hot toddy near his hand. It was an open question whether the farmer was visiting Samuel to talk or to drink the brew Emelda had prepared.

'A terrible thing.' Emelda supplied the words. Samuel certainly wasn't going to express any regret that Alastair was dead. He kept silent while his guest continued.

'Thayer's been insisting that his boy died accidentally.' Lugos leaned back and folded his hands around the steaming mug. 'Of course, whatever the townmaster says is what everybody repeats, but I think there's more than a few of us who don't believe it.'

Samuel frowned at the remark. He wondered if anybody had seen his manhandling of Alastair. He didn't think someone as proud as Alastair would have told anyone he'd been thrashed by the beasthunter, but there was always the chance that Thayer could've wormed it out of him. If that had been the case though,

Samuel was confident that the townmaster would be claiming murder rather than a mere accident.

'What do you think happened to him?' Emelda asked, giving Samuel a worried glance.

Lugos didn't notice the unspoken exchange between husband and wife. 'Well, it would be a remarkable thing, an accident like that. If there was a witch about, it might get you thinking about hexes and enchantments.' He shook his head and took another sip. 'I'm of the mind that Alastair did it himself.'

'A suicide?' Samuel let the morbid word echo through the room. Lugos nodded sagely.

'Thayer's been pushing the boy hard lately,' the farmer declared. 'Badgering him about his responsibilities. Trying to get him to surrender his indolent and wastrel ways. I think it got to be too much for him and he saw the noose as preferable to his father's persistent displeasure.'

Samuel considered the possibility, trying to reconcile that level of despair with the arrogant goon who'd tried to bully him into making Cicely marry him. There just didn't seem any way to make those characteristics agree. Unless Alastair's brain had some kind of sickness that made him capable of shifting between such extremes of personality.

'That's why Thayer's so insistent it was an accident,' Lugos elaborated. 'He doesn't want that stigma attached to Alastair.'

'More than just stigma,' Samuel said. 'If Alastair's death was suicide, his body couldn't be interred in Nagash's Garden. Pater Kosminski would have to perform rites to bind Alastair's spirit to the corpse, then cremate it and scatter the ashes into the river.'

Lugos winced at the hunter's words. 'True. If the proper measures aren't taken, Alastair may return and his vicious spirit will prey upon Felstein.' He set down his mug and curled his fingers into the sign of Nagash, invoking the dread god's intercession with the malignants.

'So Thayer won't press anything that puts the idea of an accident into doubt,' Samuel commented. It gave him a strange sort of relief to make that observation. If Thayer did know about the altercation between himself and Alastair, the townmaster would be very cautious doing anything about it. His control over Felstein wasn't so absolute that he was able to make the community put themselves in jeopardy. With the least encouragement, people like Lugos might start saying what they thought openly – and spread the idea to others about how the body needed to be disposed of. No matter whose son Alastair had been.

'He might be in mourning right now,' Lugos said, 'but Thayer's still got a mind like one of the ratkin. He'll do whatever he must to maintain his status and position.'

Samuel considered that aspect. Thayer had been Felstein's leading citizen for so long that it was almost impossible to imagine something toppling him from his perch. Emelda's reaction to the suggestion was more heartfelt.

'You can't believe that. Even of him. He's just lost his son.' Her voice cracked at the last. The Helmgaarts could relate only too well to that sort of grief.

'Perhaps,' Lugos conceded. 'Maybe he had some genuine affection for Alastair beyond his expectations for having the boy continue after him.' He sipped again at his drink. 'I still don't believe Thayer would allow any emotions to offset that calculating brain of his.'

'Emotions have never swayed Thayer before,' Samuel reminded Emelda.

'Rukh's dispossession is proof enough of that,' Lugos said. His expression became solemn. 'I was sorry to hear about little Barnabus. An awful tragedy.'

'It was an accident,' Samuel replied. For some reason, the statement sent an uneasy horripilation through him. He couldn't place why he was disturbed; he only knew that he was. It was like when he'd walk the paths of Briardark and suddenly stop only to discover a snake hidden in the brush ahead of him. A quiet warning too subtle for conscious recognition.

'Poor Barnabus cut himself and an ill humour was drawn into the wound,' Emelda explained. It was an all-too-common sort of death. At least a few of Felstein's inhabitants entered into Nagash's dominion each year after cutting themselves with an old knife or a rusty hoe.

Lugos was sympathetic. 'I lost a brother five years ago that way,' he said. 'When Nagash beckons, only the Stormcasts can ignore his summons.' He turned and locked eyes with Samuel. 'Not that anyone should be too quick to court the Lord of Undeath. We've a real problem, Samuel, if Thayer gets Pater Kosminski to bury his boy.'

'Talk will only take you so far,' Samuel cautioned. 'Are you really prepared to use action? Because I know if anyone had tried to keep me from burying Marden, no words would have kept me from it. Thayer's not going to back down just because you tell him you're afraid his son's spirit will become a malignant.'

'People won't stand for it,' Lugos said.

Samuel sighed and leaned back. 'People will stand for anything they've been conditioned to stand for. Thayer holds debts against more than half this town. Say anything against him and he'll call in those debts as retribution. Most folks won't act when there could be consequences. And you can be sure Thayer will make examples of the first ones who cause him trouble.'

'The man couldn't be that vile,' Emelda objected.

Samuel gripped her hand. 'You always try to see the best in someone, even when they're at their worst. But just think for a moment. He kicked Rukh and Anya out of their home for far less cause.' He thought of Alastair's arrogance and entitlement. These were things that he'd learned from his father. 'Maybe Thayer won't even wait for a reason,' Samuel suggested. 'If he's really hurting because of Alastair's death, he might take out his anger on anyone he has power over.' The hunter was quiet as he reflected on his own treatment of Cicely. 'If he's despondent, he might decide others need to share in his misery.'

'He can only push so far,' Lugos persisted. 'Everyone has a breaking point.' He set down his mug and rose from the table. 'If Alastair returns and starts haunting Felstein, nobody will care what kind of hold Thayer has over them. They'll start worrying about their lives and their families.'

The argument had a bitter irony to it for Samuel. It echoed what he'd been told when his neighbours had spoken to him about the dire wolf. 'Maybe,' he said, 'but the first ones to speak out will suffer for it. The individual who stands up will be punished, and it takes a long time to rally a group.'

'Be that as it may,' Lugos said as he started to leave, 'the town won't stay idle if Thayer buries his boy and the proper rites are ignored. Just think about the fear that ran rampant when everyone was worried about your wolf. People will be far more afraid if there's a *chainghast* stalking the streets.'

Samuel winced to hear the beast that killed Marden referred to as 'your wolf', but Lugos had given him something to think about. It had needed Thayer's agitation to stir the community against the hunter and demand the wolf be caught. If Alastair's spirit did return, the people wouldn't need anything else to whip up their fears. 'You might be right,' he told Lugos as he shook the man's hand.

Lugos nodded to Emelda. 'Thank you for the drink,' he said before leaving the house.

'Do you think he's right to be worried?' Emelda asked Samuel when they were alone. 'Do you think Alastair will come back?' There was a tremor in her tone. No inhabitant of Shyish regarded the menace posed by the restless dead lightly.

'If it really was an accident, no,' Samuel said. 'My brother-in-law lives in Gothghul Hollow, and he's made a study of gheists and spectres. I remember him saying that the way someone dies is nearly as much a factor in whether they come back as a malignant as the sort of life they led is. An accident, sudden and unexpected, doesn't usually create a nighthaunt. At best there might be a residual presence, more like an image or reflection than anything with any awareness within it.'

'But if it wasn't an accident?' Emelda prodded him.

Samuel sighed. 'Then things would be different. Suicide, murder, death in battle, these are the things that make a spirit resist descending into an underworld. At least, that's what Hephzibah's husband always claimed.'

'If that's true, then Thayer can't be allowed to bury his son.' Even now, there was a trace of pity for the townmaster in Emelda's tone.

Samuel held her to him and ran his fingers through her hair. 'I'm afraid no one will stop him,' he said. 'Not until it's too late.'

Unnoticed by her parents, Cicely closed her bedroom door, shutting out their voices. The essence she'd drawn off Alastair was already fading. Her affliction was returning with horrid rapidity. The terrible corruption that twisted her senses was again asserting its capricious peculiarities. She'd already noted the way light hurt her eyes while shadows became clear and vibrant. Now she felt the same maddening inversion with her hearing.

Anya and her remaining children were in the wood room, their mother trying to comfort them in the loss of their brother. There was only ten feet between her room and where her cousins played, yet their sounds were faint and muffled, as though reaching her from a great distance.

The front room, where her parents had received Lugos, was much farther away, yet Cicely had heard every word. She'd even sensed the emotions wrapped into those words with a keenness beyond mere sound. The morbid turn the conversation had taken upset her, and she wondered if it was precisely because she'd be troubled by it that her affliction made it so easy to hear. Much as she had wanted to close the door and try to blot out the voices, she knew that she couldn't. However upsetting, there was a fascination that wouldn't be denied.

By the time Lugos finally left, Cicely felt as though a millstone was pressing down upon her. All the speculation about Alastair's death and – more importantly – what would happen to his spirit oppressed her. She'd resigned herself to the youth's death, justifying it in a thousand different ways. But she'd never stopped to think about the consequences.

Killing Barnabus had been an accident, but killing Alastair had been deliberate. That was murder, a thing almost certain to provoke vengeful manifestations. Cicely could almost resign herself to such a thing if it was just herself who might be in peril. Sadly, the ways of spirits and the undead weren't so clear. She tried to imagine how such creatures, existing in that twilight between life and death, perceived the world around them. Certainly, there were enough stories about malignants seeking revenge that lacked the capacity to recognise their killer and so would attack any mortal who crossed their path. She thought of the story of the ferryman who drowned at the edge of a swamp and whose wraith haunted the area for centuries, strangling anyone who tried to cross the fens.

Such a creature haunting Felstein was a horror for which she'd be responsible. It was her hand that had killed Alastair, as surely as if she'd stuck a knife into him. She remembered something from one of Pater Kosminski's sermons, that spirits, particularly those fated to become nighthaunts, experienced revelations about their deaths and learned things unknown to them in life. Alastair, she was sure, would know he'd been murdered by magic and that she was responsible. She could imagine his wrath when he rose from his grave as one of the undead. He'd be like the ferryman, lashing out at whoever he could find.

Dread roared through Cicely's heart. She sat down and took up the tapestry. Her eyes fixed on Alastair's image. Why had she ever done it? What madness had provoked her so?

Not madness, she corrected herself. Survival. To live, Cicely needed the needle's magic. There was nothing more to it.

Agitated by what she'd heard, already weakened by Alastair's dissipating energy, an inexorable weariness fell upon Cicely. Slumber took her while she sat in her chair, the tapestry thrown across her legs like a blanket.

The sleep that crept upon Cicely was anything but restful. Foul dreams beset her. Dreams of death. Useless, senseless deaths. She saw Marden, his body ripped by the wolf's fangs. In his hands he gripped the half-finished carving. At first it was a mammoth, then it transformed into a wolf. Her brother stared at her with dead eyes, and she heard him speak. 'My life is yours,' the nightmare said.

Then she was looking upon the streets of Felstein. She saw Alastair's grave, the largest and most magnificent in the cemetery. The heavy marble slab slid away, and from the casket below, a dark shadow billowed upward, a shrouded form draped in chains. Anguished laughter cackled from the apparition as it sped into the town. The chainghast drifted through barred doors, seeking... ever seeking. At last, it descended upon her house, seeping through the wall itself. She could hear its vengeful groan as it hurtled towards her mother and wrapped its spectral fetters around Emelda's throat. Cicely flung herself at the spectre, but her fists passed uselessly through the phantom. All the while her ears were filled with her mother's croaking burble as she fought for breath, her face turning purple...

'Mother!' Cicely cried out as she snapped free of her nightmare. Her dazed eyes swept about the confines of her room, half expecting to see the chainghast crouching in one of the corners. Only a dream, or was it something more? A premonition? A warning of what would come to pass?

'No! I can stop it!' Cicely vowed. Her fingers closed about the needle. She shifted the tapestry around so that she'd have an open spot to work with. If Thayer was the one who insisted his son's death was an accident, then he was the menace that had to be eliminated. Without Thayer to influence them, the town would take a prudent approach. They'd cremate Alastair and cast the ashes into the river. There'd be nothing buried in the graveyard to manifest itself as a malignant. There'd be nothing for Felstein to fear then.

Cicely felt regret at the necessity of doing that to Alastair. Treating his body in such a fashion would condemn his spirit to wander the lowest and most ill-favoured of the underworlds, but it was the only way to ensure he wouldn't come back. She could sympathise with Thayer not wanting to condemn his son to such a fate. She was proud that Samuel had expressed an equal determination in regard to Marden.

Pangs of empathy wouldn't stop her, however. Both to replenish her own vitality and to protect Felstein from Alastair's spirit, she had to act. She set needle to thread and began to work. It wasn't as easy for her to picture Thayer in her mind. She wasn't as familiar with him as she had been with his son or Barnabus or Saint. More, there kept flashing through her brain that grotesque scene of the chainghast strangling her mother. It was a supreme effort to keep her focus. So intense did her concentration become that it seemed that her hands flew about the tapestry with a life entirely of their own.

At times a flicker of doubt nagged Cicely while she worked. She knew it was death that she was invoking. As certain and unalterable as the trickling gravesands at the edge of Shyish. She thought instead not of Thayer as a person but of all the malicious things he'd done. The hurt and pain he'd caused so many people, not just her cousins and her father. And always there was that terrifying image of her strangled mother to spur her onwards. It was in her power to keep that from happening.

The needle dove in and out of the cloth, tireless as a Kharadron machine. Cicely shifted the tapestry around as she worked, but such was the swirl of fears and fancies that sought to disrupt her concentration that she didn't truly observe what she was doing until it was done.

'Sigmar!' Cicely gasped when the needle fell still and her hands drew back from the tapestry. All the images that had tormented her as she worked faded from her mind. Nothing could be more nightmarish than what she now gazed upon. While she'd held the needle, her perceptions had been befogged by the daze of her affliction. Now there was no such veil between herself and what she'd created. She lurched to one side and vomited her dinner onto the floor.

She took up the tapestry, desperately trying to deny the evidence of her eyes. It was a trick, another of the hideous deceits brought on by her affliction. Cicely stepped to the window, letting the moonlight shine down on the cloth. She moaned as the light displayed the image of a red-haired woman instead of a bald, paunchy man. A woman with deep eyes and sharp features. Features Cicely knew as well as she knew her own.

She wiped the spew from her lips with her sleeve and looked again at the image. Without being aware of what her hands were doing, Cicely hadn't added Thayer into the tapestry. Instead, she'd completed her mother's picture. There was a heavy coil around Emelda's throat and the face was almost black. Cicely thought to the nightmare scene that had played out in her imagination. It was that scene that had been communicated into her fingers, that horrible moment she'd depicted with needle and thread.

'Please, no,' Cicely begged. She didn't care about her father's warnings now. She'd grovel before Nagash and plead that what she feared wouldn't happen. She sprang across the room and grabbed her mirror. Horror stared back at her – a face that was flush with health and rich in colour. A visage ripe with stolen vitality.

Feeling sick to the core of her being, Cicely took the tapestry and threw it under her bed. Then she turned and opened her door. The house was quiet, wrapped in the perfect silence that occurs just before dawn. The darkness wasn't quite complete when she started into the hall. She could see a flicker of light coming from the front room. A frightful compulsion took hold of her. Cicely was horrified to go further, but it was impossible to stay where she was. She had to confirm her mounting fear. To see for herself the evil she'd caused.

There was a rushlight clamped into a little tin holder standing on the table, but its glow wasn't what cast the flickering red hue about the room. That came from the hearth, where a bed of embers smouldered. Cicely stepped around the table and saw her worst fears realised. She tried to scream, but all that left her throat was a terrified gasp.

An iron stand leaned over the hearth. It had double hooks from which a big pot normally hung. One of the chains had snapped, and the pot sagged from the remaining links. The broken length was caught tightly around Emelda's neck. Cicely tried to reconstruct the weird scene. Her mother would have stirred the embers to start a fire before swinging the pot out over it. For whatever reason, she'd knelt down towards the fire again after moving the pot. One of the chains had snapped and in a freakish manner had coiled around her neck.

Cicely wept as she imagined the scene. One of her mother's hands was pulling at the chain while the other lay stretched on the floor, coated in soot. The floor showed black marks where she'd struggled to keep herself propped up. In the end, however, she'd slipped and fallen face-first into the embers. Cicely wondered how long her mother had struggled, the chain making it impossible for her to cry for help that was only a room away.

Agonised sobs quivered through Cicely as she thought of her mother's terrible death. A death she'd caused. Guilt managed what horror could not, and Cicely's ragged cry echoed through the house.

The sounds of Cicely's anguish roused the rest of the household. Anya, carrying her baby, got as far as the edge of the hallway. One glance at the figure lying sprawled by the hearth was enough to make her turn back. Firmly, she kept Amelia from seeing the body.

Samuel barely acknowledged Cicely as he dashed to the hearth. He dragged Emelda out of the fire, snapping the other chain and pulling the pot along with the body. He flipped her onto her back and frantically unwound the chain from her neck. He froze when he had it free and just stared down at his wife. A pained howl swelled up from him.

Cicely dared to look past her father at the body he crouched over. By some malicious caprice, Emelda's face was still recognisable, though it had been charred by the heat of the embers. In the flickering glow, it had a purplish cast to it. Exactly like her picture on the tapestry.

Horror compounded upon horror. Cicely felt her knees turn to jelly. The darkness that escorted her mind into oblivion was far more comforting than the accusations of her consciousness. For a moment she struggled against it, then she collapsed to the floor.

CHAPTER TEN

Carrion crows squawked from their perches on the gravestones while vultures soared through the fog overhead. A chill wind slithered across Felstein's cemetery, bearing with it Briardark's musky odour. On a rare, clear day, when the mists were low and the sun was high, the dark forest could be seen from the edge of the graveyard, ominous and brooding, as redolent of death as any tomb.

For the third time in as many weeks, Samuel found himself standing in Felstein's graveyard listening to Pater Kosminski recite the rites of the dead. First Marden, then little Barnabus, and now his beloved Emelda. As he watched the deacons lower the casket into the plot beside his son's grave, it was all he could do to keep from shouting over the funerary ritual and cursing every god he could name. Respect for his wife was the only restraint that held him back. Before the first shovel of earth was cast into the grave, he reached up to his neck and pulled at the skull-faced talisman of Nagash that he wore. The cord that held it snapped as he exerted his strength. He didn't even look at the talisman he'd worn since he was a child, just tossed it down into the grave.

Samuel was through with gods. What use was it to honour and worship them when they simply sat back and allowed such misery? From baleful Nagash to righteous Sigmar, he was done appealing to gods who didn't listen.

Cicely stood nearby, her eyes red from weeping. She looked so frail and vulnerable, pale and drawn as though her sorrow were eating her from the inside out. Samuel thought she looked even worse than when Marden had died. He knew that guilt had compounded her grief then and that his blaming of her had made it even worse. He worried now that in some way she was blaming herself for Emelda's death as well. *By Nagash, it would have been better if anyone else had found her mother*, Samuel told himself. He could just imagine the guilt she was feeling, that if she'd only been there sooner then her mother would be alive. He started to reach towards her, to offer some kind of comfort. For a moment his hand hovered near Cicely's shoulder, then he drew it back before she was even aware of the overture.

First Marden, now Emelda.

The beasthunter didn't know what he could say that wouldn't make things worse. Maybe the words would come later. Samuel prayed he would find them while they could still do some good. He turned his head and looked across the other mourners.

Anya and her children were beside Cicely. They, too, were visiting the graveyard with heinous regularity. Samuel saw them casting lingering looks across the cemetery to where Barnabus was buried.

Other relatives were gathered around as well. Cousins more distant than Rukh and Anya, an elderly uncle from Emelda's side of the family, a wandering nephew named Thorley who just happened to be in Felstein. In all, Samuel counted just over thirty mourners between relations and friends. It brought a smile to him to consider how Emelda would've reacted. She was so humble that it would have shocked her to know so many people had come to bid her farewell.

A commotion at the graveyard gates interrupted Pater Kosminski's prayers. Samuel followed the priest's gaze and was surprised to see a large group of people marching towards them. Briefly, he wondered if they, too, had come for the funeral. Then he noticed the pitchforks and spears many of them carried. These weren't mourners. This was a mob.

Pater Kosminski closed the *Nagashian Verses*, his hand tightening about the prayer book as though it were the grip of a sword. He stormed around the open grave and confronted the mob. 'What's the meaning of this outrage!' he demanded. 'You intrude upon a sacred ceremony. Begone before you provoke the wrath of Nagash!'

The mob faltered for only a moment. There was a stirring within their ranks, and Samuel was stunned when Thayer forced his way to the fore. The townmaster was cold with wrath of his own. His eyes were like chips of ice when he met the priest's glower. 'We've come for Anya Helmgaart. Turn her over to us and we'll be on our way.'

Pater Kosminski shook his head. 'This ground is sacred to Nagash–' he began. Thayer raised his voice and shouted down the priest.

'That wasn't a request, it was an order,' Thayer snarled. He pointed a shaking finger at Anya, who cowered beside Cicely, hugging her children to her. 'By the gods, we can profane this ground no worse than she already has!'

Samuel never knew who shouted the word, but he heard it rise up distinctly from the midst of the mob. A word that, under the circumstances, was the most awful sound imaginable, a thing that seemed to slither into the ear on legs of terror.

'*Witch!*'

Pater Kosminski took a step back. The priest's indignation

faltered as doubt crept into his eyes. His posture lost the defiant
confidence of a moment before and his arms dropped down to
his sides. Thayer was quick to leap upon the priest's vulnerability.

'Aye! Witch!' he yelled, sweeping his gaze from Kosminski to
the shocked mourners. People began withdrawing from Anya's
vicinity. Samuel didn't know what scared them more, the possibility that his cousin was a witch or the threat of becoming
another target for the mob. He stepped forwards, taking up the
position Kosminski had abandoned and standing in Thayer's path.

'That's absurd,' Samuel growled at the townmaster. 'She's no
more a witch than you are.'

Strangely, instead of shouting down the hunter, Thayer spoke
with sympathy. 'You don't know what she's done, do you?' A few
in the mob would have pressed ahead, but Thayer waved them
back. 'We've had our differences, Samuel, but whatever antago-
nism we feel towards one another, this is bigger than that.' He
gestured at Anya. 'She's hurt us both. She took my son from me.
She took your wife from you.'

The claim left Samuel speechless. Only dimly did he hear
Anya's cry of protest. His mind was reeling with the horror of
what Thayer was saying. He felt numb all over, shocked to his
very core.

'It's true,' Thayer said, seizing upon Samuel's silence the same
way he had Kosminski's. 'After I lost Alastair, I went to Mama
Ouspenskaya. She put me into contact with Alastair's spirit.' His
voice cracked with the weight of emotion that surged up from
inside him. 'Alastair told me he'd been killed. Murdered by fell
magics!'

Samuel stirred from his shock when he heard Cicely gasp in
alarm. His daughter's fright rallied him back to his senses. His
gaze hardened when he looked at Thayer, recalling the townmaster's dubious methods. 'So that's it, isn't it? You're so desperate
to have Alastair buried that you've concocted this story to silence

anyone who thinks he killed himself.' He thrust each word at Thayer as though it were a knife. Of all the despicable things he could envision, this was probably the lowest. 'You'll accuse an innocent woman, a mother, of witchcraft just to ease your own grief.'

'That's not true,' Thayer countered, still choked with emotion. 'During the séance I heard Alastair's voice speaking through Mama Ouspenskaya. He spoke as though from a great distance and with difficulty. But I heard him. He told me he was killed by magic.'

'Herr Greimhalt's right,' piped up Gunther, the sour-faced glass-blower who had his workshop near the town square. 'I was there. I heard Alastair's spirit say these things.'

'I'm not surprised to hear you echoing the townmaster, Gunther,' Samuel snapped. 'You were never slow to make yourself useful to Thayer.'

'She is a witch, Samuel.' The beasthunter *was* surprised when Roderick stepped forwards to support Thayer's accusation. 'With my own eyes I've seen her speaking with a raven in her yard. She would talk and it would respond.'

'Is that your proof?' Samuel growled at Roderick. 'Who in a moment of fancy doesn't speak to their animals? I used to speak to my gryph-hound. Does that make me a witch too?'

'The bird had an ill-favoured look about it,' Roderick retorted. 'Surely a messenger from the Ruinous Powers.'

'It had been mauled by some predator and only had one leg,' Anya tried to explain. 'I felt sorry for it and would give it bread crusts–'

'Shut up, witch!' someone from the crowd shouted. Anya trembled at the angry murmur that rippled through the mob. She drew her children closer to her, as though to remind the people of their presence and evoke mercy.

Thayer glared at the woman. 'You bewitched my son,' he stated.

'I found the letters you wrote to him! Why do you think I was so quick to dispossess Rukh? I thought he'd leave Felstein and take you with him. Then Alastair would no longer be distracted by your adultery and build a decent life for himself!'

For Thayer to publicly admit the affair, Samuel knew that it, at least, was true. Thayer would never have besmirched the reputation of his dead son in such a way. The shame he saw in Anya's expression verified his instinct.

'These "accidents" that have been happening with such regularity in your household, Samuel, do you not find their frequency unusual?' Thayer persisted.

'Sigmar's grace,' Samuel hissed. 'You're not going to use that to support this madness? The first to die was Anya's own child!'

'The Dark Gods demand a price for the powers they bestow on their disciples,' Roderick said.

'Barnabus to gain the power she needed.' Thayer raised his voice, ensuring the mob could hear him. 'My son to gain revenge.'

'And Emelda?' Samuel demanded. 'My wife, the woman who isn't even decently in her grave yet! Why would she want her dead?'

'Don't you know?' Thayer lowered his voice. His eyes were like daggers when he glanced at Anya. 'Rukh has left town. She killed my son. She wanted another man.'

A bestial snarl shook through Samuel. He started to lunge at Thayer, but Gunther and Roderick intercepted him and pinned his arms behind his back. The townmaster gave a regretful shake of his head. 'I don't blame you, Samuel,' he said. 'She's bewitched you just the way she did Alastair. You're not responsible.'

Thayer waved the mob forwards. Pater Kosminski retreated before them. Anya screamed as the townsfolk seized her. They pushed Amelia away from her mother and handed off the baby to Anya's aunt, who looked none too pleased to take the child into her arms. Only Cicely protested. She tried to get in the mob's way, shouting all the while. 'She's not a witch! She didn't do anything!' Someone in the crowd wearied of her interference and knocked her to the ground.

Seeing his daughter mistreated spurred Samuel to break away from his captors, but the men held him fast. 'Is this what you call justice? Is this what Felstein has become? A flock of frightened sheep ready to pounce on a neighbour when there's the least excuse?'

'We're only doing what needs to be done for the safety of the community,' Thayer declared. 'But you're wrong. I know she's a witch, but Anya will be given the chance to defend herself.' He turned and looked across the crowd. 'We'll send to Darkhaven Hill for a witch hunter to examine her. If we've made a mistake, they will know.' Thayer glared at Anya as the mob dragged her through the cemetery. 'If she's a witch – she hangs,' he snarled.

'None of this will bring back your son!' Samuel shouted at Thayer as the townmaster followed the mob out of the graveyard. Roderick and Gunther let go of him once they judged it safe to do so, and Samuel rounded on them. 'Who will you call a witch when Alastair becomes a malignant and starts killing people?' he yelled. 'What excuses will Thayer give you then that you'll cling to in your fear?' Neither man had an answer for him. They hurried to join the rest of the mob.

Samuel turned and ran to Cicely. He lifted her from the ground. She felt abnormally light in his arms and her skin was cold to the touch. He dreaded to think what hurt the mob's rough treatment had done to her in her weakened condition.

'Father,' Cicely said, her hand tightening around his metal arm. 'Anya's not a witch. She's not! You can't let them do this to her.'

Samuel glanced over at the other mourners. They looked far less convinced than Cicely did. Most of them seemed like they couldn't leave the graveyard fast enough. To her credit, the aunt who'd been given the baby took Amelia in hand when she departed. At least Anya's children would be together.

'Father, you have to stop them!' Cicely cried.

The hunter held her close. 'I can't,' he said. 'Thayer's convinced them.' The helplessness in his voice swelled into impotent rage. 'He's going to get Anya hanged just so he can bury his son, and there's nothing anybody can do to stop it.'

The townsfolk locked Anya in Balthas' barn. The slack-witted farmer had been given a small stipend to act as guard. It was a role that lent him an air of self-importance. He was oblivious to the reality that no one else wanted the job.

Balthas gave a start when Cicely walked towards the barn. He lowered his pitchfork as though it were a halberd and stared suspiciously at her. 'Who goes there?' he demanded.

Cicely rolled her eyes and sighed. 'Balthas, you know me. You've known me since I was born. I walk past your house every time I have to get more cloth from the weaver.' She sighed again when he made no reaction. 'Cicely Helmgaart.'

'Oh, Samuel's girl,' Balthas muttered, belatedly making sense of what she was telling him. 'You shouldn't be here. They're using my barn to keep the witch until the witch hunter gets here.'

Cicely stared at him in amazement. Did he really think there was anybody in Felstein who didn't know Anya had been arrested and the reason why? Never mind that Cicely had been there when the mob – of which Balthas had been a part – came to seize Anya. She decided not to remind the farmer of any of these facts.

'I wanted to see my cousin,' Cicely said.

'I wouldn't do that,' Balthas replied. 'She's a witch. Killed your mother and Thayer's boy with her hexes.' His eyes narrowed and his expression became suspicious again. 'Does Samuel know that you're here?'

'The witch hunter hasn't yet arrived to judge Anya.' Cicely let some of the fury she felt creep into her voice. Merely because Thayer had accused her, almost the entire town had turned on her cousin. Even many family members. It was a painful thing to see and even worse for her. Because she knew for certain that Anya was innocent.

'When he gets here, he'll tell us she is,' Balthas stated. 'Then we'll hang her just like they did Natalia Kolb way back when.'

'They haven't even decided who to send to Darkhaven Hill,' Cicely persisted. She calmed herself when she saw that her anger was only making Balthas more resistant. 'Please, think of how alone she is. Think of what she's suffering. If it's proved she isn't a witch, all of this cruelty will be unjustified.'

Balthas dug in his heels. 'I don't make the rules. I just do what I was told.' He waved his hand as if to dismiss Cicely.

'And what were you told?' Cicely asked.

'I don't let anyone in the barn,' Balthas said, throwing back his head and puffing out his chest. 'Nobody goes in or out.'

Cicely pointed to the barn. 'I'll only be a few minutes,' she said. Balthas shook his head, his expression firm. 'Just let me talk to her.' She gestured to the window at the side of the building. 'I won't go in. I'll just talk to her from the window.'

Balthas scratched his chin and mulled over her proposal. For a moment Cicely thought he was going to deny her request, but at last he gave her a nod. 'Keep it short,' he said. 'And remember that I'll be watching you.'

Cicely returned the farmer's nod and hurried over to the side of the barn before he could change his mind. She pulled back the wooden shutter and peered inside.

Her eyes needed no time to adjust to the darkness within. Cicely's affliction was asserting itself again, altering her perception. What she saw, however, was more terrible than her own plight, and it hit her with the impact of a physical blow. Anya was lashed to one of the barn's supports, the ropes tied so tightly that she could see them biting into her cousin's flesh. Her clothes were torn and her skin was bruised. A crust of blood covered one side of her face, further evidence of her harsh treatment by the mob. Her head hung down, her chin resting on her chest, but her eyes were open. Cicely had never seen such a terrible look of defeat before.

She took a moment to compose herself and tamp down the monstrous guilt she felt. The crimes Anya was accused of were her own, but it would accomplish nothing if she let her cousin even suspect the fact. Thayer wouldn't permit himself to admit to a mistake. All that might happen would be for Cicely to be arrested too. And then how would she stave off the malady that threatened to overwhelm her?

'Anya?' she called out. She saw her cousin stir slightly, so she called to her again. This time Anya raised her head and looked towards the window. The look of relief that crossed her features was both heart-wrenching and pathetic.

'Cicely!' Anya gasped. 'What have they done with my children?' Even in her grim circumstances, her first thought was for the children who'd been taken from her.

'They are well,' Cicely replied. 'Aunt Viktoria is looking after them.' She didn't want to add the great reluctance with which Viktoria had taken them on or her efforts to locate Rukh and send the children to him. Cicely could see how vital it was for Anya to believe they were both safe and well looked after.

Assured of her children, Anya's thoughts turned to the crimes she was accused of. 'Please tell me you don't believe these things they're saying about me,' she implored. Her entire body shuddered with revulsion at the murders attributed to her.

Cicely tried to muster what she hoped was a reassuring smile. 'I know you couldn't have done these things. Even if you could work magic, you'd never do something to hurt Barnabus or my mother.'

The words did offer the prisoner some succour. Anya relaxed in her ropes, reducing the strain on her body. She stared down at the floor. 'It doesn't make sense. How can they accuse me of witchcraft?'

Cicely's temper flared up at the despondent words. 'It's all Thayer Greimhalt's fault,' she spat. 'He's desperate to convince people Alastair didn't kill himself.'

'Alastair,' Anya whispered. There was an awful wistfulness in her tone that disturbed Cicely. 'I really did think he loved me, but he didn't do anything when his father kicked us out of our home.' Quickly she turned and looked to the window. 'But I didn't kill him. I swear to Sigmar, I didn't kill him!'

'I know you didn't,' Cicely replied. 'The only people who believe that are those Thayer has bribed or bullied.' She felt a cold rage rising inside her. 'It's all Thayer's doing, your being here. He's the one making Felstein embrace this farce.'

Anya sagged back down in her ropes. 'He's the townmaster. We're just common folk. What can we do?'

Cicely was glad Anya wasn't looking her way at that moment. Because she'd just decided what could be done and was worried that her new determination might be betrayed by her face. 'Justice has a way of attending to itself,' she said. 'Keep hope.'

Cicely left the window when she heard Balthas walking towards the barn. The farmer had his old clay pipe nestled in the corner of his mouth, greasy smoke rising from its bowl. He made a sweeping gesture with his pitchfork. 'All right, you've gawked at the witch long enough,' he grumbled. 'Go home now.'

Balthas didn't need to repeat the command. Cicely was eager to get home. There was something she had to do there.

The needle darted in and out of the tapestry as Cicely worked a new likeness into the cloth. She fixed in her mind the face of the man she would destroy. No distractions this time. No mistakes.

She concentrated upon the tapestry with the utmost intensity, letting it become the focus of her entire being.

Dimly, she was aware of her father moving through the now empty house. Samuel was devastated by her mother's death. She regretted that she couldn't offer him her support right now, but the work she was intent upon was too important to brook any delay. Once someone was sent to Darkhaven Hill to bring back a witch hunter, it would be too late. If she could've confided in her father, she knew he would understand. Doing so, however, was impossible. It would mean admitting she'd accidentally killed Emelda.

Guilt over her mother's death spurred Cicely on. The figure she was adding to the tapestry now was the one that should have been there instead of Emelda. Thayer had escaped the needle's magic before because of her inattentiveness and lack of caution. There would be no such mistakes to save the townmaster this time. This time he would die, and his death would save not only Cicely but Anya as well.

Hate drove the needle again and again into the cloth. Cicely was adding fires around the townmaster's shape. The memory of her mother's face burned in the hearth's embers had made her decide a fiery death was the only fitting fate for Thayer. It was the finish that awaited Anya after she was hanged, her body cremated and the ashes scattered. Thayer would suffer the same end, only without a noose to ease his suffering. Oh yes, she'd make the swine pay!

The stitches that formed each finger of flame were exacted with loving detail. Cicely thrilled to the play of orange and red, the shift to bright yellow and black smoke. She could almost imagine she heard the crackle of the fire as she worked. Thayer's screams as he was consumed. When he learned that not all his wealth or power could save him.

As she applied the finishing touches, Cicely smiled down at

her work. She stared at the picture of Thayer surrounded by flames, his mouth open in a cry of abject horror. He would die in agony, exactly as she'd depicted. The onyx needle's awful magic would make it so.

Panic seized Cicely when, before her eyes, the tapestry began to change. The threads, like living things, undid themselves and reconstituted themselves in new patterns. The leaping flames remained as they were, but the figure they devoured was transforming. Cold horror pulsated through Cicely when she saw Thayer's image undone and in his place that of her cousin Anya.

By what monstrous trickery this thing had come to pass, Cicely didn't know. She only knew that it had happened. Even now she felt her body being invigorated. She thought of Anya and the cruel flames she'd woven around her cousin's picture.

Cicely was rushing to the door of her room when it was thrown open and her father appeared. His face was gripped by horror. She could see Balthas standing in the hallway behind him. The farmer's clothes were singed and his skin was black with soot. Faintly, she could hear the sound of the bell in Felstein's town hall ringing an alarm.

'There's a fire!' Samuel shouted, grabbing Cicely's arm and rushing her through the house. As they ran into the street, Balthas jogged after them.

'I didn't mean to do it!' Balthas groaned. 'I only closed my eyes for a minute. I was so tired. My pipe must have fallen and caught some of the straw...'

As they ran through the streets towards the barn, they could see people hurrying to the building with buckets of water. Cicely knew they'd do no good even before she saw the size of the conflagration. The entire barn was wrapped in flames, a thick pillar of smoke billowing into the night. From somewhere inside, she could hear Anya's shrieks as the fire devoured her.

Cicely clamped her hands to her ears, trying to block out

the screams. In her mind all she could see was the tortured image of her cousin on the tapestry. The image that had transformed from her intended victim into that of the person she'd tried to save.

CHAPTER ELEVEN

Samuel inspected the pack, studying each item he'd added to it. He wasn't entirely happy with the state of the oakbread – it felt stale already – but his other supplies looked to be in good order. A heavy bedroll and blanket that would fend off the Shyishian chill-fog. A good supply of water in three goatskins. An ember box to ensure he could light a fire when he needed to.

That last bit of equipment brought him to bitter contemplation. The fire at Balthas' barn had consumed it utterly. There wasn't anything left of Anya to find afterwards. Already there were some whispering that the witch had caused the fire with one of her spells so she could escape. Oddly, Thayer hadn't joined in those speculations. Perhaps the townmaster was experiencing some belated remorse.

What did he know of black magic, witches or curses? Samuel was a hunter. Give him an adversary he could track through a forest, a beast he could face with spear and axe. Not this. Not this nebulous menace that was at once everywhere and nowhere.

The ordeal facing the town was beyond his abilities to understand, much less fight.

'Why do you have to go?' Cicely asked as he finished check-
ing his packs. It felt to Samuel like the hundredth time she'd
put that question to him.

'Whatever's going on, someone has to stop it,' he told her.
'What's been happening... all of these deaths... they can't be
coincidence. Something is going on. Something unnatural.'

'But why do *you* have to go?' Cicely insisted. The fear in her
eyes was painful to Samuel. He knew his daughter was still weak
from all they'd been through. Some days she looked as healthy
and vibrant as she ever had, but there were other times when
she seemed perilously frail and sickly. With the deaths of Marden
and her mother, the two of them were all that was left. The only
ones to support each other. He felt his daughter's worry, her fears
of abandonment. Of being left all alone.

'Your uncle Aaric is a learned man,' Samuel explained. 'He's
studied much on the subjects of magic and the occult, things I
know little about. If there's some supernatural agency preying
upon Felstein, he'll know how to find out what it is.' The hunter
retrieved his spear from where it was leaning against the wall.
His hand tightened around its haft. 'He'll know how to track it
down and put an end to it.'

'You really think he can help?' Dread filled Cicely's voice. With
the tragedies they'd suffered, Samuel could understand why she
was reluctant to entertain any kind of hope. There was little
that was crueller than a hope denied.

'Hephzibah was my sister and Aaric was her husband,' Samuel
said. 'That makes us family, and the ties of family might sway
Aaric where any other appeal would fail.' He nodded, trying to
convince himself with his own words. 'He'll listen to me.'

'But Gothghul Hollow is so far away,' Cicely objected. 'The
roads are too dangerous.'

Samuel rested his arm on his daughter's shoulder. 'This thing... whatever it is... it killed your mother. Maybe it even caused Marden's death. I owe it to their spirits to do all I can to stop this killer. The best way I know to do that is to bring Aaric here.'

'I don't want you to go.' Cicely hugged her father, her arms wrapped about him tightly. Samuel winced to feel the coldness of her body and the ill odour in her breath. She was getting sick again.

He eased her away. Fear raced through him. Fear worse than when the skullsnapper had his arm in its mouth. Emelda and Marden were gone. Cicely was all he had left. If she were lost to him now, he didn't know if he could go on.

'You know I love you,' the hunter told her, trying to keep any worry from his voice. 'Never forget that, even if it might seem that I've forgotten.'

'Father,' Cicely sobbed, 'I thought–'

'Don't,' Samuel interjected. 'Don't ever think that way. You're not to blame.' His mind turned to when his daughter was born... and the circumstances around that birth. 'Never think you're responsible.' His expression grew firm. 'We're all we have now. There's nobody else. We've got to stay *strong*.' He emphasised the last word as though he could will her back to health. Concern for Cicely's welfare warred with his deeper worry – that whatever blight was afflicting Felstein might set its sights on her.

'I should be gone no more than a week,' Samuel said. 'I won't tarry in Gothghul Hollow. Aaric or no, I'll be back here as quick as I can.'

Cicely gave him a weary nod. It seemed she'd worn out her capacity for objections. An air of resignation clung to her as she helped him with his pack and held the door open for him when he stepped from the house. Samuel looked back to see her in the doorway, tears in her eyes, her body trembling with anxiety. He quickly turned away. He hated to put her through this, but there wasn't anything else he could do. Some fiendish power was at work in Felstein, and whatever it took, he was going to see it destroyed.

Despite what he'd told Cicely, Samuel wasn't at all certain he'd be able to induce Aaric to investigate murder in Felstein. He'd only met the man perhaps half a dozen times and not at all since the death of his sister, Hephzibah. There had never been any especially warm regard between them, though neither did he think there was any bad blood. The bonds of family were stretched thin between them, and it might be too much to expect that link to sway Aaric into action. Still, he'd been honest when he'd said he had a better chance than anybody else in town of convincing the occultist to help them.

Fog once again hung thick over Felstein, obscuring the sun and limiting his vision to just a few yards. Samuel didn't like to think how much greater his awareness would be compromised once he was beyond the environs of his community. He could skirt past Briardark and take the wagon track to Rattlepath. There'd be coaches to hire at the village, situated as it was midway between Darkhaven Hill and Gothghul Hollow. He'd feel a good deal less vulnerable once he was inside a coach. He tried not to think of the stories of spectral hounds that liked to chase after wagons and which would devour anyone inside should they run down their prey. Black Gaston, the ogor highwayman, was another menace. He'd waylay travellers by strangling their horses, and if his victims didn't have enough to satiate his greed he was known to carry people off to add to his larder.

There were any number of perils that *could* happen on the way to Gothghul Hollow. Ones that Samuel was aware of and others he was certain were unknown to him. Yet as he looked about Felstein, watching familiar buildings rear up at him from behind the fog as he neared them, he appreciated that any feeling of security here was mere illusion. The power that had killed most of his family was abroad and unchecked. It could strike out again at any time. No one was safe.

Samuel turned and looked back in the direction of his house. He felt like a cur for leaving Cicely behind when this danger persisted. But he'd seen her repeated relapses into sickness. Though her body felt cold, outwardly she seemed healthy, but what would happen if she became seriously ill while they were away? Taking the risk that travel would further upset her delicate constitution wasn't something he could accept. He'd been forced to calculate which choice offered less immediate threat to his daughter.

If he were still capable of putting any faith in the gods, Samuel would have prayed he'd made the right choice.

Cicely had carefully folded the tapestry and pinned it together so as to hide the fiery image of Anya. Now she undid the pins and rolled out her handiwork across her bed. Her eyes fixated on something lying on the floor beside her chair.

It was the carving. The one that had been in Marden's room. The one that had changed into a wolf. She stared down at it, feeling its silent accusation. *'My life is yours.'* She seemed to hear Marden's voice echo through the room. Only it wasn't Marden's voice. There was a strange reverberation to the ghostly sound. As though several voices were simultaneously saying the same thing.

Cicely seized the little carving and threw it against the wall. It bounced off and landed upright in the middle of the room, as though mocking her anger. She sprang from her chair and took the carving in hand, smashing it against the floor until it had been splintered beyond recognition. She sank back into her chair, trying to catch her breath after the violent exertion.

It wasn't her fault! She could truly say that this time. She'd concentrated on sewing the image of Thayer. It was the needle's perfidious enchantment that had spoiled her intention. She would have wrought justice and removed a callous villain from Felstein. It was the onyx needle's treachery that had brought about Anya's death. She wasn't to blame.

But will Uncle Aaric see it that way? How desperately she'd tried to stop her father from going to Gothghul Hollow. She'd pleaded with him as much as she could without arousing his suspicions. She really did fear for his safety on the long journey, but she feared even more what would happen if he brought Aaric back.

Through her mind raced the vision of what would happen if she was discovered. Felstein had turned upon Anya with the most vicious cruelty, a woman innocent of the murders credited to her. How much worse would be their fury when they had the one who was truly guilty within their grasp? Anya had been beaten and imprisoned with no more than Thayer's accusations and the hearsay of a few farmers. Aaric would be able to give them evidence. His knowledge of the occult would expose Cicely.

The onyx needle was in her hand once more. Cicely's eyes went to the splintered carving on the floor. The thought came to her that she could destroy the needle too, destroy it and be done with it.

And by doing so, destroy her only chance for life. The only thing keeping her from destruction.

She started to bind a thread into the needle's eye. It was in her power to stop Aaric before he even started. It wouldn't be murder to add him to the tapestry. She'd simply be defending herself. No different than when she'd fought the dire wolf. It took her some time to quash her conscience. She couldn't afford to be sentimental. She had to act before it was too late.

But she couldn't act. Even when she was firm in her resolve, Cicely found she lacked the ability to carry out her intention. She'd only ever seen her uncle twice, and those occasions had been many years ago, when she was a small child. Try as she might, she couldn't call up a mental picture of him from her memory. She didn't have an image to sew into the tapestry.

'You don't know what Uncle Aaric looks like,' she hissed in disgust. Horror churned in her gut when that thought was quickly followed by another. She did know what Samuel looked like. If her father never reached Gothghul Hollow, it would be just like killing Aaric...

Horror roared through Cicely at the murderous idea. How had such a thing ever squirmed into her brain? 'I'm not a monster,' she whispered. 'It's not me.' She glared at the shiny black needle.

Cicely threw the tapestry across the room, the needle sticking out of it with its loose thread. She was sick from the profane idea, the horrible plot that had to have come from the needle's fell magic. It had been an accidental matricide, but if she acted upon this abominable urge, she'd bear the stain of patricide in full. Pater Kosminski said that such people became the most wretched malignants when they died, gheists shunned and despised even by the nighthaunts.

'*My life is yours,*' the ghostly voice whispered to her. Now it wasn't Marden's tone that was prominent, but that of another. Weak and uncertain, as though speech was strange to the speaker. Cicely was certain she'd never heard such a voice before. Just as she was certain she knew who was saying the words. Someone without a name, without a face.

On the floor, the smashed carving stood upright, a wolf once more. There wasn't the least chip to suggest the destruction Cicely had wrought upon it. The sight of it broke the last strands of her courage.

'What can I do?' she groaned, rocking back and forth on the balls of her feet in a fit of agitation. She looked at her hands. The skin had the merest hint of pallor to it right now. The essence she'd drawn from Anya would sustain her for another day at most. Then she'd need to claim another sacrifice.

She glanced at the wolf. Its carved fangs grinned at her, challenging her. Defying her to be brave. But she couldn't be brave. Cicely wouldn't let her life slip away while there was a chance to save it.

If she dared. After what had happened when she'd tried to target Thayer, Cicely was afraid of what would happen when she used the needle again. The threads might weave themselves into the semblance of anyone. She'd rejected the killing of her father, but might the needle's treachery not accomplish the deed without her volition?

Cicely sprang to where she'd thrown the tapestry. She tore the needle from the cloth. For a moment she considered burning it in the same hearth where her mother had died. The idea quickly evaporated. If she did that, Cicely knew she was lost. The needle's magic was all that kept her from fading away completely.

'I need answers.' Cicely's fist tightened about the needle. She felt it dig into her palm. The pain as it bit into her skin, the blood that oozed from her cut, had a soothing effect upon her. She was still substantial enough to feel these things. What she had to do now was find out how to stay that way. She needed to know what laws governed the needle's capricious magic. There was only one person who might be able to tell her.

'Verderghast.' The name dripped from Cicely's lips like a basilisk's venom. She grabbed her cloak from her wardrobe and hurried from the empty house.

Fog smothered Briardark in a grey veil, chilling Cicely even as it strove to blind her. As she picked her way between the skeletal trees with their clawed branches, as her cloak caught in the thorn-bushes, she felt the hopelessness of her situation. The heavy mist let her see only a few yards ahead. That abnormal perception that came with her affliction was only gradually asserting itself again as her health waned, but the fog confounded it in ways shadows couldn't. She was as lost as anyone would be under the forest's shroud.

'Verderghast!' Cicely called out. She could hear her voice echo among the trees, distorted and twisted by the woods. She recalled the tales of the malicious woodfolk, of the dryads that would use such tricks to lure people to their destruction deep within their forest enclaves. The bodies of lost travellers would become fertiliser for their forbidden groves. She was thankful that of the many dark legends attributed to Briardark, none claimed the place as a haunt of the Sylvaneth.

Gloom drew close all around her as she walked still deeper into the forest. Faintly, she could hear the sounds of small creatures crawling through the underbrush. Sometimes she'd hear the flapping of wings as some bird or bat flew nearby. Always these sounds were moving away from her. An ominous sign that she tried to dismiss, but couldn't. She had the impression of being marked, that all the denizens of Briardark were avoiding her because some fearsome beast had selected her as its prey. Even now it might be stalking her through the fog.

Suddenly, a flight of silver-furred bats flittered down at her from the treetops. Cicely's ears were filled with their shrill chirps as the rodents dove towards her. She could see their blood-smeared mouths, the rows of sharp teeth eager to rip her flesh, the red eyes shining in the blackness.

Cicely crouched low and swung her arms above her head, trying to fend off the flying vermin. She felt furry bodies and leathery wings brush against her hands, clawed feet snag in her hair, rough teeth scratch at her skin.

'No!' Cicely cried out, but it wasn't the touch of the bats that provoked her outburst. It was the shrill cacophony of the flock, their piercing shrieks that stabbed through her ears to her very brain. The squeaking had intensified to a tortuous magnitude. She doubled over, all but prostrate on the ground. She expected to feel the vicious creatures swarming over her, tearing at her with their claws and teeth.

The bats, however, didn't press their attack. Instead, she could hear them flapping away into Briardark's depths. Cicely lifted her head, amazed to find the air around her no longer alive with rodents. The flock had fled. Fled from *her*.

Cicely tried to dispel the fears that raced across her mind. Of course the forest animals were avoiding her. The only reason a human normally entered the forest was to hunt. To collect meat to supplement whatever the farms provided. Or else perhaps to gather ingredients for medicine or one of Mama Ouspenskaya's rituals. Whatever brought a person into the woods, it was prudent for the animals to avoid any interaction.

Cicely was sent sprawling when she stumbled over a tree root. For a moment, she lay stunned on the ground, then she felt the earth heave up beneath her. She watched in petrified fascination as the soil churned and shuddered. Roots, thick as her arm or slim as a needle, were shifting and squirming, pulling and tearing, as they tried to reposition themselves. As they did, the ground lost its solidity, was whipped into the consistency of mud. Cicely's paralysis was broken by an even greater shock. She was sinking!

The ground was losing all cohesion, drawing Cicely down into its gelid morass. Frantic, she scrambled away on hands and knees, but the quagmire continued to expand. She grabbed one of the slithering roots, the only thing of any firmness. It rolled in her grip, as though to wrest itself free of her touch and send her tumbling back into the sucking mire.

Drowning in the dirt, entombed beneath Briardark. Cicely dug her fingers deeper, so deep that sap spurted over her hands. She would not die like that. Frightened desperation renewed her strength. She surged forwards and snatched another root, using it to pull herself across the churned ground. Her body was sinking into the earth; only her hold on the roots kept her from being dragged down now.

'*My life is yours,*' the phantom voice crackled. Now there was only the least trace of Marden in the spectral chorus.

The voice magnified her horror and spurred Cicely to greater effort. She pulled herself onward and threw out her arm to grip another writhing root. Seizing it, she repeated the process. Again and again, lunging forwards to seize a root, dragging herself within reach of the next. Finally, she felt solid ground under her hands. With a final push, she freed herself from the deadly morass.

Breathing hard, Cicely turned to look at the horrible trap she'd escaped from. She could see a huge tree, its branches especially thick but coated in sharp red leaves. The trunk was twisted, coiled like a corkscrew. She watched as it contorted still further, as if it wanted to shift away and escape her notice.

Cicely felt relief at the nearness of her escape and wondered how it was that her father had never spoken of such a terrifying phenomenon before, a tree that tried to trap victims in the soil beneath its roots. She was fortunate to have escaped becoming its next meal.

Yet still there persisted a nagging feeling of dread, the echo of that tormenting phantom voice. Cicely felt as she had that terrible night, pursuing the wolf with Marden unaware that as they hunted it, it was hunting them. The hairs on the back of her neck stood on end, goosebumps rippling over her skin. She almost turned back, but she feared what would happen if she did. 'Verderghast!' she called out again.

The scratch of a foot against stone caused Cicely to spin around. She could make out a dim shadow behind the fog. Just the impression of a shape, but after a moment she realised it wasn't tall enough to be the man she was looking for. Her heart throbbed with horror when the figure came bounding forwards.

She felt her body freeze, unable to move as the thing charged out from the fog.

That dreadful night was replaying in more than just her mind. Out of the mist emerged a gigantic dire wolf, its fur peeling away from its rotten flesh, the bone of its muzzle exposed in a skeletal snarl. Cicely was back in that moment when the beast had appeared on the rocky shelf, turning the tables on its hunters. She saw the eerie light within its sockets, that ghostly glow that served the undead in lieu of eyes. Visible wounds removed any last doubt of the wolf's identity. It was the same creature that had attacked her before. The killer of Marden, the beast in the carving, risen again into a semblance of life.

The dire wolf glowered at her and took a few menacing steps towards Cicely. As she felt its enmity, she wondered if this was the reason Verderghast didn't answer her. Had the beast tracked him down after it revived, and killed him? A part of her refused to believe it, but as she watched the wolf start to circle her, she realised it wouldn't matter. Alive or dead, the physician couldn't help her. This time she didn't even have her brother's knife to defend herself from her enemy.

Its eyes fixed on her, the wolf continued to circle Cicely. Its long fangs were yellow and pitted with decay. Its rotten tongue lolled from its jaws, and it panted hungrily as it licked its chops.

Cicely expected the wolf to pounce. 'Get back!' she shouted at the beast. She threw out her hand to protect her body from the animal's teeth – even if for only a moment. Terror of the wolf ruled her mind, but not so completely as to keep her stomach from turning when she saw the near transparency of her skin. She could see the bones and veins beneath her flesh.

Instead of pouncing, the wolf froze. It cocked its head to one side, as though perplexed. It took a single step towards her, its muzzle lifted, its nose snuffling at the air. The beast's green eyes narrowed. Cicely thought the creature was studying her, really seeing her for the first time. A low, grating sound squeezed itself up from the wolf's decayed throat. With a sense of disbelief, she recognised it as a frightened whine.

The wolf backed away from her, the glow of its eyes shrinking to mere pinpoints. The flesh of its hackles shivered and the remains of its tail were drawn down between its hind legs. The beast shrank back into the fog, changing once again into an indistinct shadow behind the mist. When she lost the flash of its eyes, Cicely dimly heard the scrabble of bony paws across rocks. The dire wolf had fled into the forest. The undead had fled from her!

Wonder gripped Cicely. She was amazed at her good fortune, the incredible escape she'd experienced. Then a feeling of horror blotted out her relief. She looked at her hand. It was fading, translucent once more.

Terror dogged Cicely as she ran from Briardark. The wolf's retreat heightened the ghastliness of her affliction. The change that was coming upon her was so monstrous that even the undead recoiled before it.

Her hand was tight around the onyx needle. She had to get back to the tapestry, add another figure to the cloth before her condition could worsen any further.

She had to get back to Felstein and find another victim.

Cicely kept the hood of her cloak drawn up so that nobody in the square could get a good look at her. It wasn't a question of concealing her identity – the cloak had been made from a stag's hide her father brought back from one of his hunts. What she hoped to do was conceal her worsening condition from the townsfolk. She wasn't confident that the powder she'd used would be enough to conceal her pallor. It was common knowledge that she'd been sickly following Marden's death. Her fear was that some good-intentioned neighbour might notice her paleness and try to help her.

There was only one help for her, and that was the onyx needle in her pocket. It wasn't murder. It was survival. She bore no malice towards the target she'd chosen. He was simply vulnerable.

Jurge was a vagabond who'd wandered into Felstein a year ago. He survived by doing odd jobs in exchange for food and shelter. He never stayed with anyone for long though, offering his labour to whoever might need another hand. 'Flighty' was the best word to describe his nature. 'Drunkard' would be the best way to evaluate his character, for whenever he could, he'd repair to the Skintaker's Swallow and try to bum drinks from the patrons. Today he was engaged in that customary activity, oblivious that he was being closely studied from a table near the back of the inn's common room.

As Jurge drank up whatever a generous touch might offer him, so Cicely was drinking up every detail of the vagabond's appearance. Every nuance of his face, every shift of expression, she was committing to memory. She concentrated on Jurge as she'd never concentrated on anything before. Her memorisation was literally a matter of life and death.

After some hours, Jurge finally left the Skintaker's Swallow. Perhaps he'd hit the limit on what he could extract from the townsfolk for today and so decided to find himself some shady spot to sleep. Cicely waited only a little while before she also quit the inn. She resisted the desire to race back to her house and start her work. Haste might draw prying eyes and undue attention. What she had to do, she had to do alone.

'It isn't murder,' Cicely repeated to herself when she was inside and had removed her cloak. 'I don't have anything against Jurge. I don't bear him any wish for harm. So it isn't murder.' She quickly moved down the hall to her room. At least Samuel's absence eliminated the possibility of discovery now that she was home. The solitude was cheerless, but it did offer some benefits.

'I'm sorry,' she whispered as she drew out the needle and attached a thread to its eye. She took up the tapestry and began to work. Diligently, she drew up the vagabond's appearance and translated it into the stitches. His image gradually began to appear. She hesitated only when she was nearly done. How should she try to direct the hand of Death? She didn't want something too painful to happen to him. At last, she decided that she'd make it so that he'd merely drunk too much. It was a finish that was only too likely for him anyway. She added a bottle in his hand, then leaned back to survey her work.

Twice Thayer had escaped her intention to kill him. *That* would have been murder, for she bore him nothing but enmity. Perhaps that was why the tapestry had rejected his image and the needle's magic had changed victims. But then why had it allowed her to add Alastair? She had just as much hate for the younger Greimhalt as she did the elder. Maybe it was some strange power that protected Thayer. Whatever the cause, she wasn't going to risk trying to kill the townmaster again. Jurge was safe. He was a vagabond, a nobody. No one would be too upset when he died.

Cicely started to smile to herself as she gazed down at Jurge's image. She stopped smiling when she saw the threads start to undo themselves. Just as they had before. She hurriedly clamped her hands down on the tapestry, as though she could hold the threads in place. Like a nest of writhing worms, she could feel them squirming under her touch. She knew they were going about their hideous purpose, changing her intention and choosing for themselves another sacrifice.

Even when the threads fell still, Cicely was too frightened to look at what they'd done. She kept her hands pressing down until the growing warmth that coursed through her body told her that the magic was revitalising her. Someone was dead and their essence was replenishing her. All she had to do was remove her hands to find out who.

Her heart drummed against her chest as fear compounded upon itself. 'Please, not father,' she prayed. At last, the tension became unbearable. Not knowing had become worse torture than she could have believed. She had to know. She had to see.

When she pulled back her hands, Cicely knew Jurge was still alive. His picture had changed, taking on a familiar aspect. A shudder passed through her, but with it there was a grim sense of relief.

She hadn't added Samuel to the tapestry. It was Aunt Viktoria who'd become her latest sacrifice. Soon she was certain someone would come to the house to tell her about an awful accident. Maybe her aunt had consumed bad water or contaminated milk. However it had happened, she was certain the woman was dead.

First Thayer and now Jurge. It made no sense to Cicely why the treacherous needle kept shifting targets, swapping out intended victims for people from her own family.

Unless *that* was the reason. Cicely collapsed when she made that realisation. The needle had never changed victims when she tried to sacrifice family members, as poor Barnabus showed. Alastair too! She recalled something her father and mother had been discussing once. It was about Hochmueller's estate and how it would be divided when he died. It seemed that Hochmueller had a mistress once, years ago. They'd each gone their own way after the dalliance, but according to the town charter, the affair made her part of his family. The needle must work on similar lines. Anya's involvement with Alastair had, by the twisted logic of magic, made him a member of their family. A legitimate sacrifice.

Cicely stared at the onyx needle. She almost felt like it was laughing back at her. She'd unravelled its secret and with it brought upon herself a horror she was only now beginning to appreciate. To survive, she'd have to prey on her own family.

She sobbed and clasped her hands to her eyes. She should let herself die. Otherwise, she'd be left with no one. She'd be little more than a wraith anyway, haunting empty rooms, wandering through a lonely existence while she watched others truly living. What was the point of being alive if she was all alone?

Even as she asked herself that, Cicely knew there was that part of her so afraid of death that she'd cling to life even on such terms.

At some point she might even be desperate enough to sacrifice her own father.

CHAPTER TWELVE

'A coach, Cicely! Just think of it!' Lucilla tugged at Cicely's arm as they hurried down the lane. All of Felstein was abuzz with excitement, everyone headed to the square to see for themselves this unusual visitor. The arrival of a coach was a remarkable event. The community was too small and isolated to warrant attention from those who travelled in such luxury.

'I saw a coach once before,' Cicely told her friend as they jostled through the crowd. 'Oh, it must have been when I was six or seven. Markgraf Diemien came through Felstein on his way to find the Gravehold of Tarn.'

Lucilla curled her fingers together in the sign of Nagash. 'You shouldn't talk so,' she warned in a subdued tone. 'It's bad luck to mention one of the wight kings. They might put a curse on you!'

Cicely smiled at her friend's caution. She doubted if any wight could place a curse on her as terrible as the one she was already suffering. Today was the first day in five that she'd felt well enough – and looked presentable enough – to visit Lucilla or walk the streets in daylight. That's because she was still flush with the energies she'd drawn out of her cousin Sebastian. The townsfolk had fished his body from the mill pond only yesterday.

'A curse would be better than a chill,' Cicely quipped, drawing her cloak more tightly about herself. She wasn't actually cold, but she thought it better if her neighbours believed she was. That would explain why she went about so heavily muffled. Right now she was fine, but she knew her vigour wouldn't last and there would come a time when she'd again need to conceal her affliction from everyone.

Lucilla frowned at Cicely's morbid humour, but rather than scolding her, she simply changed the subject. 'Oh, I wonder who it could be?'

Cicely could have answered that question. There was only one person she could think of who was so prosperous that he'd have a coach at his command and might be expected to pay Felstein a visit. Uncle Aaric Gothghul. She felt relief at the idea her uncle was here, because it meant her father had made it safely to Gothghul Hollow and would be back now. She also felt uneasy knowing the scholar was in the town. Knowing that there was now someone in Felstein who might discover what she was doing.

'Let's hurry before the square is too full,' Cicely said. 'Then we'll see for ourselves who it is.' Now it was her turn to speed Lucilla down the street, squeezing past people intent on the same objective.

A large crowd had gathered in the square. People craned their necks, eagerly whispering to one another as they awaited the arrival of the coach. When the clatter of hooves became audible, a hush fell upon the crowd. People scrambled aside to clear a path for the brace of huge demi-gryphs that emerged from the fog, the blue plumage of their feathered heads standing in marked contrast to the sleek black fur of their bodies. Behind them they drew an ornately carved coach with a colour somewhere between old ivory and saffron. The coachman was a massive, powerfully built man heavily muffled by the high-collared coat he wore. Upon the doors of the carriage a silver griffon rampant was depicted, the heraldry of the Gothghul lineage.

The two women watched in fascination as the coach circled around the hanging tree and stopped before the town hall. While the demi-gryphs stamped and shifted in their harness, the coachman jumped down from his seat and stepped back to unhook a set of wooden steps that dropped down before the door. This he then opened before stepping aside.

Lucilla gasped. 'Why, Cicely, isn't that your father?'

Cicely's heart leapt when she saw Samuel emerge. He was outfitted in clothes much finer than those he'd worn upon lea- ving Felstein, though still of a rugged and hardy cut. The leather gauntlets had been reinforced with bands of viperskin along the fingers and palm to provide a better grip. His boots were edged with studs of steel, and as he stepped down from the coach, she could see that the soles were hobnailed. His coat was trimmed in fur and hung down past his knees, silver buttons depend- ing from the hooks that could close the garment tight about his figure. Breeches, shirt and vest gave a similar effect of richness mixed with durability. Samuel's appearance was such that an impressed murmur spread among the crowd. Many turned their heads to consider their townmaster and found Thayer's ostenta- tion less impressive by contrast.

The crowd fell quiet when another man stepped down from the coach. The style of his clothing was much like Samuel's, but of a uniform black except where silver clasps and chains spar- kled amid their sombre settings. He wore a broad-brimmed hat adorned with a bright red feather. Beneath this were the long curls of a russet wig, draping his shoulders in twisted locks. The stranger looked across the crowd with a gaze that Cicely thought was both weary and studious, a seeming conflict that couldn't reconcile itself in her estimation. He was advanced in his years, but there was a harsh strength to his features that belied his age.

'Who is that?' Lucilla wondered, poking Cicely with her elbow.

'I'm certain I don't know,' Cicely replied listlessly. It was an untruth. This, she felt certain, was her uncle Aaric Gothghul. It took only a moment for her suspicions to be confirmed.

The man in black addressed the crowd, effortlessly project-ing his voice across the square. 'Citizens of Felstein. The plight of your community has been communicated to me by one of your own.' He laid his hand on Samuel's shoulder and swept the crowd with an imperious gaze. 'I have come among you to investigate these strange deaths that afflict this town.' He paused and drew a deep breath. 'The spectres of witchcraft and sorcery have been raised.' He paused again, and a cold smile curled his mouth. 'Such allegations carry the utmost severity. It is unwise to bandy them about flippantly.'

Many in the crowd looked towards Thayer. The townmaster paled when Aaric followed the direction of their gaze. Cicely thought Thayer would wither under the scholar's scrutiny. Without commenting, Aaric turned away from Thayer and addressed the gathering as a whole. 'I cannot say how long my investigation will take. Samuel Helmgaart has graciously agreed to play host to me while my task keeps me in Felstein.' Again he paused, letting his audience anticipate his next words. When he spoke them, Cicely felt her blood curdle. 'If this community is beset by dark magic, I will expose it. You may content yourselves with knowing that wherever the weed of witchcraft has taken root, I will find it out.'

'What's wrong, Cicely?' Lucilla asked, concern in her eyes.

Cicely didn't answer. She could feel the intensity of her uncle's eyes, as if he'd already singled her out.

'Wherever this evil hides itself,' Aaric declared, 'I will expose it.' He raised his hand and tightened it into a fist. 'And destroy it.'

'There's no need to go to such extravagance on my behalf, niece,' Aaric said as Cicely hurried to spoon more carrots onto his plate.

'You're our guest, Aaric,' Samuel reminded him. 'It's our duty to ensure your comfort.' He gave his daughter an encouraging smile. Cicely nodded and settled back into her chair. She seemed to him more concerned with keeping her uncle's plate full than she was about emptying her own. If she'd taken more than two bites it would be a surprise to him. He worried that her illness was returning.

Some sign of worry must have shown on his face, but Aaric misconstrued its cause. 'Do not fret about my comfort,' he told Samuel. 'I'm quite used to privation. When I was first engaged in my studies under Master Jeremias, I'd sometimes forget to eat for days on end. Not until my body reached that tipping point where I was so ravenous I'd be ready to eat a tuskgor's gizzard boiled in a grot's brainpan.' He raised his spoon so it was just under his nose and inhaled the aroma. 'I can assure you, this is a marvellous repast,' he told Cicely. 'While I might call your labours unnecessary, do not think they go unappreciated.'

'I thank you, uncle,' Cicely replied, not quite able to hold Aaric's gaze.

Samuel thought he guessed the reason for his daughter's unease. 'That was a very impressive speech you made in the square,' he declared. 'I wonder how many in town think you're an agent from the Order of Azyr.'

Aaric leaned back and smiled. 'I merely made a few statements and left others to draw their own conclusions.' He winked at Samuel. 'After what you told me about the redoubtable Herr Greimhalt's activities, I felt it would be useful to let your neighbours think of me in such terms. It reduces the chances of your townmaster sending for a real witch hunter.'

'Then you aren't a witch hunter?' Cicely asked. There was a hopeful note in her voice that Samuel found surprising. Then again, with the sinister reputation some of the less discriminate and overzealous witch hunters attained, it was understandable that she'd have some qualms about sharing a roof with the Order of Azyr.

'No,' Aaric said. 'I've had cause to work with witch hunters on rare occasions, but I have no official standing with their society.' He pursed his hands together. 'It is an error to believe that the Order of Azyr are the only ones who seek to defend civilisation from the dark powers that would devour it. The sepulchrists, for instance, work to find ways to harness the magic of Shyish for the betterment of mankind. Sigmar's mighty Sacrosanct Stormcast Eternals include the unravelling of sorcery among their duties to the God-King.' He nodded and tapped a finger against the table. 'Even some of Nagash's creatures are devoted to the persecution of those who trade with the Ruinous Powers, for the Great Necromancer is no friend to Chaos.'

The word brought a gasp from Cicely. Samuel's hand reached to his neck for the talisman he'd once worn. *Chaos.* Of all the horrors a mind could contemplate, it was those inflicted by the Dark Gods that had to be considered the most malefic. They brought not merely death but corruption, a perversion of all that was natural. Those who succumbed to Chaos were beset by mutation and madness. They were consumed in body, mind and soul. By their very existence they spread the contagion of their corruption, warping the world around them by malign degrees, gradually drawing it into the infernal dominion of daemons.

'Do you think that is what menaces us?' Samuel asked, hoping Aaric would dissuade him of the hideous possibility.

'I don't know,' Aaric admitted. 'From what you've told me, I wouldn't dismiss it out of hand.' Again he tapped his finger against the table. 'Your account leads me to believe that there's a deliberate system in play. From that evidence alone we can discount coincidence.' He shook his head. 'Coincidence,' he repeated. 'The most irrational conclusion any mind can reach. It means a pattern that is incompatible with pre-established belief and expectation. A placebo to discard the inconvenient.' He smiled and dipped his head in apology. 'We'll have no talk of coincidence in this matter.'

Cicely looked up and struggled to hold her uncle's gaze as she posed a question to him. 'What do you think is happening?'

'These deaths are certainly not random,' Aaric stated. 'The factors that appear random I'm convinced are simply because we don't know enough to understand how they fit. The differences in age and occupation, the gaps between when these deaths occur, all of them must be determined by criteria we've yet to establish.'

'There's also the randomness of how–' Samuel was rebuff by an irritated look from Aaric.

'As I've said before, when first you brought this matter to my attention, that is only an illusion.' He picked up the knife on his plate and made a thrusting motion with it. 'If I stab you, then the weapon was this knife.' He turned the blade around and made a sweeping swing. 'If, however, you're slashed, the weapon remains the knife. Only the nature of the wound has changed, not the instrument. So, I am convinced, are these killings. The "accidents", as they seem, are but wounds. The instrument that inflicted them is some pernicious magic.'

'You sound very certain of that,' Samuel objected. 'Surely you need to know more before drawing so firm a conclusion.'

Aaric's visage darkened before he made his reply. 'There's a pattern that is too terrible to deny, yet you're too close to it to see it. Or you don't want to see it.' Samuel noticed the look of horror on Cicely's face when her uncle pointed to her. 'There have been two more deaths since you left. A woman and a young boy. They were known to you?'

Samuel's insides turned cold. He knew now what Aaric was driving at. 'Emelda's sister, Viktoria, and my nephew Sebastian. You're telling me this malign power is targeting my family.' He shook his head, desperately rejecting the idea. 'You forget Alastair. He wasn't part of our family.'

'But what of Thayer's allegations?' Aaric said. 'Perhaps Alastair and Anya were married in secret. It wouldn't be the first time a clandestine marriage took place.'

'But there's also Saint and Octavia,' Cicely suddenly interjected.

Samuel sighed at Aaric's confused expression. He started to ask about these other murders, but now it was the hunter's turn to interrupt him. 'My gryph-hound and Anya's cat,' he explained. 'Both had accidents.'

'Fatal accidents?' Aaric probed. Cicely nodded, and a satisfied look appeared in the scholar's eyes. 'These deaths happened before the first human casualty... the child Barnabus?'

Now it was Samuel who nodded. He didn't understand what Aaric was building towards, but it seemed this confirmation supported his theory.

'Don't you see? The animals *are* connected. Whoever or whatever is perpetrating these murders had to make a test first.' Aaric warmed to the theory, pushing ahead with eagerness. 'That the animals belonged to your family is important. It meant they were connected to you. That gave this unknown malefactor a hold upon them. Sorcery is at its most potent when it can form sympathetic bonds, a kind of arcane resonance. By attacking the animals first, it was establishing that connection.'

Cicely dropped her spoon onto her plate. Samuel was stunned to see how pale she looked. He thought he recognised the onset of another attack. She excused herself and quickly withdrew to her room.

'I'm sorry,' Aaric said. 'I let my excitement overcome my judgement. When I focus upon a problem, I sometimes lose sight of how others will react to the conclusion I draw. I apologise for upsetting my niece.'

Samuel was quick to reassure Aaric. 'She's been unwell ever since her brother died. These attacks come upon her sometimes even before she's aware of them.'

Aaric frowned at the reminder. 'That was after they were both attacked by a wolf in Briardark?'

To hear the event described in such a tone by the occultist set icy dread into Samuel's heart. 'You're not thinking that it was an ulfwernar and she was infected?'

Aaric smiled and made a placating gesture. 'Ease yourself, Samuel. I've studied greatly in dark subjects others are afraid to confront. In all my research, I've yet to find a substantiated report of anything like an ulfwernar. To be certain, you do find stories, but they're just that.' He pointed to the stand where their coats were hanging. 'Besides, one of the first things that happened when you received me into your house is Cicely took my coat and hung it for me. If she were an ulfwernar, she'd never have been able to touch it. Silver is as toxic to that breed as troggoth bile is to us.' His smile broadened. 'At least, if you believe the legends. As I said, I've seen no proof of such things.' He sighed, and the humour left his features. 'It will always be a mystery to me why, with all the real horrors in Shyish, people see fit to invent further ones.'

Samuel felt some relief to have that particular fear allayed, but there was still the grim spectre Aaric had raised regarding the pattern to the mysterious deaths. 'You are convinced these tragedies are being directed against my family?'

'Aren't you? The evidence certainly lends itself to that conclusion.' Aaric chewed on a spoonful of stew before elaborating. 'If we set aside the death of Alastair Greimhalt, the rest are certainly connected to you. Right down to the animals. There's a systemic quality there that can't be ignored.' He set down his spoon and leaned forwards. 'Tell me, Samuel, have you made any enemies? Anyone who hates you enough to try to destroy everything around you?'

A bitter laugh was the first reaction Samuel gave. 'I'd have said Thayer, but the man would never strike his own son. Allowing, of course, that he even had access to the kind of witchcraft you're describing.'

'Thayer knew enough to explain why Anya would kill her own son with magic,' Aaric cautioned. 'Sacrifice is a common means by which those who would beg power from the Dark Gods prove themselves vile enough to be given what they seek. There are records of the most depraved outrages performed for the express purpose of propitiating the Ruinous Powers. No, what Thayer said is established precedent in the arcane.' The scholar scowled and scratched his head. 'But it doesn't fit. If Thayer did sacrifice his son, then it wouldn't explain the earlier deaths... and I'm convinced none of them were an accident.'

Samuel clenched his fists. 'If I knew who was behind this, I'd strangle him with my bare hands and leave his body to the corpse-rats!' He closed his eyes and rapped his knuckles against his brow. 'But I can think of no one. No one who could hate me or my family that much.'

'There is, of course, your cousin Rukh,' Aaric said. 'If he knew of his wife's dalliance with Alastair, that would be reason to kill them both.' Even as he warmed to the possibility, Aaric discarded it. 'Why persist in the killing though? And, as you pointed out, would he be so determined on revenge that he would kill his own son?'

'Then what is the answer?' Samuel wondered. 'Some murderous malignant seeking revenge for wrongs done to it by my ancestors?'

Aaric mulled that over for a moment, but then rejected it. 'If it were any form of undead, your priest would have recognised its presence. I don't know what sort of man your Pater Kosminski is, but the priests of Nagash generally fall into two camps. There are those who seek to foster harmony between the living and the dead. If Kosminski were of that sort, then he would be seeking to appease this spirit and protect your community.

'But if he were of the other sort, those who simply seek power for themselves, then Kosminski would try to exploit the malignant's outrages to aggrandise himself.' Aaric waved his finger at the ceiling as he made his point. 'He'd preach a cadence of terror to your town that would paint him as their only salvation from this scourge. You tell me that he's done neither, which in turn leads me to believe that Kosminski has failed to detect any trace of necromancy at work here.'

'Which leads us back to where we began,' Samuel groaned. 'This is worse than trying to track a beast in the forest. At least on the hunt I have some idea of what I'm hunting. Here we don't even know what we're looking for... or if it even exists at all!'

The scholar's face was grim. 'Oh, it exists. Of that much I can assure you. What it is, its absolute nature, these are things I can't tell you.' He reached across the table and gripped Samuel's arm. 'But there's a way that we could find out. If you have the courage to permit it.'

'What are you proposing?' For some reason he couldn't explain, Samuel was afraid. There was a suggestion in Aaric's voice that went beyond any demand for mortal courage. Something beyond the mere risk of life and limb.

Aaric maintained his grasp and locked eyes with Samuel. 'You told me that Thayer consulted a spirit-speaker, a medium.'

'Yes... Mama Ouspenskaya.' Samuel could perceive now what Aaric was leading towards. 'You can't... It wouldn't be right.'

'The spirits learn things in death that were obscured to them in life,' Aaric stated. 'The quickest way we can discover the path we must investigate is to consult Ouspenskaya and have her conduct a séance.' Sympathy crept into his face, and his tone was regretful when he added the part that Samuel railed against. 'Emelda's spirit would surely answer if you called to her, and the circumstances of her death would certainly be known to her.'

Samuel shook his head, horrified by the proposal. 'Don't ask this of me.' Tears formed in his eyes and started down his face. 'I couldn't do that. I couldn't listen to her voice... knowing.' He stiffened and wrenched his hand from Aaric's grip. 'Can't you see? To hear her again, to know she was near but also to know... Gods! It would be like losing her all over again!'

Aaric was quiet. He gave Samuel a moment to compose his grief. 'You know that I've gone through what you've gone through. Your sister... I...' His expression hardened and there was an edge to his voice. 'But it isn't our dead we must think of. It isn't our own anguish and misery. We can't be so selfish. What we must think of now are those who are in danger. Forget about the dead and focus on the living who are threatened!'

Samuel did. He thought of Cicely, the only child left to him. He imagined her being struck down by sorcery. He looked into Aaric's eyes with a steely gaze.

'I'll do it,' the hunter agreed.

'The best ones to tell us who killed them,' Aaric said as he leaned back in his chair, 'are the victims themselves.'

CHAPTER THIRTEEN

The spirit-speaker, Mama Ouspenskaya, had been an institution in Felstein for as long as anyone could remember. Samuel could recall his grandfather speaking of her as already old when he was a young man. There were some who claimed she'd learned something of the necromancer's art to extend her life. Others whispered that the medium wasn't truly alive but was in fact one of the undead herself.

Samuel took a more pragmatic view. The Mama Ouspenskaya of today wasn't the same woman from his grandfather's time, but rather just the latest spirit-speaker to adopt the name and mantle. It was much easier for a medium to assume the legacy of another than it was to build their own reputation.

The medium's residence was situated on a dreary side street, a half-timbered structure of two storeys whose most notable features were the iron gargoyles perched atop its gabled roof and the assorted hex signs painted across its facade. The buildings to either side of it were in advanced stages of dilapidation, derelicts that had been uninhabited for decades. Only the desperate would take up residence adjacent to the spirit-speaker, fearful that some apparition called up during a séance might be unwilling to return to the underworld and would continue to haunt the area. Those who made a try at it would invariably quit after a few months, their nerves worn thin by the outré goings-on. Strange lights and eerie noises were often found emanating from Mama Ouspenskaya's house.

'Do we have to do this?' Cicely stopped outside the front gate, one hand gripping the iron railing. Her voice was tense, her expression pleading. Samuel felt sorry for her, remembering the first time he'd gone into the medium's house. That had been when Cicely's grandmother had lost a family heirloom and thought the spirits could tell her where to find it. Any doubts he might have had over the medium's powers were settled when the ring was discovered exactly where the séance told them it would be found.

'I'm afraid it's the quickest way,' Aaric said. He frowned as he regarded Cicely. Samuel could guess the reason for his concern. She was looking less robust than she had yesterday. The old complaint was sapping her strength again.

'You don't have to go,' Samuel told her. 'Your uncle and I can do this. You can wait for us at home.'

'I've done enough waiting already,' Cicely retorted, annoyance in her voice. 'You've only just come back from Gothghul Hollow and the dangers of that journey. I'm not going to sit back now and let you assume more risks.'

Aaric tried to offer some comforting advice to his companions. 'In a séance, the risks are entirely assumed by the medium. Remember that she is the foundation for any manifestations. The spirits that appear aren't independent, like malignants. They remain tethered to the underworlds, unable to truly leave. The degree of their interactions in the mortal world is wholly dependent on how much energy the séance provides to them.' He raised a warning finger. 'Remember, it is your fear that is the greatest threat. The spirits can't hurt you, but *you* can hurt yourself. I have been present at a séance where one of the sitters was so frightened that his heart failed him and he collapsed dead at the table.' A contemplative look came upon the scholar, and he added, 'It would have been amusing had the medium been able to bring his spirit through while we were still present.'

Samuel gave Cicely another worried look. He wasn't confident her mind was composed enough for this. 'You don't allay my concerns with that story,' he told Aaric.

'I repeat, then, that the real risk is that undertaken by the spirit-speaker,' Aaric said. 'She will be using her body as a gateway by which the spirit can slip away from the domain Nagash has judged it to belong in. As the example of the various undead shows, those who've passed on feel both a desperate longing and a bitter loathing for the realm of the living. It is this all-consuming conflict within themselves that renders the undead so inimical to us, even when they were known to us in life. Spirits called in a séance can exhibit the same obsessions. When they do, instead of merely seeing the medium as a conduit through which they can manifest and communicate, they treat her as prey.'

'If Mama Ouspenskaya is the only means by which they can manifest, how can the spirits threaten her?' Cicely asked.

Aaric glanced at the house with its gargoyles and hex signs. 'Those are protective wards,' he said. 'Designed to oppose occult energies, repel any amethyst magic that could seep through and permit a spirit to strengthen itself. When you see Mama Ouspenskaya, she'll no doubt have many rings and charms intended to shield herself from the same arcane influences. A sufficiently powerful spirit could fasten upon her and seek to draw her soul into the underworld.'

'Wouldn't that end the spirit's manifestation?' Samuel wondered. 'If Mama Ouspenskaya is the only link between worlds, breaking that link would send the spirit back.'

'Typically,' Aaric agreed. 'An angry spirit won't take that into consideration or simply won't care. Sometimes removing the medium's soul won't be fatal and the body will live on as a mindless husk... or as a shell of which the spirit can take possession.' An uneasy expression entered his eyes. 'There are also those very rare times when the spirit is malevolent enough that it can strip away the medium's energies completely and use them to transform into a wraith.'

Samuel saw the way Cicely flinched. The recent fears over Alastair returning as such a murderous apparition were still fresh in everyone's memory. Even more with Anya's tragic accusal and death.

'If I didn't feel it was absolutely necessary, I wouldn't suggest this action,' Aaric said. 'Time, however, is vital. The force that is preying on your family could strike at any moment.' He unlatched the gate. 'Whatever risk you believe awaits you here, remember what we hope to learn. Remember that if this malefactor is left at liberty, the next victim could be one of you.'

No doubt the gravity of the situation justified Aaric's curt summation, but a sidelong glance at Cicely caused Samuel to interrupt the scholar. 'You should go back,' he told her again. She just shook her head, that mix of fear and distress etched across her face. What was it, exactly? Anxiety, or anticipation? Samuel thought he understood. This was a chance, perhaps a final chance, for her to speak to Emelda. He abandoned the idea of coaxing Cicely to leave. However afraid she might be, what daughter could walk away from the chance to speak to her dead mother?

As that thought came to Samuel, he embraced something he'd tried to resist acknowledging. Aaric kept speaking in pragmatic terms, about what they might learn. He'd lost sight of the human connection beyond its usefulness as a way to attract the spirits. It wasn't just some nameless spectre they'd be communing with if everything worked as intended. It would be Emelda. Cicely's mother. His wife of twenty years.

Samuel hung back a moment as Aaric walked across the yard to the door. He needed to compose himself, rein in his emotions. In a few moments he'd be speaking with someone who was lost to him.

Before that happened, he wanted to figure out what he wanted to say. What clumsy words could express the sorrow he felt and communicate the emptiness inside him now that she was gone? He wished he had Aaric's education. Then maybe he'd know the right words.

'Then again,' Samuel whispered to himself as he and Cicely started towards the house, 'maybe I wouldn't.'

Cicely's entire being was filled with trepidation when Aaric rapped on Mama Ouspenskaya's door. The final fragile hope that somehow they'd be thwarted at the last moment and the spirit-speaker would refuse to see them vanished when the portal opened and an ill-favoured servant regarded them with strange, amber-coloured eyes. Despite the scarf wrapped about the lower half of the woman's face, Cicely was certain she'd never seen her before. The shock of crimson hair that flowed across her narrow head, the almost ethereal grace with which she moved, these were things Cicely was certain she would have noted even in more mundane surroundings.

'We have come to consult Mama Ouspenskaya,' Aaric announced imperiously. The servant regarded him with a look that was anything but servile. She treated Samuel with the same surliness, but when her weird eyes turned to Cicely, the expression in them became quizzical. For an instant she drew back and seemed about to slam the door in their faces. After a moment, though, she stepped aside and motioned for them to enter.

The hall into which they were led was wreathed in black hangings that pooled into piles of cloth at the base of each wall. A single light burned from the ceiling, but the illumination it gave wasn't the cherry glow of flame. This was a pale blue flicker exuding from a crystal sphere about the size of Cicely's hand. When she let her eyes linger on the globe, she could discern a spectral shape trapped inside, pawing at the transparent walls of its prison with bony fingers. It was from this entity that the ghostly luminescence was transmitted.

A shudder passed through Cicely. The fate of the trapped spirit struck too close for her. If she faded completely and lost her corporeal form, would some medium condemn her to such a fate? Locked forever inside a crystal, alone and forgotten.

The servant preceded them down the hall. She moved with a strange gracefulness that was both enchanting and unsettling. Cicely wondered at the harsh sound each time the woman took a step, imagining the noise could only come from wooden sabots or perhaps hooves. There was a musky, animal smell in the building that seemed more pronounced when the servant was near.

Still maintaining a surly silence, the woman stopped midway down the hall and drew back a section of the hanging to reveal a doorway. She pointed inside before stepping back.

The precise dimensions of the room within were impossible for Cicely to judge, even with her abnormal perception. Like the hallway, the walls were heavily draped in black. A sphere similar to the one she'd seen earlier floated up near the ceiling. By its glow they could see a large round table surrounded by chairs. A cabbalistic design was carved into the wood and highlighted with some golden application, though she couldn't tell if it was gilding or merely paint. Around the table, across the floor, a complex design had been chalked. Three intersecting rings with strange glyphs filling each spiral. A narrow span left the circle incomplete, leading from the outer room to the table itself.

'Step only along the path,' Aaric said, gesturing at the chalk ring. 'Disturbing the circle could be dangerous.'

Samuel followed the scholar's advice, but Cicely found herself unaccountably reluctant to draw closer than she already was. It took a puzzled look from her uncle to provide the motivation to overcome the peculiar aversion. She hurried along the path and fairly jumped into the chair next to her father. She furtively watched Aaric as he joined them, hoping he'd think her reluctance to stem from natural fear rather than the occult affliction that held her in its grasp.

'You've come to consult the spirits.' The voice, creaking with age yet still conveying a sense of terrible authority, rose from only a few feet away. Cicely whipped her head around, shocked to see that they weren't alone at the table. Across from Aaric, a shape was huddled in one of the chairs. A figure that Cicely couldn't swear hadn't been there when they'd entered but which in her gut she knew had materialised in their midst by some arcane means when no one was looking.

Even a glance was enough to reveal that the old woman at the table was Mama Ouspenskaya. An aged crone, her face was cobwebbed with deep wrinkles and the skin hung loose about her bones. A few blackened teeth yet kept hold within her curled mouth. Her eyes flanked a knife-like nose that came to a sharp point just above her cracked lips. One eye was milky with blindness, as pale as a frog's belly. The other was dark, of such a profound blackness that it seemed to be all pupil. Strands of lank silvery hair swept down from the medium's scalp, dangling across the shoulders of the colourful shawl she wore over her dress. Her arms, scrawny as rails, were festooned with a confusion of jewelled bangles and bands that jangled together whenever she moved. Each stick-like finger was adorned

with at least one ring, with many so overladen that they covered the first knuckle.

'We have come here to seek wisdom only the dead can bestow,'
Aaric replied.

Mama Ouspenskaya cackled with amusement, the sound echoing through the séance parlour. 'There is always a price when
petitioning the dead. Before you pay it, know that those who
consult the spirits only rarely hear what they want to hear. Truth
is seldom what we'd like it to be.'

Cicely watched her father reach into his pocket and remove
several items of jewellery. She recognised several of them as
pieces her mother had owned. When Samuel pushed them across
to the medium, the crone disdained all of them. Her fleshless
claw closed on the hunter's hand. One long nail tapped against
the wedding band he wore.

'This,' Mama Ouspenskaya hissed. 'This is the price you must
pay. I will accept no other.' Her dark eye gleamed in the wisp-
light's glow. Challenge crept into her tone. 'Will you pay my
price?' Again, her nail tapped the ring. 'How sorely do you want
to speak to your wife?'

Samuel pulled his hand back. Cicely saw the anguish in his
face, but after only a slight hesitation he pulled his marriage ring
free and gave it to the spirit-speaker. Mama Ouspenskaya coldly
removed one of the rings she was already wearing and threw
it away. She replaced it with Samuel's ring. Despite the skeletal thinness of her finger, somehow it didn't fall off her hand.

'The price is paid,' the medium stated. Cicely felt there was
an ominous note to those words, as though they signified the
completion of a ritual in itself. A compact between themselves
and the spirit-speaker. Mama Ouspenskaya wagged her finger at
each of the three sitters. 'You will remain seated until the séance
is ended,' she dictated. 'It will be dangerous for you to leave.'
She nodded at the chalked ring that surrounded the table. Cicely

gasped to see that the open path was now shut and covered in cabbalistic signs.

The medium glanced at Aaric and gave him a gap-toothed grin. 'The danger is not only for myself,' she said, as though aware of his words outside the house. 'Should anything happen to me because one of you broke the circle, my helpmate wouldn't be very forgiving. She has a vengeful streak that cannot be appeased. A bit of advice you should take to heart.'

'What other instructions do you have for us?' Aaric asked. Cicely thought he looked less confident than he had before. Something about this séance parlour wasn't what he'd expected.

Mama Ouspenskaya nodded. 'You will keep your hands linked, arm through arm, until the sitting is concluded.' She clasped her own hands before her, with elbows spread wide apart. They followed her example, Cicely linking arms with her father, Samuel looping his other arm with Aaric. 'Good,' the medium crowed. 'No matter what you may see or hear, keep that grip. Your protection comes from unity.'

'And what of you?' Aaric posed. 'A medium typically holds hands with the sitters.'

'I have my own protections,' was her enigmatic response. She shifted in her seat and swept her gaze around the table. 'A last chance to leave. When this moment has passed, it will be too late.'

Cicely turned a hopeful look to Samuel, but she could see he was firm in his intention. Aaric, too, was resolute. She tamped down her own anxiety. If they were to go on, then she had to remain. She had to know whatever they learned.

Mama Ouspenskaya bowed her head. 'That is settled then. We will begin.' A bitter smile wormed onto her face. 'Whatever happens, remember that you were warned.'

The atmosphere within the séance parlour had been cold from the moment they came into the room. Samuel was impressed that

Cicely gave no indication of discomfort, but he knew she must feel the shiver rippling through his arm. When Mama Ouspenskaya began the sitting, the chill grew still more marked. Samuel doubted he'd be able to detect his daughter's trembling from his own, so greatly was he effected. He could tell from the quiver of Aaric's lips that the scholar wasn't immune to the mounting cold.

'By the ten thousand treacheries of Olynder, Lady of Sorrows, do we command indulgence,' Mama Ouspenskaya cried out. Her beringed hands curled into arcane gestures as she continued the incantation. 'Let no malignant enter our circle or seek unto itself a fleshly vessel. By the six hundred scourges of Reikenor, Hunter of Shadows, let no gheist desire to hide itself within mortal frame. By the ten dread names of Nagash, Lord of Undeath, let all souls shorn of life be bound by his tyranny and cower before his might.'

The fitful glow of the wisp-light faltered as the medium invoked the name of Nagash. Mama Ouspenskaya fell back in her chair, her head lolling, her mouth gaping open. 'Spirits of those who have passed to the underworlds, I call upon Maltrix the Reviled to be my guide. Heed me, you accursed, and bear unto me those with whom these visitors would have discourse.'

Samuel felt Cicely's arm tighten as tension raced through her body. For a time he didn't understand her agitation, but then he became aware of what she'd perceived moments before. There was a dark shape hovering behind the medium, so dark that it stood out from the blackness of the room. He could discern a head encased in some spiked helm, but there wasn't a face within that frame of spectral steel. He could see thin shoulders and arms, but no legs to support the apparition.

'Maltrix, traitorous wretch, damned by deed and design, obey me now!' The spirit-speaker writhed in her chair as though wracked with pain. 'Heed the authority of those even you dare not defy.' The pained spasms relented. Samuel thought the phantom behind her chair grew less distinct, though it remained present.

Mama Ouspenskaya leaned forward again, her eye fixating on Samuel. 'You've paid the price. Let yours be the first to draw near.' A knowing smile formed on the medium's withered face. 'Name her, and say to her what you would say.'

A knot formed in Samuel's throat. His tongue felt like lead in his mouth. It dawned on him that only in the most abstract way had he appreciated what would happen in the séance parlour. As desperately as he wanted to speak to Emelda, a part of him was crippled by fear of doing so. He felt helpless, frozen with indecision. It was only when Aaric pulled at his arm that he knew he must speak.

'Emelda Helmgaart,' Samuel whispered. The instant he did, he saw the phantom behind Mama Ouspenskaya wink away into nothingness. It was gone for only a moment. When it reappeared, it seemed to clutch a ball of light in its hand. The orb drifted away and sank down onto the medium's chest. No, Samuel corrected himself, not onto, but rather into, for soon the sphere had vanished inside the old woman.

'Saaaamuuuul,' the medium groaned. She closed her eyes and her hands felt across her body as though unaware of what they were attached to. 'Huuusbaaaand...'

Aaric's arm tightened on Samuel's, as though to convey unspoken warning, but the hunter was filled with too much emotion to be restrained now. The voice hissing out of Mama Ouspenskaya wasn't that of the crone. Distorted as it was, he could recognise it as Emelda's. No, it wasn't just the sound – he *knew* it was his departed wife. He could feel her presence as surely as he'd ever felt anything before.

'I'm here,' Samuel gasped. 'I'm here, my love!' He looked aside to Cicely, saw the anguish on their daughter's face. 'Cicely's here too. We're both here!'

Mama Ouspenskaya began to shudder in her chair. From her open mouth, a deep, grating moan arose. 'Cicely? Cicely!' The voice cascaded into a piercing scream, filled with all the torments of the unhallowed realms. The medium thrashed about as the screams persisted.

'Emelda! What is it? How can we help you?' Even Aaric's and Cicely's grips weren't enough to keep him from standing, and only their restraint kept him from lunging across the table. He didn't know what was happening, he only knew that the medium had drawn Emelda here and that his wife's spirit was in pain.

'Samuel, don't be a fool!' Aaric cried. The gravity in the scholar's tone snapped Samuel back to reason. He sank back in his seat, trying to control the urge to action that gripped him.

At the sound of Aaric's voice, the screams rising from Mama Ouspenskaya suddenly changed. Samuel saw the orb that had been drawn into her emerge from her mouth like a glowing bubble. This exploded into twinkling fragments that swiftly vanished.

A kind of ominous anticipation now held sway. Samuel saw another orb manifest, but this time it didn't appear in Maltrix's hand. Rather, it came shooting into the room from behind the black drapery. The helmed phantom moved to intercept the rogue sphere, a shadowy sword billowing between its outstretched fingers. The orb nimbly dodged the spectre's guard and slipped past it to sink into the spirit-speaker's body.

Now a new voice rose from Mama Ouspenskaya. Unlike Emelda's, there was no confusion in its tone, but a firmness and surety that was commanding. 'Aaric! Hear me while you can!'

Samuel glanced over at his brother-in-law. The voice sounded familiar, but he wasn't certain until he saw the shock on the scholar's face.

'Hephzibah!' Aaric gasped.

Samuel looked back at the medium. Her head was sagging forwards, but now there was a strange veil across it, a distortion that increasingly assumed the appearance of another face. A transparency through which the crone's wrinkled features could still be detected. It was this double image that caused Samuel a moment's delay before recognising his sister's visage.

'I'm here, Hephzibah!' Aaric said. 'This is Felstein. We sought answers to the–'

'I know what you would learn,' Hephzibah's spirit pronounced. 'Those answers are veiled in terror. A terror of which our family has already partaken.'

Again, Samuel felt Cicely's arm grow tense. Her face was shivering with dread, her teeth clamped firmly on her lower lip to keep from crying out. His heart surged with pity for her fright, but he knew they had to keep going.

'What is this evil that plagues this community?' Aaric asked. Samuel could see from his expression that there were any number of other things he wanted to say but that even in a situation like this, he was trying to focus on the danger they hoped to put an end to.

The spirit growled, a malicious intonation that crackled through the room. As it was spoken, blood started to seep from the medium's nose. What it meant, Samuel had no understanding, but it was readily apparent that Aaric wasn't so ignorant.

'Even here its evil has spread?' The scholar shuddered.

'You must guard yourself, Aaric,' Hephzibah cautioned. 'You must make unto yourself a talisman. Three stalks of grave-reed from the tomb of a child. A branch from a tree where a witch was hanged. The spittle of a one-eyed toad. Twelve hairs from a fell bat's wing. Bind these in the skin of a gryph-hound's paw. Do this and you will be protected from the evil that threatens you.'

'But what is this evil?' Samuel cried out.

A piteous moan rose from the spirit, and it seemed to writhe in agony.

'What form has it taken?' Aaric demanded, his eyes wild and his voice strained. 'It has fixated on your family here! How is it killing them? What instrument is it using?'

The spirit moaned and its voice gradually died away. The orb left Mama Ouspenskaya as the other had, but this time the shrouded apparition of Maltrix lunged for it. The spectre's sword spit the sphere upon its tip. Samuel could sense the phantom's obscene delight as it drew back with the glowing orb impaled on its blade. Its satisfaction lasted only a moment. With stunning abruptness, Hephzibah's spirit detached itself and went speeding away. Maltrix lifted its helmed head back in a silent shriek, then charged after the fleeing soul. Before it could pursue it into the wall, the wraith was arrested as though held back by invisible chains. It spun around, and Samuel could sense the enormous hate it directed at Mama Ouspenskaya. Raising its sword once more, it flew at the spirit-speaker to which it was tethered.

'Begone, Maltrix the Reviled!' the medium pronounced, rising from her chair and pointing at the phantom. 'Return from whence you came!' At her injunction and before it could reach her, Maltrix vanished into nothingness.

Mama Ouspenskaya collapsed back into her seat, visibly exhausted by the ordeal. When she reached to her face and found blood streaming from her nose, she turned an angry eye towards the sitters. Whatever the spirit-speaker had expected, it was obvious that the séance hadn't gone as she'd intended.

'Begone,' she rasped, flicking beads of blood from her fingers. Her ancient body shivered as though suffering a palsy. Her eyes were wide, the anger receding into raw terror. She slumped down against the table, her head thumping against it. 'Leave my house, accursed wretches,' she groaned. 'You would challenge an evil even Great Nagash could not fathom! I want no part in the damnation that pursues you.'

A bestial, animal smell filled Samuel's nose. He spun around to see the medium's servant standing behind him. She made an impatient gesture towards the doorway. Quickly, the visitors left the table.

'Do not come here again,' Mama Ouspenskaya called after them, her voice a thin groan. 'Abomination has attached itself to you. If you try to bring it into my house again…'

Samuel didn't hear the rest of the spirit-speaker's threat. At that moment, his eyes had dropped to catch a glimpse of her servant's feet.

They were hooved. The feet of something as inhuman as anything conjured up within the séance parlour.

The servant leaned close to them as they were shown to the door. As they crossed the threshold, she spoke a single word. Her voice was melodious and vibrant, more so than any human voice, but there was an air of unspeakable evil in what she said.

'Mhurghast.'

CHAPTER FOURTEEN

'Some of the items detailed by Hephzibah's spirit I've acquired from Felstein's herbalist... or by other means.' Aaric's pause told of his reluctance to resort to what he considered criminal methods. Cicely could tell from the awkwardness of his tone.

She sat in her room, having retired there after the séance. It was easy enough to convince her father that she was sick. But instead of resting, she kept her door cracked open and listened to the two men as they discussed what they were going to do. She needed to know their plans before making her own.

'The fell bat hairs will be the problem,' Aaric stated.

'There are always a few to be found in Briardark,' Samuel told the scholar. 'I regularly have to go in and cull them when they start straying from the forest.' Cicely could picture her father shaking his head. She thought she heard a faint sigh. 'Try as I might, more always show up and I have to go hunting the new ones.'

'Let's just hope that some are there now and that we can find them,' Aaric said. 'We must act upon this warning.'

'If only I'd been able to get through to Emelda,' Samuel groaned. By the sound of his voice, Cicely thought there must be tears in his eyes. 'You don't think she's suffering?'

Cicely felt as though her heart would crack to hear that question. Bad enough to know she'd caused her mother's death, but to think that Emelda's spirit had been sent to some torturous underworld was too horrible to bear.

'No,' Aaric replied. 'I think her distress was provoked by the séance. Once she departed from the circle, there'd be no further harm done to her.' Cicely felt there was something duplicitous in her uncle's voice. He was making claims he couldn't confirm in hopes of easing Samuel's mind. Clearly her father wasn't showing signs of being convinced, because Aaric continued to elaborate. 'You saw that the sitting was peculiar, shocking even Mama Ouspenskaya. Some force was trying to disrupt the ritual. Afraid we'd learn too much.'

'But we've learned nothing.' Cicely heard the impact of Samuel's fist against the table as he struck it in frustration. 'We've no more idea who or what killed Emelda than before.'

'We do know something,' Aaric said. 'We now know how we can protect ourselves. When I have the fell bat hairs, I'll make the talismans at once. Then, at least, we'll be protected from this malefic power. Nor, I will add, can such protection come too soon. The enemy might strike at any time, and we cannot be certain who will be its victim.'

Cicely winced at her uncle's words, guilt and fear uniting in equal measure. *She* was the enemy, the unknown they were hunting. The power they sought protection from was that of the onyx needle. But what else could she do? Submit to her affliction? She imagined the phantasmal spirit guide at the séance parlour, that vicious shadow enslaved to the medium's will. An existence of that sort was far worse than death. To wander Shyish as a malignant, a nighthaunt. No! While she yet lived, she had to fight against becoming such a monster. Whatever it demanded of her, she had to fight.

'...we'll hunt the fell bats,' Samuel was saying when Cicely refocused her attention on the men. 'It'll be easier to deal with them by day, but they'll be easier to find at night. Maybe too easy.'

'The bats, at least, are foes that can be fought openly,' Aaric commented. 'You've dealt with them before and come back alive. The evil that menaces our family is a different matter.'

'*Our* family?' Samuel asked, having caught Aaric's choice of words.

'I think our enemy casts a wide net. The list of victims shows that.' Aaric hesitated a moment. When his speech continued, there was an edge to it. 'I might as well confess to you that I do know something of this enemy. Little that is of benefit to us, but I've encountered the name Mhurghast before.'

Mhurghast. The name evoked a feeling of revulsion in Cicely. It was as if she were again in Briardark with the wolf's hungry gaze fastened upon her. A sense of immediate menace more pronounced than ever before seized her and set her limbs shaking.

Cicely quietly closed the door, blocking off the men's voices. She looked over to the chair where she'd set the tapestry. The carved wolf was there again, sitting on the floor.

'*My life is yours.*' There was little of Marden now in that phantasmal voice. It was now almost entirely that *other*. The one she'd never heard but which she *knew*.

There was only one thing to do, but it took her some moments before she could quash her own reluctance. She was not yet so inured to murder that she was able to resign herself easily to the deed. Yet she could see no other way.

She was Aaric's quarry, and if she were to protect herself, her uncle had to die. Die before he gained the means to protect himself from her. Then she could go farther afield. She could leave Felstein, go to Gothghul Hollow, where Aaric's family lived. A fresh hunting ground.

Cicely retched at the thought. Another place where she'd sow death and destruction to sustain herself. But otherwise she'd die, and there was that within her that refused to accept death. She'd be betraying something that wouldn't be denied.

'*My life is yours,*' the spectral voice moaned.

The tapestry was soon resting across her lap and the onyx needle again in her hand. Cicely fixed Aaric's image in her mind. How fortuitous that he was a relation, someone that the occult laws of the needle put within her power to destroy. There was a sardonic sense of fortune that events should have contrived to make things so. Not for Aaric would there be the arcane misdirection that had allowed Thayer to escape destruction.

Intent upon her work, Cicely failed to note the sound of footsteps in the hall until they were nearly at her door. Panic seized her when she realised her father was certain to check on her before starting out on a hunt. She heard a rapping against the portal and realised with a start that she'd failed to bolt the door.

Her father was certain to hear her if she dashed over and locked it now. That course was lost to Cicely. She glanced down at the tapestry. Thus far she'd only sewn a single foot of her uncle's image, but even this made her anxious. The foot blazed accusation back at her, like the bloodied dagger of a murderess. Folding the tapestry back, she used the onyx needle to pin the guilty image back so that it was hidden.

Another knock. Cicely knew that next Samuel would try the door. Quickly, she sprang from the chair and dropped onto her bed. She'd just covered herself with a blanket when she heard the door open.

'Cicely?' Samuel called out. She kept her eyes closed, feigning sleep as she listened to him step into the room. His footfalls were followed by another's, and she knew Aaric was with him. She sensed her father standing over the bed, looking down at her. She could feel his concerned gaze searching for any sign of illness.

'Asleep,' Samuel told Aaric. A pained sigh followed the declaration. 'She sleeps much too much these days. Ever since the wolf attack, her constitution has been weak. Some days I can barely make her take food.'

'Her complexion is pale,' Aaric said. 'You should have a physician see her. Nagash knows there are enough pestilent miasmas in the land to test even the hardiest.'

'I've considered it,' Samuel confessed, 'but sometimes she seems to improve and I think this malady has passed. Then it will come stealing over her again.' A note of guilt entered the hunter's voice. 'Maybe I'm just afraid to hear what a healer might say. I keep remembering my cousin Anya's face when she learned there was no hope for little Barnabus.'

Cicely dug her nails into her palms, trying to use the pain to mitigate the sorrow that rippled through her. She'd never meant to hurt anyone, only to save herself. She'd accepted the suffering of others in an abstract fashion, but now she was listening to her father describe the awful turmoil these losses brought upon the survivors. Adding to her wretchedness was to hear him express his fears for her welfare. If Samuel knew the truth, she was certain he'd suffer no agonies about her. But to confess what she'd done by accident... what she'd done by design... was a horror Cicely couldn't face.

Still feigning sleep, Cicely heard the tapestry rustle. A moment later, Aaric was commenting on it. Icy dread filled her heart to know that the investigator held the key to everything in his hands... if he only recognised it for what it was. How extensive were his occult studies? Enough to discern the tapestry's importance? Enough to expose her crimes and denounce her? Hardly daring to breathe, she listened to her uncle's observations.

'Your daughter does remarkable work,' Aaric said, admiration in his voice. The tapestry continued to rustle as he adjusted his grip.

'She's been earning extra for the household with her sewing,' Samuel explained. 'That's something different. Something for herself. A family portrait.' Cicely noted the sadness in his voice and could picture him looking at the tapestry and seeing her mother's image.

'This man doesn't resemble anyone I know,' Aaric stated. Cicely's blood seemed to freeze. She knew he was looking at Alastair, rightly questioning why his image would be present. When she'd folded the tapestry, she'd managed to hide Anya's picture, but not that of the hanged youth.

Samuel's voice was heavy when he answered. 'That's Alastair Greimhalt.'

Cicely dreaded to hear the inevitable question her uncle would ask. It was the key that could expose everything.

'Why would your daughter depict him in a family portrait?' Aaric wondered.

A low sigh rose from her father before he replied. 'Thayer was putting pressure on me to be replaced as beasthunter. At the same time, Alastair was trying to court Cicely. He offered to mitigate Thayer's activities if they were wed.' The tapestry rustled once more. Cicely sensed that it was now her father, not her uncle, holding it. 'She had no love for the boy but must have resigned herself to the marriage in order to help me.' Samuel's words cracked with emotion. There was a heavy thud as he dropped the tapestry to the floor.

'Evidence,' Aaric pronounced. Cicely bit down on her lip to keep from crying out. He'd fitted the key to the lock! Her uncle knew!

Terror held Cicely for only a heartbeat.

'If Alastair was intent on the marriage and Cicely resigned to it,' Aaric said, 'then that may have been enough for the occult force being used against your family. Without any connection to your cousin, Alastair's aspirations may have been enough to expose him to the same enemy. The laws of magic are not so rigidly bound by the limitations of space and time. If he were to become part of the family in the future, then that could also make him such in the present. At least within the auspices of this curse.'

Cicely felt flush with relief. Aaric had come to the wrong conclusion with his evidence.

'We have to get the protection of these talismans,' Samuel said, his voice dripping with fear.

'Then let's start,' Aaric stated. Cicely heard him walk to the door. 'The sooner we find a fell bat, the sooner we can guard ourselves.'

She listened as the two men stepped out into the hall. Cicely waited until she could pick out the faint sound of them leaving the house before stirring from her bed.

She picked the tapestry up off the floor. The needle was still in place, hiding where she'd started to work on Aaric's image. The urge to hurry and complete the picture gripped her. She withdrew the needle and held it between her fingers, staring down at the work she'd barely started.

Guilt surged up within her. She thought of the anguish she'd already brought to so many. Broken families left to grieve their murdered dead. She couldn't cause more suffering. It was better to let Aaric discover her, force a revelation of her crimes. If she couldn't do it herself, then he'd have to. Once he had what he needed to make the talismans, he'd be safe from her power.

The tapestry lay draped across Cicely's knees, her hands smoothing out the cloth. She noted how pale they'd grown, the underlying veins visible through the translucent skin. She was losing substance, growing more ethereal.

Her fingers tightened around the onyx needle. Cicely tried not to imagine the hideous fate ahead of her, to fade into a spectral malignant. Worse than death, an afterlife existence of torment.

Cicely closed her eyes, trying to will herself to her resolution. No more lives to sustain her own. She wouldn't do it!

Yet the urge for self-preservation was already whispering to her, chipping away at her determination. *'My life is yours,'* the phantom voice echoed in the depths of her soul.

How long could she endure, watching herself gradually fade when escape, however abominable the price, was within her grasp?

'I won't,' Cicely vowed. Even as she said it, she knew the words were a lie. It was only a matter of hours before she'd resort to the onyx needle's magic. She'd kill again to preserve herself, and when she did, Uncle Aaric would be her next victim.

The gloom of Briardark engulfed them like the suffocating waters of a mire. Samuel couldn't recall a time when the forest had felt so sinister and overwhelming.

'What we're looking for will be roosting in the trees,' he reminded Aaric. 'But don't ignore what's around you either. Never forget that while we're hunting our prey, other things will be hunting us.' His mind turned back to the wolf that had killed Marden and how it had stalked his son even while he was tracking it.

'You're the expert,' Aaric said. 'In this arena I bow to your judgement.' His hand slapped the bag slung over his shoulder. 'Finding a fell bat will be your task. Putting it to use once we've got it is my job.'

'Just keep quiet and follow my lead,' Samuel instructed. He kept his boar spear held up at his side, its barbed head poised so that it was above his own. He'd seen fell bats strike at prey from above and hoped to thwart such a strategy by the threat of being skewered. To get around the spear, a bat would have to swoop low and come directly at him, thereby giving him more warning. Enough warning that he'd have time to react, he prayed. Usually when he went looking for fell bats, he'd have the spear held across his body and protect himself from a murderous dive by wearing a spiked helm. That piece of gear, however, had been given over to Aaric along with a spare spear. Inexperienced as he was, Samuel felt the scholar needed the better outfit for their hunt.

Furtive sounds crackled through the forest as small creatures scurried through the underbrush. Once, Samuel caught sight of a thorncat creeping away with some rodent in its mouth, but otherwise none of the forest's denizens revealed themselves. The trees, with their craggy bark and skeletal branches, were utterly devoid of either life or the gruesome unlife that permeated the lands of Shyish.

A spot of white at the base of a tree caught Samuel's eye. He drew Aaric's attention to it and motioned for silence. The object was a skull, that of a ram or goat. Other bones were littered around it, evidence that something had been scavenging meat from the carcass. The situation of the bones was suggestive to the beasthunter. He studied the trunk, looking for any traces of discolouration left by dripping blood. He couldn't be sure, but he thought there were some suggestive streaks running down the side.

Holding his spear fast, Samuel lifted his gaze, following the possible streaks upwards. He caught Aaric's shoulder with his free hand and arrested the scholar's attention. He pointed at a spot very near the top of the tree.

'I don't...' Aaric started to whisper. His voice trailed off when he finally saw what Samuel wanted him to see.

Clinging to the trunk, its leather wings furled and the hooks of its fingers digging into the bark, was an enormous bat. It had a charcoal colouring that blended well with the wood, but

Samuel's practised eye had noticed the white tufts of fur on its ears, and having spotted them, he was soon able to pick out the animal's outline. The creature's body was as large as that of a gryph-hound and its wingspread would be somewhere between twelve and twenty feet. A true monster beside the small bats that pestered people in Felstein. It was poised so that its head was facing down towards the ground. Samuel could see the crusted blood around its fanged mouth.

'There might be others nearby,' Samuel advised Aaric, keeping his voice low and his eyes on the fell bat. 'They'll sleep until nightfall, as this one does, unless something disturbs them.'

Aaric whispered, 'Do you think we can take this one without rousing others?'

Samuel gauged how high up the creature was. He'd hoped to find one that occupied a lower perch. A fell bat was too big to reliably take down with an arrow, but a solid cast of a spear could incapacitate one… if it was close enough. 'I don't know. It's too high up. If we want to take this one, I'll have to lure it down to us.'

'Time could be critical,' Aaric reminded him. 'I think we should try for this beast.'

'All right.' Samuel nodded. He rested his spear against his side and reached to his belt, drawing his knife from its sheath. With his other hand he opened a pouch on his belt and caught the animal inside. A little white mouse. Bait for the sleeping predator.

The mouse squirmed in Samuel's grip. A quick slash of the knife ended its struggles. He could feel its blood dripping over his hand. He waited until he felt the gore running down onto his wrist, sure that the scent saturated his flesh. Arcing his arm back, he fixed his gaze on the sleeping bat. A powerful throw sent the dead mouse flying upwards. The tiny carcass glanced off the bat's head, spattering its face with flecks of crimson.

The smell of blood more than the impact of the mouse stirred the fell bat from its slumber. Its upturned nose twitched as it detected the scent. The mouth opened in a hungry yawn, the sharp tongue licking across the gleaming fangs. As it awakened, the monster's eyes stared down at the forest floor. Samuel could see the irises dilate as the creature focused on him.

'Be ready,' Samuel said, taking hold of his boar spear. He couldn't afford to take his attention away from the bat to see what Aaric was doing. The animal might take wing at any moment.

The bat continued to regard Samuel, its nose twitching as it caught the smell of mouse blood from his hand. It kept its body still, but one eye snapped shut while the other kept watching him. A moment later and the predator reversed the process, so that in quick succession it had made a separate study of him with each eye. Samuel knew the beast was gauging the distance between itself and the hunter, trying to calculate the best angle of attack.

Even though he was expecting the bat to launch itself into action, when the creature did it still managed to surprise Samuel. One instant it was utterly still, the next it had released its grip on the tree and was hurtling down at the hunter. Before it crashed into him, the bat suddenly opened its wings and turned its fall into a dive.

Samuel could smell the reek of the bat's breath as it dove at him. It chirped in anger when it spotted the spear. Dipping one wing, the creature wheeled away. It turned its dive into a glide and arched between the trees. Samuel cursed under his breath and lowered his spear, ready to rush after the bat.

Before he could move, the fell bat came swooping back at Samuel. The hunter had only an impression of bared fangs and red eyes before he threw himself flat against the ground. He felt claws snatch at his clothes as the creature flew past his prostrate form.

A shrill howl echoed through the forest. Samuel rolled onto his back to see Aaric thrusting his spear at the bat. The point ripped through the membrane of its left wing, tearing it like old parchment. The injury failed to knock the beast down, and a buffet of its other wing spilled the scholar to the ground.

Before the bat could attack Aaric, Samuel lunged. He slashed his spear at the beast, forcing it back. It gave another angry chirp, a sound sharp enough to shatter glass. The animal tried to climb back into the air, and by doing so made a fatal mistake. The torn membrane crippled its ascent, slowing its rise. Samuel didn't give the fell bat an opportunity to change tactics. With a mighty heave, he threw his boar spear at the monster. The cast struck it in the middle of its body with such force that the head and several inches of the shaft were driven into its flesh.

A pained shriek rang out. The bat flapped its wings furiously, trying to keep itself aloft. The grievous wound it had taken quickly eroded its command of its own body. Unable to coordinate its wings, the beast plummeted to the ground. The impact drove the spear still deeper into its body, and the barbed tip erupted from its back. It made one last effort to rise, beating its wings hopelessly against the ground. Bloody froth spilled from its mouth when it lifted its head and gave Samuel an accusing glare. Then the beast slumped against the earth and was still.

Samuel helped Aaric to his feet. The scholar looked to have suffered no serious injury from the bat's attack. 'Well, there's all you'll need and much to spare,' the hunter declared, waving his hand at the dying monster.

'Would that I had enough of the other ingredients, I'd be able to make talismans for every soul in Felstein,' Aaric said. The prudent thing to do would have been to wait until the fell bat was completely finished, but the scholar argued once more that time might be vital. Handing off his spear to Samuel, he rushed over to the creature and slit its throat.

Samuel watched on as Aaric quickly set about harvesting what he needed from the fell bat's wings. He opened his bag and began combining the hairs with the other components, wrapping it all within the dried gryph-hound skin. The hunter felt regret at that last inclusion, for to secure it he'd had to exhume Saint's body and take the loyal creature's paws.

'This is for you,' Aaric said when he'd finished the first talisman. It was a grisly, bag-like affair with a cord fixed to one end so it might be looped over the neck of the person it was to protect.

Samuel started to reach for it, then shook his head. 'You need the protection more than I do.'

'I have enough materials to make three more,' Aaric told him, waving his hand over the components.

'All the more reason for you to keep it,' Samuel persisted. 'If time is as vital as you say, then we can't take the chance that the enemy has set its sights on you and may strike at any moment.' A chill crawled down the hunter's spine when he made the conjecture. A feeling not unlike those times when he'd been stalked by some beast in the forest. It was the sense of a hostile awareness being directed at him. Still, he insisted Aaric keep the first talisman. 'If you were struck down, I lack the knowledge to make more of them. You need the protection more than I do.'

Aaric reluctantly accepted Samuel's logic and put on the talisman. 'I'll hurry,' he promised as he set to making the second.

Never had time passed so slowly for Samuel as it did while he watched Aaric work. The unease that wore at him swelled with every heartbeat. He knew their enemy was fixated on them, aware of what they were doing. Any moment he expected it to strike, and if it couldn't get Aaric, then it would seek another victim.

'Be sure to make one for Cicely,' Samuel enjoined the scholar. If death did suddenly fall on him, he would rest easier knowing his daughter was safe. Right now, that was more important than anything.

To know that Cicely, at least, was safe.

The onyx needle was jolted from Cicely's fingers, provoking a gasp of pain. She looked down at the nearly completed image of her uncle, then glanced at her hand. The flesh had become almost vaporous, the bones stark beneath the gossamer veil of her skin. Panic thrummed through her. She'd resisted doing what she needed to do for far too long. She had to hurry or it would be too late for her.

She retrieved the needle from the floor. An awkward task, now that her fingers were practically invisible and nearly devoid of any tactile sensation. It took an inordinate degree of concentration just to maintain a grip on it. Hurriedly, she brought it back to the tapestry and tried to continue to work.

Again the needle was jolted from her hand, unable to even finish a single stitch. Half expecting such, now Cicely was more aware of what had happened. It wasn't her deteriorating condition that had knocked the magic needle from her grip. It was an outside force. Trying to drive the point into her uncle's incomplete picture was like stabbing at a wall.

Cicely used the thread still attached to the needle to draw it back to her. She considered the strange obstruction and at once realised what had happened. Indeed, she'd vainly tried to resist saving herself for far too long. Her delay had given Aaric time to protect himself with the talisman he was crafting. He was immune to the terrible power that was at her beck and call. The power that alone could prevent her death.

Cicely undid the thread and fumblingly attached another to the needle's eye. She had to forget about Aaric now. She had to choose a different victim and pray she had enough time to complete their image before it was too late.

It would have to be a small figure. Something she could finish quickly. Cicely thought of the delicate shape of the infant Anya had left behind. She hesitated for only a moment. 'Poor thing,' she muttered, 'to go through life without your mother. It's a cruel existence and one that it's merciful to spare you.'

Resigned to her course, Cicely quickly began to work. There was no guarding power to turn her needle this time, only the threat that her fingers would become too phantasmal to complete the picture before it was finished.

CHAPTER FIFTEEN

'I'm so sorry to tell this to you, but your cousin's youngest child is dead.' Hochmueller gave that report to Samuel as he and Aaric left Briardark and headed back into town through the man's fields. The farmer's visage was grave, his eyes tinged with fear as he related what he knew of the accident that had claimed still another member of Samuel's family.

To every emotion there comes a threshold at which it can be sustained no longer. There was no more room in Samuel's heart for sorrow. The news that little Enoch, Anya and Rukh's infant, had died was unable to add to his grief. He took the information as dispassionately as he would hearing Hochmueller tell him about the weather. It was just a fact to be filed away in his mind, not a tragedy to be registered in his soul.

'These are ill tidings,' Aaric said, disrupting the strained silence from Samuel's lack of reaction. He nodded and added in a sagely tone, 'Too many accidents to be accidents.' Hochmueller had already reached the same conclusion, but at the scholar's words,

203

the farmer made the sign of Nagash and pressed the bone amulet he wore to his lips.

'Mortarchs have mercy,' the farmer hissed. 'Thayer was right. There is witchcraft!'

Samuel gripped Aaric by the arm and drew him towards town. 'We waste time tarrying here,' he said as he urged him along. He didn't care overmuch what impression their abrupt departure made on Hochmueller.

Samuel's focus had to be on who could be saved, not on what was already lost. There was nothing he could do now for Enoch, but it was possible to still save others from the witchcraft running rampant in Felstein.

'Give me another talisman,' Samuel told Aaric as they started down the narrow road and Felstein's buildings began to emerge from the fog. 'I want one to protect Cicely.'

'I knew that you would,' Aaric said, proffering the grim article to his brother-in-law. He closed his hand around Samuel's as he started to take it. 'I was only able to make four, and even that was a strain of resources. You must emphasise how vital it is that she keep the talisman safe. She must keep it with her at all times.' He raised his finger for emphasis. 'At all times.'

Samuel drew his hand free of Aaric's grip. 'Of course,' he said. 'Do you think I'd take any chances with my daughter's life? That's why I must be the one who gives it to her. She'll do what I tell her.'

Aaric nodded. They were passing through the square now, with the gruesome hanging tree at its centre. The Skintaker's Swallow had a small crowd gathered outside. Conversation died away when the group noticed Samuel. From their uneasy looks, the beasthunter could guess that he'd been the subject of their discussion. One way or another.

'Fear breeds strange ideas,' Aaric said when they were past the tavern. 'The longer fear lingers, the stranger the ideas. But it is panic that makes people act on those ideas. So long as we can prevent the fear from germinating into panic, we can maintain some control of the situation.'

'And how do we do that?' Samuel demanded, anger in his voice. He'd already seen Felstein descend into panic, and Anya had been the one to pay the price. Who might suffer when next the town lost control was a question he didn't want to think about.

Aaric turned, a grim cast to his expression. 'By learning. By observing.'

There was that in Aaric's manner that curdled Samuel's blood. He didn't know what provoked such a feeling, he only knew that he felt it. A menace, a danger that Aaric wasn't ready to put into words.

'Come, we must hurry to Cicely,' Aaric said, almost visibly pushing aside the subject he'd started to broach. The idea so terrible he wasn't ready to share it with Samuel.

'My mind will be at ease once she has protection,' Samuel said, hand tightening about the talisman. He wondered how long such relief would last. How long before Aaric disclosed his suspicions.

The house was dark when they reached it. The gloom hovered about the place like a shroud. It was strange to remember what it had been with Emelda and Marden there, old Saint curled up in the yard. All gone. All the light and cheer. Only Cicely now, lingering in the empty home like a shadow. What he wouldn't give to restore even a small part of happier times, just to draw his daughter from the melancholy that hounded her.

Samuel hesitated on the threshold, his hand upon the latch. He felt his pulse quicken, but the blood that coursed through him was cold as ice. 'What if...' he muttered. He choked on the rest. To even say it was anathema. The sorcery abroad in Felstein, ravaging his family. He turned desperate eyes to Aaric. His fear burbled forth in a whispered sob. 'What if Enoch wasn't enough? What if it's taken Cicely?'

The scholar gripped his arm in sympathy. 'Whatever is past, you cannot change. All you can do is what's left to be done.' He pulled on the latch and bowed Samuel into his home.

Inside was dark. Not so much as an ember glowed in the hearth. Cold shadow engulfed everything, leaving only the vaguest outlines. Fear clawed at Samuel. *She's gone*, it told him. *Enoch wasn't enough and the evil has taken her. You were too late.*

Samuel stood just inside the threshold, frozen like a statue, fear hammering at his heart, despair tearing at his soul. Aaric pressed on him, trying to urge him onwards. Not even on the worst of his hunts had he found it so difficult to move. It was like trying to shift blocks of lead to lift his feet. Every step was an effort that made sweat drip down his face. Cicely was all he had left. If she was gone too...

'I'll start the fire,' Aaric said. 'Light is what this place needs.'

The scholar drifted away from Samuel. By now his eyes had adjusted somewhat to the dark. He could see Aaric leaning over the woodbox to retrieve a few logs. Something else caught his notice, visible now that his vision was accustomed to the gloom. There was someone sitting in one of the chairs. He started forward with a gasp. He could discern the pale skin and dark tresses of his daughter.

Samuel could see more clearly when he got closer. Cicely had a dazed, weary look to her, staring fixedly at the table. He was almost beside her before she shifted her gaze and noticed him. A strange, indefinable emotion showed in those eyes. He couldn't decide if it was relief or guilt or alarm. Perhaps all three at once trying to find release.

The hunter's gasp brought Aaric hurrying over. It was only a matter of seconds, but by then Cicely had composed herself. She gave her uncle a tired smile. 'I'm sorry, I was dozing. I didn't hear you come in.'

Aaric chuckled and shook his head. 'That would explain the

dark house,' he said, gesturing at the cold hearth. 'It caused us some trepidation, thinking something happened.'

'Something has,' Cicely replied, her voice cracking with grief. 'Little Enoch is dead. Lucilla came and told me about my cousin and I just couldn't stop crying.' She turned an apologetic look to her father. 'I must have cried myself to sleep.'

Whatever might have happened, Samuel knew that wasn't true. Cicely had been awake – brooding, perhaps, but awake. There was an insistent undertone to her speech. She obviously didn't want Aaric to know she hadn't been sleeping. For the moment, he decided to support her lie. It was a small thing to balance against his relief that she was all right.

'I… was worried about you,' Samuel said, leaning beside Cicely's chair. He held her hand in his, relieved to find that it felt warm under his touch. There were times when she seemed impossibly cold, an effect of the recurrent malaise that had settled upon her since Marden's death.

'I'm so sorry,' Samuel told his daughter. 'I treated you so badly after Marden died. I didn't think. I didn't try to think.' His voice cracked as regret poured out of him. 'I'd take all of it back if I could.'

'I'll light the fire,' Aaric declared, returning to the hearth and giving father and daughter their space. He put the logs in place and set them alight with a bronze-coloured device he drew from one of his pockets. Samuel could see a duardin rune embossed on its side.

As light threw back the shadows, Samuel reached into his own pocket and grabbed the extra talisman. He held it towards Cicely. She wrinkled her nose and drew back. He could sympathise. The wrapping of gryph-hound leather was pungent enough and some of the things Aaric had bound inside it were still more noxious. He pressed the talisman into her hand and closed her fingers around it.

'Uncle Aaric made this for you,' he told his daughter. 'It will protect you.'

Cicely gave him an uneasy smile. 'I'll be all right,' she said, trying to reassure him.

Aaric walked over and leaned against the table. 'Making that talisman was no easy thing,' he stated. 'But it will protect you from this evil that is abroad. Sorcerer, witch or vampire, whatever fiend has been set loose on... Felstein... will be balked by this.' He reached to his neck and displayed an identical bundle hanging there by a cord.

'Keep it with you all the time,' Samuel told his daughter. His tone grew hard when he detected hesitance. 'Promise me. Promise me you'll keep it with you.'

Cicely lowered her head and stared at the floor again. 'I promise,' she whispered.

Samuel hugged her to him. 'I need to know that you're safe. If anything happened to you, I don't know what I'd do.'

As soon as she was able to excuse herself, Cicely hurried to the seclusion of her room. The moment she was alone, she dropped the talisman to the floor and kicked it under her bed. The thing was foul to the touch, viler than anything she'd ever encountered. The dire wolf's rotten tongue would have been less revolting. It had taken all her self-control to keep from hurling Aaric's bundle of garbage into the fire.

No, it wasn't just self-control. It was also the intense faith her father put in the talisman. She could see the worry drain out of him when he gave the thing to her. She couldn't reject something he had so much trust in.

Cicely shuddered and dropped down in the chair. Her fingers plucked at the edge of the tapestry resting across its arm. 'He's right to trust the protection of Aaric's talismans,' she whispered. That strange refusal of the onyx needle to obey and complete

Aaric's image. That could only have been the talisman's power at work, striving against her. She'd had no problem at all with Enoch's picture.

'And maybe that's why the thing disgusts me.' Her eyes strayed to the narrow gap between her bed and the floor. The talisman's purpose was to guard against the magic she herself was using. Why should it be so strange that the conjuror herself should be repelled by its power?

Her stomach turned when Cicely wondered about a very different possibility. She sprang to her feet and grabbed the rushlight from its holder. By the flickering flame she studied her hand, the one into which Samuel had pressed the talisman. Around the palm and the insides of her fingers it was almost transparent. Any vitalising essence drawn into her by the needle's magic had been pulled back out again.

For some time, Cicely just sat and gazed at her hand. She scrutinised it with the most intense study, trying to spot the least advance of her affliction. By the rushlight, she couldn't quite decide if there was a slowly creeping pallor or not. At last, she took the step of raking her skin with her nail and creating a mark by which to measure her fear. Long minutes passed before she let out a relieved sigh. The regression was confined to just the one hand.

'Still, I cannot go about with one hand looking as if I've drawn it out of the grave,' Cicely said. There was also the concern of what would happen if the regression was allowed to go too far. If her hand faded away completely, what would that do to the rest of her? She could remember when animals in the village were injured and the wounds became necrotic, how the cut on a leg would poison the entire sheep and cause it to die. Could that happen to her?

'No, because worse than death waits for me,' Cicely reminded herself. It wasn't simply the grave that loomed ahead of her, but a transition into a state of discorporate existence. An unheard echo cut off from even the shadows of the spirit realm.

'*My life is yours,*' the spectral voice whispered at her mind, but she couldn't decide if it was threat or warning. All Cicely knew was that it demanded she act.

She tightened the fingers of her afflicted hand, wincing when she could only vaguely detect them pressing against her palm. She couldn't risk waiting. Enoch should have been enough for a long time, but Aaric's meddling had spoiled that. She needed another victim now. And Cicely knew just who it would be.

Cautiously, Cicely cracked open the door and pressed her ear to the gap. She could dimly hear her father and her uncle talking in the other room. Would they never retire for the night?

As she caught more of their conversation, mere snatches of words here and there, Cicely realised she'd have to be patient. Samuel and Aaric were going out again. Some errand that revolted her father but one on which Aaric was most insistent. The scholar finally prevailed and gained the beasthunter's acquiescence.

Fear pulsed through Cicely as she listened to the men leave. Whether she liked it or not, she was going to have to wait now. Then an icy calm settled upon her. Perhaps this was even better. The men had been hunting in Briardark most of the day. Now they were going out again. When they did come back and finally settle down, they'd be exhausted.

All the better. Because for what she had to do, she needed them both to be sound asleep. Incapable of reacting until she'd done what needed to be done.

The moonlight sent strange shadows swirling about the grave-yard. An owl hooted off in the distance, its eerie vocalisations drifting through the fog. Samuel kept turning as some furtive motion caught the edge of his vision. A trick of the eyes, he told himself when he could find nothing but the grey tombstones. He didn't want to believe it could be anything more. Not with the loathsome task ahead of them.

'If Pater Kosminski finds us here, the consequences will be dire,' Samuel reminded Aaric.

'We're not grave robbers,' Aaric replied, shifting the shovel he carried over his shoulder. 'We'll take nothing, and we'll leave everything just as it was before.'

Samuel shook his head. 'It's still desecration. That'll be enough to enrage the priest. If Thayer were of a mind to, he could use that to have us both exiled from Felstein.'

'You told me your townmaster was becoming a recluse.' Aaric paused to inspect the inscription on one of the gravestones.

'Thayer has been keeping to himself,' Samuel conceded. 'But I don't think guilt about what happened to Anya is the cause. He's probably waiting for the witch hunters he sent for. That way, whatever happens, he can deny responsibility for it.'

Aaric frowned. 'It might be he's mourning his son. When anger has no focus, sorrow can quickly unseat it.' He cast his gaze across the cemetery. 'Where is Alastair buried?'

The seeming innocence of the question didn't deceive Samuel. 'I appreciate the thought, but if we're going to do this, then it must be my way.'

'Wouldn't it be easier if we visited Alastair's grave?' Aaric pressed. 'There certainly wasn't any affection lost between you when he was alive.'

'That's why we leave him alone,' Samuel said. 'I've no right to disturb him, nor to add another measure to his father's grief. You're right, I've nothing but contempt for the Greimhalts, but that doesn't justify abusing them.' He gestured with his bronze arm to the right, to a patch of the graveyard he knew only too well. 'This way.'

The two men crept between the stones, seeking out the plots where Samuel had buried his family. If someone had told Samuel

he'd ever concede disturbing these graves, much less partic-
ipate, he'd have called them crazy. Now, he knew, the one
thing more important than who he'd lost was who he might
still lose. To protect Cicely, he'd countenance even the profane
deed ahead of them.

'Here.' Samuel's voice was low when he stood over Emelda's
grave, staring down at her stone. He looked over at Aaric and
saw the hesitation in his face. It was ironic that after the scholar's urging, it was he who should hesitate. 'We have to do it this
way if we're going to do it at all.'

Aaric nodded. 'There have been so many victims. We could
still choose someone–'

'The dead sleep lightly.' Samuel quoted the old admonition
his own father had impressed on him after he'd been caught
trespassing in the cemetery as a child. 'But if we're to disturb
the spirits, it would be better to disturb that of someone who
would sympathise with our reasons. Someone who might forgive this desecration.'

'She will,' Aaric assured him. He thrust the spade of his shovel
into the soil. Again he paused. 'I can do this alone,' he suggested.

Samuel shook his head. 'I appreciate your consideration, but I
have to see this through.' He looked across the cemetery. 'Besides,
someone has to keep lookout and warn if Pater Kosminski comes
around.'

'I know what it means to lose a wife,' Aaric said. He gestured at the grave. 'To watch this... That is something else. Now
that we're here, I don't think I could let it happen if our roles
were reversed.'

'Yes, you would,' Samuel told him. 'You'd do it to protect your
daughter the same way I am to protect mine.'

The point struck home and Aaric bent himself to the task at
hand. The shovel ripped into the plot, breaking the hard-packed
soil and dispersing it in a heap beside Emelda's grave.

Samuel circled the excavation, keeping his attention on the graveyard around them. A thin mist crawled among the tombstones and tiny wisps of light danced through the weeds, spectral energies that were sometimes called corpse candles when they appeared in Briardark and beckoned the unwary into the marshes. He was vigilant for any hint of a lantern. The only person likely to stumble on them was Pater Kosminski, and he knew the priest would be carrying a light if he were making a late-night inspection of the cemetery.

The sound of shifting earth became like the pad of a predator's step to Samuel's ears. Each dig of the shovel felt menacing and sent a tingle of alarm down his spine. 'Forgive us,' he whispered, his hand closing about the empty air at his neck where the icon of Nagash had once hung. Even he wasn't sure if his words were meant for the grim god or for Emelda's spirit.

'I've reached the coffin,' Aaric called to Samuel in a subdued tone. The hunter turned around to see the scholar using the edge of the spade to pry open the lid. He winced at the groan of each nail as it was wrenched loose. It seemed an eternity before Aaric had worked it free and lifted it away.

'Sigmar's mercy!' the scholar gasped as he leaned over the casket and peered at what was inside. When Aaric instinctively recoiled from the repugnant sight that greeted him, Samuel was able to see what had provoked such horror. He fell to his knees as a feeling of sickness threatened to overwhelm him.

Among the inhabitants of Shyish there was a custom that any corpse which showed signs of unnatural preservation was proof that it had become a vampire. Such bodies were treated in different ways according to cultural traditions. Samuel had heard there were places that celebrated these occurrences and would seek to propitiate the supposed vampire with blood sacrifices, installing the corpse in its own house as though it were a living thing. Others would tie the preserved body to the back of a horse and chase it away into the wilderness, hoping by such means to send the vampire elsewhere. In Felstein, the more widespread custom of burning such bodies was maintained, to destroy the undead before it could come into the fullness of its terrible power.

Emelda's body, however, exhibited an opposite condition. It wasn't unnaturally preserved. It was unnaturally decayed. Only a bit more than a month in her grave, yet she looked as though she'd been there for many years. The corpse was shrivelled, little more than skin stretched taut across bones.

'This can't be Emelda,' Samuel hissed, unable to accept the ghastliness of the scene. Yet the skeletal husk was wearing the same grave clothes; around its finger was the same wedding band. The skull was missing the same tooth. Desperate as he was to deny it, he knew this indeed was the remains of his wife.

'Withered,' Aaric stated, regaining some of his composure. The scholar used a small copper rod he withdrew from his belt to inspect the corpse. He prodded and poked at it for some time, lifting its rigid arms, peeling back its mouldering rags. 'More than just the life has been extinguished. Something else has been drawn out of her.'

Samuel struggled to turn his mind away from the grisly sight. 'What has happened to Emelda?' he managed to ask.

Aaric shook his head and replaced the lid on the coffin. 'I can't tell that until I've seen another body. I have a suspicion, but I need another specimen to confirm the idea.' He held up his hand, and Samuel lifted him out of the grave. Together, they reburied Emelda.

'Anya is over here,' Samuel said when they'd finished their task. He led the scholar to his cousin's grave. With his augmented arm holding the shovel, the work proceeded much quicker. When the lid was pried away, the body had the same withered look to it, far beyond the work of the flames that had killed her.

Aaric leaned over his shovel when they'd filled in Anya's grave.

'I can say now that what has been done is more terrible than we'd supposed. The means of death, as I said, is inconsequential. Whether by fire or noose, the true cause of the killing is the sorcery that produces it.' He paused and wiped his brow, a shudder passing through him. 'Murder, however, isn't the motive. Or, at least, the only motive. The killer is draining the victims of their very life essence, drawing it away like water from a well. That is why the corpses become husks. Even after death, the essence continues to be extirpated.'

Samuel blanched in disgust. 'To what end? Isn't killing them crime enough for this fiend?'

'Fiend indeed,' Aaric nodded. 'For only the most debased practitioner of magic would resort to these methods. I have read of necromancers who, to preserve their own lives, will leech the life from others, fattening upon it in the same way a vampire fattens upon blood.' He shook his head, and his expression grew even more disturbed. 'We may have to rethink what we believed. The culprit behind this horror may not be concerned with revenge. This could all be simply a ruthless effort to preserve their own life. Though I shudder at the sort of spells they use to accomplish their ends.'

'Killing so many people,' Samuel growled, coming to grips with the hideous theory. 'So much misery just to keep one sorcerer alive.'

'That's just it,' Aaric said. 'If the villain's means is simply survival, then there shouldn't be so much killing. The spell being used must be far different from anything recorded before. Primitive and inefficient, demanding continual sacrifices.' His face paled as he cast his eyes back to Anya's grave.

'There's something else,' the scholar continued. 'Even in death, the spell doesn't end. I tell you that even now the bodies are still being drained. More slowly, to be certain, but they're diminishing nonetheless.' Aaric's voice dropped to a horrified whisper.

'Eventually, they may be completely consumed. Utterly vanish from this world.'

'Vanish?' Samuel seized on the word. 'Vanish to where?'

There was raw terror in Aaric's eyes when he replied. 'I wish I knew, Samuel. I wish I knew.'

CHAPTER SIXTEEN

Cicely held the carved wolf in her hands, caressing its unfinished body in a ceaseless, monotonous motion. As she did so, over and over, she could hear the spectral voice. Or rather voices, for it was always as though a chorus were speaking in unison. Sometimes she could pick out Marden, sometimes it was Emelda or Anya or some other victim of her spells. Always, however, there was that *other*. Prominent and hauntingly familiar, yet also strange and alien.

Cicely wasn't sure how long she'd been lost to the repetitive action and the voices. A noise in the yard outside finally broke her from her trance. As her mind stirred, she realised she couldn't feel the wolf in her hand. There was a complete lack of sensation. She could see her fingers gripping it, but she couldn't feel them.

Cicely dropped the carving to the floor. Her hand was a stark reminder of what would happen. What was at stake. The image of her body fading entirely filled her mind.

'No, that won't happen,' she vowed. If she simply surrendered, then all those who the magic had killed would have died for nothing. She had to sustain herself so that their sacrifice wasn't in vain. *'My life is yours,'* the spectral chorus said. Cicely couldn't throw that life away.

'If I can just stave off Uncle Aaric's threat,' Cicely told herself. 'I'll find Verderghast and demand answers from him. There has to be a way to stay alive without killing anyone.' It was a desperate hope she'd repeated to herself until it had become almost a mania. Once Aaric was gone it would be safe enough to venture into Briardark and find the fugitive physician. She'd have her answers then. But first she had to deal with the immediate danger.

The night advanced, falling into the ghostly hours before the dawn. Cicely was too tense to feel fatigue. Where had they gone, and would they ever return? She had seen for herself how exhausted the men were. They couldn't have gone far. Whatever their errand had been, it couldn't have taken them away from town.

Finally, to her sharp ears, there came the sound of the front door being opened and boots scraping on the floor. Cicely listened intently as the men lingered in the front room for a moment. She heard someone, likely Samuel, put something away in the closet. Only a few muffled words passed between the two before she heard footsteps in the hall. The door to her parents' room opened and was quickly shut. Across the hall, the door to Marden's room, where Aaric was staying, did the same. She wasn't sure if her hearing had really become so sensitive or if it was mere imagination, but she faintly caught the rustle of bedclothes being shifted as the men retired.

Cicely forced herself to wait. Desperate to act, she retained enough wariness to know that the thing most apt to spoil her plans was to move before the men were asleep. Weary as they must be, it shouldn't be long. She determined to be prudent and allow even more time to pass. She began counting off her own heartbeats, using her pulse to gauge the falling minutes. The process eased her mind, almost letting her slip into a trance. The immediacy that nagged at her was quieted by the calming redundancy.

When the numbers grew so large as to become unwieldy, demanding concentration that shattered the numbing tedium, Cicely decided to move. She had to allow Aaric time to sink deep into slumber, but she also had to be mindful of the nearness of dawn. Felstein would stir with the sun, and there was danger some sound from the awakening town might disturb her uncle.

Softly, Cicely eased her door open and slipped into the hall. A mouse would have made more noise as she crept towards Marden's room. Her hand paused on the handle. She drew in a breath, holding it tight in her lungs. What if the wood had swollen, or some debris had caught under the door? What if it refused to open or in opening made a sound that woke Aaric?

The fears of the moment held her firm. Uncertainty weighed down on her, adding its burden to the guilt she'd tried to rationalise away. Cicely was on the verge of retreat. It was the cold, dead feel of her afflicted hand that kept her where she was. A vivid reminder of what awaited her if she didn't stay the course.

The door slowly eased open under her touch. At first only a crack, to which she pressed her eye. The darkness of the room offered small obstacle to her vision. She could make out the bed against the far wall, the shape of her uncle beneath the blanket. Keeping her gaze fixed on Aaric, Cicely shifted the door inward, pausing every time the gap widened by another inch. The least movement from her uncle would have sent her scrambling away, but the insensate man didn't stir.

When the opening was wide enough, Cicely slipped inside. She drew the door close behind her, mindful that she also had to worry about being discovered by Samuel. She knew his hunter's senses were keen and apt to rouse him at the least disturbance.

Cicely waited a few minutes, nerving herself for what she had
to do. Despite the regression done to her hand, she was thankful
her father had given her a talisman. It let her know exactly what
she had to find now.

She didn't waste time looking about the room. Aaric would
keep the talisman on him so it could protect him. Even asleep,
she knew her uncle must have it with him. Careful to make no
noise, she moved towards the bed. Her hand trembled when she
reached out to grip the blanket. Conscience reared its objection
for an instant when she looked down on Aaric's face. This was
the man she was going to kill.

Survival throttled her hesitation. Aaric was a scholar, and his
knowledge was a dire threat. If she were to live, he had to die.
Cicely slowly tugged the blanket away from Aaric's shoulders,
drawing it down the bed as she studied the sleeping man. The
scholar was a bit older than her father and his frame wasn't
nearly so robust. His nightshirt hung loose about him, and where
it was open around his neck, she could see a leather cord.

Cicely let the blanket fall slack around Aaric's waist. She could
see something underneath his shirt over his chest on the left side.
Instinct, or something near enough to it, informed her that it
was the talisman. He'd fastened it to the cord and was wearing
it over his heart.

Now Cicely did make a brief search of the room. She caught up
one of Marden's hunting knives and quickly returned to the bed-
side. The blade felt heavy in her hand as she leaned over Aaric.
She could plunge it into his breast and eliminate the danger he
posed right now. The idea flashed through her brain, abhorrent
and malignant. Necessity had made her a killer, but she wasn't
a murderess. She couldn't stab him in the dark like an assassin.

Deftly, Cicely pulled open Aaric's shirt and slipped her other
hand underneath. She knew the horrible feel of the talisman,
the same as the one Samuel had given her. The impulse to

recoil from the foul thing was strong, but the urgency of her task was stronger. With great care, watching Aaric's face for the least trace of awakening, she pulled the talisman away from his heart. She let the shirt fall back against the man's chest. She was wary enough to keep the talisman close so that the cord wouldn't grow taut and rouse her uncle. Instead, she let it lie on his breast while she curled the cord against the knife blade and raked it against the edge.

Aaric's eyes opened. Cicely froze in horror. Her uncle was looking right at her.

'Hephzibah,' the scholar whispered. Though his eyes were open, they were glazed and unfocused. After a hideous moment, he closed them again. Cicely waited until his breathing fell back into the regulated pattern of slumber before she dared to stir. Slowly, she began to drag the knife across the thong again.

Minutes elapsed, but finally Cicely sawed through the leather. Biting down on her revulsion, she caught up the talisman and made her way back across the room. She continued to watch Aaric's face and felt her blood freeze when his features began to twitch. The tics became ever more pronounced. A nightmare of some sort, bedevilling her uncle. If they grew any more intense, she was certain Aaric would wake.

Haste displaced caution and Cicely fled from the room. She hurried across the hall to her own and hurled the talisman under her bed to join the other one. She leaned back against her door as she shut it. For the first time in what felt like an eternity, she allowed herself to draw a full breath. It left her in a ragged sigh.

'The task is only half done,' Cicely whispered as her gaze turned to the chair and the tapestry.

And the onyx needle.

'Uncle Aaric's picture is almost done,' she reflected, leaving the door and walking to the chair. She picked up the needle and threaded its eye. 'Only a moment or two, and I can finish.'

She frowned when she noted that both of her hands now had a chalky transparency about them.

'Everything will be better when I finish,' Cicely said as she dug the needle into the cloth.

Samuel woke with a start, no drowsiness nagging at his mind. Every speck of his being was alert, keyed to a razor's edge. He didn't know what had snapped him from sleep, but he trusted the instincts he'd honed through so many years hunting the wilds around Felstein.

Doubt was dispelled a moment later when he heard a scream of fright and the sound of glass shattering. Samuel didn't wait to question, he simply lunged out of bed and grabbed up his axe. He left his room and was across the hall in a matter of heart-beats. A kick of his foot opened the door to Marden's room – the source of the disturbing sounds.

Moonlight streamed through the splintered ruins of the window. A tree, one Samuel had thought sturdy, had fallen and slammed into the side of the house. One of its branches had stabbed itself into the room like a blood knight's lance, impaling the bed with its jagged tip. He gasped and hurried forwards, horrified to think what he'd find lying in that bed. He was as relieved as he was puzzled when he saw that the bed was empty.

'I've had a very narrow escape.' Aaric's voice spun Samuel around. So intent had he been on the destruction at the window and bed that he hadn't seen the scholar in the opposite corner. He was bleeding from several cuts where shards of glass from the window had sliced him, but he was very much alive.

Samuel gestured with the axe at the branch piercing the bed. 'Nagash! If you'd been asleep...'

'I *was* asleep,' Aaric corrected him. He trembled as he spoke. 'I should have been another victim of an accident. Like so many in Felstein.' A glint of steel came into his eyes. 'Only we know these aren't accidents. We know someone is employing the blackest magic to commit these murders.'

The beasthunter reached to his neck, to the talisman Aaric had made. 'But we're supposed to be protected,' he said, a hint of accusation in his tone. If Aaric's talisman had failed, then why should any of them work? His hope that Cicely was safe...

'It *did* protect me,' Aaric replied. He held out his hand and showed Samuel the talisman he held. Then the scholar's visage darkened. 'Or, I should say, *this* talisman protected me. It's the extra one. The one I made for myself is missing.'

Samuel shook his head. 'That's impossi–' He didn't finish what he was saying. His eyes had dropped to the floor and noticed something. Stooping, he picked it up. Holding it in the moonlight, he saw that it was a leather cord like the one he wore around his own neck. The cord, he was certain, from Aaric's talisman.

'It's been cut,' the hunter reported, curling his fist around it.

'The removal of the talisman was no accident,' Aaric emphasised. 'Our enemy knew about it and took action.' He tapped his finger against the replacement. 'This has rather spoiled things for them.' A haunted look came over him. 'This... and a nightmare.'

'Nightmare?' the hunter asked.

A sad smile pursed the scholar's lips. 'In lieu of what's happened, maybe more than a dream. I thought I heard Hephzibah calling to me. She was crying my name from a place so bleak neither light nor darkness would lay claim to it. She was compelling me to stir, to rise before it was too late.' He scowled at the branch. 'I woke with a scream and found my talisman gone. I leapt to see if the extra was also stolen. I'd just put my hand on it when the tree fell into the room.'

Samuel glanced back at the tree. 'You'd have been killed like all the others. Without the talisman to protect you.'

Aaric laid his hand on the hunter's shoulder. 'Our enemy knew about my protection and tried to take it away.'

Terror crackled down Samuel's spine. 'They were here! Inside the house!'

'Yes,' the scholar said. 'They were inside the house.'

'Cicely!' Samuel pushed past Aaric and hurried into the hall. A matter of a moment and he had his daughter's door open and was standing in her room.

For an instant Samuel's heart froze. Where was his daughter? Then, as his eyes adjusted to the deeper darkness of the room, he saw her shape lying on the bed under the blankets. A tide of relief left him in a low sob, and he had to hold on to the chair to support himself.

Aaric appeared in the doorway, a rushlight smouldering in his hand. He took a look around and his eyes narrowed on his niece's bed. 'Asleep? Through all of this noise?'

The suspicious note in the scholar's tone provoked Samuel. He turned and fixed Aaric with a warning glower. 'Cicely's been sickly since her brother's death and that of her mother. She often secludes herself in a deep sleep.'

'Until she's recovered?' Aaric remarked. There was an insinuation wound within his speech.

'Be careful,' Samuel growled.

Aaric offered him a sneer in reply. 'I will.' He looked over at his sleeping niece. 'Here isn't the place to say such things.'

Samuel's temper flared. 'Say what you have to say.' Though the scholar's meaning was clear enough, he wanted to hear it for himself in Aaric's own words. When the man hesitated, Samuel's temper grew worse. 'She's asleep, I tell you. Not even the trumpets of Azyr could rouse her.'

The scholar looked far from convinced, but he was too proud to be quelled by Samuel's harangue. 'We know that the culprit is using sorcery to drain away the life essence of their victims. Subsisting on it like some obscene vampire.' He pointed at the bed. 'What if they need that energy to stave off sickness? When they claim a victim, they seem to recover. When they let too much time pass, the illness saps them until there's no choice but to act.'

'You dare make such accusations under my own roof?' Samuel hissed.

'Look at the facts,' Aaric persisted. 'Someone got inside to steal the talisman from me. What could be easier than for someone already inside the house to sneak into my room...'

'This fiend has already been proven a student of dark magic,' Samuel countered. 'Why not use a spell to spirit it away?'

'Would a spell need to cut the cord?' Aaric asked. He tapped the replacement talisman he now carried. 'Magic that could take one talisman could surely take all of them. No, it had to be someone inside who physically removed it... and didn't know where to look for the other ones.'

'The other ones.' Samuel latched on to the words, a quiver in his voice. He turned from Aaric and hurried to the bed. He drew back the blanket, pausing for a moment to see if Cicely would wake. She remained asleep, such was the depth of her slumber. He hastily examined her, horrified to find the talisman was gone.

'It isn't here!' Samuel moaned. The animosity of only a moment before was forgotten as he turned back towards Aaric. 'Cicely's talisman has been taken!'

Aaric was standing beside the chair, peering intently at the tapestry folded across its arm. 'She's been quite busy here,' he said.

Samuel stormed over to him. 'Damn your accusations, didn't you hear me? Cicely's talisman is gone. She's without protection.'

'She hardly needs protecting from herself,' Aaric stated. He held the rushlight down towards the tapestry. 'Isn't this your cousin Anya?'

'And there's Emelda.' Samuel pointed his bronze finger at the image of his wife. 'Are you going to tell me she cast a spell on her own mother?'

Aaric hesitated for a moment. 'I can't change the evidence I see–'

'A suspicious mind sees what it wants to see,' Samuel snapped back, barely glancing at the picture. He turned and went back to the bed. He lifted the talisman from around his neck and leaned over his daughter.

'Don't!' Aaric cried. He forgot his examination of the tapestry and hurried over to the hunter. He grabbed his arm to keep him from setting the talisman around Cicely's neck. 'You'll be without any protection. You saw for yourself what almost happened to me.'

Samuel pulled free of Aaric's grip. 'You've convinced yourself she's a witch, but think if you're wrong. That means Cicely's the one without any defence against this sorcery.'

Aaric tried to make one last appeal. 'Let's say that I am wrong.' He tried to make his tone conciliatory. 'That still means you need to protect yourself. If not Cicely, then someone else stole into this house. There will be another attempt unless the fiend is stopped. I need *you* to help me bring an end to this.'

'Oh no you don't,' Samuel said. He slipped the cord around Cicely's neck and drew the blankets back over her. 'Not after what you dared to say to me. To accuse my daughter of these outrages. No, Aaric, you don't need my help, and you won't have it.' The beasthunter pointed at the door. 'I'll suffer your company this night, but tomorrow you should return to Gothghul Hollow. It was a mistake to bring you here.'

Aaric started to speak but must have recognised the futility of mere words. 'I'll leave your house in the morning,' he said. 'But I'll not leave Felstein until the danger is over. I'll find this fiend, and I won't let sentiment stand in my way.'

Samuel watched the scholar retreat into the hall. Aaric was wrong. He had to be wrong. Cicely had no such powers.

But at the back of his mind was a note of uncertainty, a whisper that Samuel couldn't silence.

What if Aaric's right?

* * *

It took all of Cicely's willpower to maintain a pose of sleep while her father and uncle were in the room. She bit down on her lip to keep from screaming when Samuel set the talisman around her neck. If anything, it felt more disgusting than the others, like a slimy newt crawling across her breast. More than anything, she wanted to rid herself of the revolting thing, but she knew the least motion on her part might instigate a situation she wanted to avoid.

Uncle Aaric's speech was enough to horrify her to the core. She'd been right to target him, but much too late in doing it. A dark providence protected the man, and she knew she'd never get the other talisman away from him. There was a bitter irony in that. He'd made four of the things, and all of them were in her control except the one she most desperately needed.

Her father lingered in the room after Aaric left. Cicely knew Samuel was keeping watch, trying to protect her. She agonised over the worry he must be under. He believed in her, and it pained her to appreciate how misplaced his trust was. How could he know the small steps that had escalated events the way they had? The horrible accident that led to matricide. The ghastly affliction that forced Cicely to murder.

Cicely focused her thoughts on the course she would have to take. She knew Aaric would stay in Felstein, with or without her father's support. He'd be watching her, searching for the least evidence to try to convince Samuel. When she started to fade again – as she knew must happen – Aaric would be looking for the signs. If someone died and she became vigorous again, that would banish any lingering doubt her uncle had. He'd act, even if he had to do so without Samuel.

Keeping still under the blankets, Cicely fixated on a way to bypass her uncle's vigilance. There would be a way. There had to be a way. Finding the answer to that puzzle occupied her through the night until she finally heard Samuel leave. When the door shut behind her father, she lost no time ripping the talisman away and throwing it to the floor.

'Disgusting.' She rose and walked over, ready to kick it under the bed with the others. She hesitated when she lifted her foot. Maybe that was the wrong approach to take? Her uncle knew so much – perhaps he also had a suspicion regarding how the talismans would affect the witch they were meant to guard against? If she wore the hateful thing, it might make him doubt himself.

Cicely took a needle and thread from her box of supplies. Briefly, her hand brushed against the onyx needle. She'd hastily stuffed it at the bottom of the box after she heard the commotion in Marden's room. Seeing it now made her wonder about the tapestry. She turned and flipped it over. The image of her uncle was there, but it wasn't so complete as it had been. The threads were frayed and loose, as though they'd pulled themselves free from the cloth. As it had before, the talisman had unmade her work and broken the spell.

Turning the tapestry over again, Cicely approached Samuel's talisman lying on the floor. Controlling her revulsion, she brought the little copper needle against the leathery skin and undid the stitches that bound it together. The oddments Aaric had stuffed it with came spilling out onto the floor. She barely glanced at them before she was sweeping them under the bed with an old dress.

Once the insides were hidden, Cicely set to refilling the leather bag. Rags and strips torn from the old dress went inside, as did a few smooth stones Marden had given her years ago. The stones would provide some rigidity and simulate the little bones that had originally been part of the talisman. When she was satisfied the bag resembled what it had been before, Cicely sewed it shut again. She carefully inspected her handiwork. It was a good resemblance, one that she was certain would pass even Aaric's scrutiny.

As she finished mending the talisman, Cicely stared at her

hands, noting their hideous pallor. Powder would let her hide the true condition, but it would still lend her a sickly look. Something Aaric would be watching for. Worse than that was the awareness that she'd need to replenish herself with someone's essence soon. Something else her uncle would be vigilant for.

Cicely turned towards the tapestry, dark thoughts swirling through her brain. If she struck at any of her relations, Aaric would uncover her. The only way to proceed was to claim a victim he'd never know about. Yet she couldn't just choose anyone. The onyx needle would only work against those its enchantment deemed part of her family. And it would have to be someone she knew well enough that she could recreate their image from memory.

Cicely sank into the chair and puzzled over the problem. Looking over the tapestry, she made note of Anya and the children. It was then that the answer came to her. Someone Uncle Aaric would never know about. Someone who wasn't even in Felstein.

Taking up the onyx needle, Cicely started to weave Rukh's picture into the tapestry.

CHAPTER SEVENTEEN

Samuel couldn't help the feeling of self-satisfaction when he walked into Felstein's square with Cicely and saw Aaric outside the Skintaker's Swallow. The scholar from Gothghul Hollow had been as good as his word. After leaving the Helmgaart household, he'd accepted the hospitality of Thayer Greimhalt. The townmaster was eager to bring an end to the killings and expose Alastair's murderer. Samuel had spent a terrible day worrying about what Aaric would say to Thayer and how attentively the despondent father would listen to him.

It was time to make the scholar eat those words. Aaric had seen Cicely two nights ago, when she was so sick and frail that she didn't even stir when they were arguing right beside her bed. Now she was hale and hearty, with a flush of rich colour in her face and the old keenness in her eyes.

'Spinning any tall tales for Thayer?' Samuel asked as he walked up to the scholar. Aaric gave him only a brief glance, then fixated on Cicely. He gave a start, confusion visible on his face.

Samuel turned to his daughter. 'Why don't you go visit Lucilla? I have things to discuss with your uncle.'

Cicely gave Aaric a surly look. 'I'd rather stay. I'd like to know why there's this rift between you now… and how I'm the cause of it. If Uncle Aaric has been saying ungracious things about me, I'd like to hear him explain himself.'

The venom in his daughter's tone, Samuel felt, was justified. If she knew the full extent of Aaric's insinuations, she'd be far more upset than she already was. For this reason, he was determined that she wouldn't be privy to the discussion. Not when it meant being accused of matricide.

'Do as I say,' Samuel told her, perhaps a bit more harshly than he'd intended. Cicely gave him a pained look, but after a moment she turned on her heel and withdrew across the square and back into the little lane that led home.

Samuel waited until he was certain Cicely couldn't hear them before he turned back to Aaric. 'Well? There's no denying she's recovered her vigour. According to you, that means she must have used witchcraft to kill a member of our family.' He jabbed a finger into the scholar's chest. 'Nobody's died in Felstein, relative or otherwise. Nobody's even missing, in case your twisted mind is trying to rationalise how your theory can still hold.'

Aaric shook his head. There was regret in his expression when he met Samuel's eyes. 'I don't know how this can be, but I would never have made such an accusation unless I was convinced.' He ran his finger across the talisman he wore. 'She's the only one who could have stolen my protection. You're desperate to disbelieve me, but you're blinding yourself so you can see only what you want to see.'

'Someone stole her talisman too,' Samuel snapped.

'To work her dark magic, she would have needed to get rid of it,' Aaric stated. He paused, his own words spurring a thought. 'The talisman may even have disrupted the stolen essence she's drawn from her victims. Another reason to rid herself of it.'

'Only she hasn't. She wears the talisman you made for me. She's wearing it right now.' Samuel scowled at the scholar. He still feared what Aaric could do with a few wrong words in Thayer's ear. 'Cicely is protected from this sorcerer. Now it is you that menaces her. Swear to me you'll not spread this vile delusion of yours to other people.' He felt the colour rushing into his face as he growled a warning. 'I'll see you dead before I see her taken by the witch hunters.'

'Thayer says the witch hunters should be in Felstein at any time,' Aaric said. 'He's nervous about what will happen when they arrive... as he's right to be. Some witch hunters aren't concerned about collateral damage when seeking their prey. Some feel it is better to burn a hundred innocents than to let one sorcerer go free.' Now it was the scholar who gave warning. 'I've kept my thoughts to myself and mentioned nothing about Cicely to Thayer, but if it looks like innocents are threatened, I'll tell all that I know.' He thrust his finger in Samuel's face. 'I'll do the same if there are any more victims. You might tell your daughter that.'

'Damn you,' Samuel hissed. His balled fist caught Aaric by surprise. The scholar was knocked off his feet and crashed into one of the tables outside the tavern. He lay there for a moment, sprawled over its surface. A trickle of blood oozed from the corner of his mouth. When he rallied, he wiped the stain away with the back of his hand.

'Short-sighted for someone who wants discretion,' Aaric commented. The altercation was drawing attention from the townsfolk in the square. A crowd was starting to gather, people glancing uncertainly at the two antagonists, wondering which of them deserved their support.

Samuel backed away, forcing his temper to subside. If he forced matters to a crisis now, it would only succeed in doing precisely what he wanted to avoid. The threat remained in his eyes when he met Aaric's gaze, but for the moment there could be peace.

'I must have been mad to bring you to Felstein,' Samuel said.

The scholar gave him a condescending smile. 'On the contrary, it was the only sane thing you've done. Come back to reason, Samuel. Don't cling to something that's already lost.'

A withering retort was on Samuel's tongue, but it went unspoken. Across the square, commotion was growing. People flocked towards the town hall, then just as quickly recoiled in fright. A presentiment of doom came over the hunter, a crawling dread that set its claws into his soul. The crisis had come.

Samuel pushed his way to the forefront of the crowd, dimly aware that Aaric followed in his wake. A wide gap was left open between the spectators and the town hall. In this space, a pair of riders sat atop their steeds, but neither were like anything seen in Felstein before.

The steeds were fleshless animals with six bony legs and long, spindly tails. Bare ribs hung from exposed spines. Elongated neck-bones supported the barren skulls of the brutes, narrow heads that suggested to Samuel aspects of both horse and hound. Rigid saddles were bolted rather than strapped to the gruesome creatures, metal fastenings that were dull with age and use.

The riders were as grim as their steeds. They were skeletal beings, but far more than simply human corpses drawn up from their graves. Their bones were bulky and thick, suggestive more of a crustacean's armour than decayed remains. Sharp spurs projected along their forearms and up their calves. Their skulls were sheathed in helmet-like protrusions of bone that encased all; the only suggestion of a face to be hinted at were the burning green embers that shone through the sockets of their featureless masks. Heavy cloaks, blacker than night, drooped from their shoulders, and buckled to their exposed bones were many pouches and bottles. Hanging from chains fitted to their hips were curved swords with dun-coloured blades and box-like arbalests that seemed carved from ivory.

'Mercy of Sigmar,' Aaric whispered in a tone of both awe and terror. 'You told me Thayer sent for witch hunters, but these aren't from the Order of Azyr. They're templars of Nagash!'

Samuel shuddered. Fearsome as was the reputation of the Order of Azyr, at least its agents were mortal. Those dispatched by the priests of Nagash were undead constructs crafted by exacting and secretive magics. They couldn't be appealed to or bargained with. Once set upon a task, they would see it through regardless of things like compassion and mercy. Sigmar's witch hunters, even the most ruthless of them, still had some notion of protecting the innocent. Nagash's templars were only interested in destroying disciples of the Dark Gods.

'He must have been mad to send–' But even as Samuel started to speak, he bit back his words. Among the onlookers, only one man approached the skeletal riders. He knew it was the man who'd sent for them, the only man who would dare to. Thayer had made a terrible mistake by impinging on the sanctity of the cemetery, bringing a mob to disrupt Emelda's funeral. He'd forced Pater Kosminski to take matters into his own hands.

The priest of Nagash held a subdued conversation with the templars. Samuel couldn't hear what Kosminski said to them, but he knew the undead understood him when they would nod in agreement or make a negative chopping motion with their hands.

'I think Felstein will need a new townmaster,' Aaric observed. On the steps of the town hall, Thayer watched the proceedings with marked unease, a ghastly pallor stealing over him.

'Thayer,' Samuel hissed. Why hadn't it occurred to him before? Thayer Greimhalt could be the sorcerer, striking out as a way to discredit Samuel and his supporters. Perhaps Alastair had opposed his father's plans and had been eliminated out of necessity.

Even as he warmed to the theory, Samuel saw one of the undead templars twist around and cut something free that was tied to the back of its steed. A body crashed to the ground. It rolled onto its side, its face turned towards the beasthunter. Samuel gasped when he recognised the dead man through the patina of gore.

Aaric caught Samuel by the shoulder. 'You know that man?'

Still shocked, Samuel answered before he was aware he was even speaking. 'My cousin Rukh. Anya's husband.'

Pater Kosminski turned away from the grisly riders and addressed the crowd. 'The principatuum found this man's body on the road only a few miles from Felstein.' He gestured at the corpse. 'This was your friend and neighbour Rukh Helmgaart.' He pointed at the templar whose steed had carried the body. 'The principatus tried to question Rukh's spirit but could elicit no answer.' The priest's eyes flashed with cold fury. 'There can be no doubt but that sorcery caused his death, sorcery foul enough to silence his spirit even when it was rendered into Nagash's dominion.'

Panicked murmurs rippled through the assembly. Pater Kosminski raised his arms, appealing for calm. 'The principatuum are here to root out this evil. They will unmask this murderous servant of Chaos.' The priest turned and looked up at Thayer. In that moment, Samuel understood that he wasn't the only one who was suspicious of the townmaster. 'The fiend will be found, wherever he hides.'

'They *will* find the villain,' Aaric told Samuel, something between a warning and an appeal in his voice. 'Do you want that to happen?'

As he watched the skeletal templars unhook themselves from their saddles and dismount, Samuel could feel the pitiless menace they represented. When he looked at Rukh's body, his refutation of Aaric's accusations brought a bitter taste into his mouth. Cicely *had* recovered and a member of their family *had* died. The one relative she knew was beyond the boundaries of Felstein. Rukh must have heard about his wife and children and was coming back when he was struck down.

'The templars won't stop,' Aaric persisted. 'They won't relent until they find who they're looking for. They will find her.'

Samuel's body was numb with horror. 'She's my daughter,' he groaned.

Aaric motioned him to silence and pulled him back through the crowd. 'She can't be saved, but you can spare her from the templars. That's still something we can do.'

The hunter pushed Aaric away with his bronze hand. 'You have no proof,' he insisted, but there was no conviction in his voice. 'I'll take her away from Felstein. Far away.'

The scholar's expression wasn't without sympathy as they headed into a side street. 'That wouldn't do any good. You could take her all the way to Carstinia and the templars would follow. They aren't gryph-hounds that can be shaken from a trail. There's nowhere you could go and be safe from them.' Aaric shook his head. 'Nor do I think Cicely would give up this foul magic. I don't think she can.'

'Please,' Samuel implored. 'You don't know for certain. It could be someone else.'

Despite the hunter's plea, Aaric had no words of comfort to proffer. Silence held the two men as they walked back to Samuel's home.

'Cicely,' Samuel called out. The name echoed strangely through the house. He could feel the emptiness of the place. Sensed that she wasn't here.

Aaric sensed it too. 'She's gone,' he said as he started down the hallway. Samuel hurried after the scholar.

'Lucilla could have told her about the templars. Or she might have been drawn to the square when they arrived. Everyone's afraid of them, but they're curious all the same.' Samuel's words sounded desperate even to his own ears.

'I don't doubt that she knows the templars are here,' Aaric said.

'She also knows what they brought back with them. Her ruse is spoiled. We know she's killed again. We know that's why she looks so vigorous.' He pushed open the door to Cicely's room and stepped inside.

'We don't know,' Samuel objected. 'You only suspect. You aren't sure.'

Aaric walked through the vacant room. He inspected a carving that had been left on the floor. Samuel recognised it as one of Marden's. His son had always been whittling animals from bits of wood. This one looked like it was going to be a mammoth... had his son ever finished it.

'I'm sure,' Aaric said as he set down the mammoth. His eyes locked with Samuel's. 'You are too. That's why you're so afraid.'

Samuel scowled at the scholar. 'You've no proof. Only circumstance and conjecture. You've no proof.'

Even as he spoke, the beasthunter noticed something lying on the floor near the bed. It was the engraved skull of a shroud toad – one of the constituents of Aaric's talismans. The scholar noted the direction of Samuel's gaze. He stooped and picked up the tiny skull, then turned to the bed. He dragged it away from the wall, exposing the floor beneath it.

There, to Samuel's undisguised horror, was the rest of what had been sewn inside the talisman. Worse, he saw two intact talismans lying on the floor. He knew they could only be the ones that had been stolen by what he'd insisted must have been an intruder.

Aaric retrieved one of the intact talismans. 'She couldn't abide the touch of them, otherwise she'd have taken them somewhere to dispose of them.' He kicked the litter of ingredients with his boot. 'She took apart your talisman after you gave it to her, to try and allay suspicions.'

'I won't believe it,' Samuel groaned. His knees felt weak, and he had to grab hold of the chair to keep from falling. His mind groped for something, anything, to explain away what they'd found. Cicely couldn't be a murderess. A monster.

'You'd better believe it,' Aaric snapped. He thrust the talisman into his hands. 'Cicely will be desperate now. There's no telling when she'll strike.' His gaze became as grim as that of the undead templars. 'Or at whom she'll strike.'

Samuel clenched the talisman tight. 'It can't be,' he said. 'There has to be an explanation.' As he spoke, his hand brushed against the tapestry lying across the chair. It spilled to the floor. Aaric bent over to recover it. As the scholar started to lift it, his eyes narrowed and he drew it close, staring at it with marked interest.

'Who are these people?' he asked, holding the tapestry out to Samuel.

'Our family,' the hunter replied, puzzled. 'I told you that before.' He tapped his finger on the figure of Alastair Greimhalt. 'Cicely added Alastair because she thought she could help my position in the community by marrying him.' Just mentioning the incident brought a sick feeling.

Aaric shook his head. 'There's something wrong here.' He hurried from the room. Samuel followed after and found his brother-in-law near the hearth, starting a fire. When he had a blaze going, he held the tapestry before it. After a moment, an expression of sombre triumph fell across his face.

'Look here,' Aaric called. 'See what the light exposes.' He drew the hunter's attention to the figure of Anya. It took a moment, but Samuel began to see flames licking about his cousin. The effect had been cunningly rendered with different threads, but how it could have gone unnoticed before struck him as impossible. The hair at the back of his neck prickled.

'She couldn't,' Samuel gasped. But as his eyes scoured the tapestry, he saw other peculiar manifestations. A noose around Alastair's neck, blood spilling from Saint's crushed skull. Emelda's face blackening into a charred ruin. 'Not her mother. She couldn't.'

'She might not have known,' Aaric said. 'Your wife would have been one of the first victims, and Cicely might not have understood the demands of the spell.' He waved his hand over the tapestry. 'All of these couldn't be an accident though.'

'You can't be right.' Samuel pointed at the incomplete images of himself and Cicely. 'You might say that the image needs to be complete to work the spell.' He shifted his hand and indicated Aaric's picture. 'But she finished yours and you're still alive.'

'That shows her cunning,' the scholar replied. He stared intently at the tapestry. 'She *did* try to kill me, but the talisman thwarted her. But she finished the image.' He pondered the problem a moment, then nodded to himself. 'The thread looks the same, but there are differences in technique. Oh, so very clever of her. Another effort to throw me off the track by finishing my picture. See, she's even used the same thread, but the weave is different.' He snapped his fingers. 'A different needle! It's the needle she uses that works the spell.'

Samuel took the tapestry from Aaric and tossed it into the fire. 'We'll burn it and prevent her from doing any more harm. Maybe the templars won't–'

Aaric shook his head as he watched the flames consume the cloth. 'The needle's the key. That's why she took it away with her and left the tapestry. She can always start a new one so long as she has the needle.'

The scholar laid his hand on Samuel's shoulder. 'We have to find Cicely before she can hurt anyone else. She's your daughter. Where would she go if she wanted to run away?'

Samuel's heart groaned with the agony of his situation. Cicely was the only child left to him. Whatever she'd done, he still loved her. He couldn't betray her.

'It's better if we find her than the templars of Nagash,' Aaric reminded him, noting his hesitation.

The hunter slowly nodded, his eyes bright with emotion. 'There's only one place she'd go. One place where she knows almost no one would follow her.' He watched as the flames consumed the tapestry, blotting out Emelda's figure.

'No one would dare follow her there,' Samuel told the scholar. 'No one except me.'

Cicely felt her heart hammering against her chest, but the blood pumping through it was cold. The chill of the grave was creeping into her again, just as her skin was losing its healthy colour. Rukh's essence hadn't sustained her for nearly as long as she'd hoped. It was Aaric's accursed talismans. She was certain they'd done something to repulse the needle's preservative magic.

'You thought yourself so clever,' she berated herself as she hurried through Hochmueller's fields. 'You should have worried that Rukh would come back.' The forest was just ahead. She could lose herself in there. If her uncle denounced her now, it would avail him little. No one would go with him into Briardark to track her down. She was certain of that much. 'Papa won't help him, and there's nobody else.'

She tried to take some measure of security from her father's devotion, but Cicely wondered what would happen if the templars forced him to follow her. She shuddered to think of those deathly avengers on their gruesome steeds. She'd been afraid of Uncle Aaric, but she was terrified of the templars.

Even reaching the forest didn't ease the thought of the templars in her mind. Briardark might offer refuge from the mortals of Felstein, but it would hold no fear for the undead hunters. Once they found her trail, Cicely knew they would follow it to the end. Her end.

Her eyes roved across the ground, seeking even the least sign of tracks. 'I must find Verderghast.' The outcast physician had been on the run for a long time. He'd certainly know a way to throw off pursuit, even from hunters like the templars.

More importantly, Cicely had to get answers from him about the onyx needle. Verderghast was her only hope. She needed the needle's magic to keep herself from fading, from becoming naught but a wraith. The physician must know something of its sorcery, a way by which she could make use of those powers without killing.

'*My life is yours,*' the spectral voice said, goading her on, demanding she find the physician.

The grey mantle of Briardark closed in around Cicely. The trees with their drab trunks and barren branches reined her in on every side. The misty fog crawled through the boughs and settled like a shroud. Colour was blotted out, everything subdued beneath the forest's cloak.

Cicely recognised the dismal surroundings only in an abstract way. To her afflicted senses, the forest became more vibrant the thicker the mists of Shyish engulfed it. She had no difficulty picking her way through the woods. The beasts of Briardark avoided her approach. She could hear them skittering away through the brambles or flying off through the trees.

'Verderghast!' she cried as she ran. Even in her chilled state, with the morbid taint overwhelming her senses, she felt dread when she recognised the rocky shelf along which Marden had tracked the wolf.

'Verderghast!' Cicely called again. 'I need you!'

She hurried along the rocky shelf. Now she was near the place where Marden had died. The site where she'd been corrupted by the dire wolf's bite.

'Verderghast!' she yelled, listening to her voice echoing through the trees. She slumped to her knees, despair overcoming her. She'd heard her father speak of how vast Briardark was. The physician could be anywhere... if he hadn't left the forest altogether.

'Verderghast!' Cicely shouted, this time with a note of futility in her cry.

'I am here,' a cold voice answered from the shadows.

Cicely recognised the physician's voice, but far from bringing relief, it only magnified her dread.

'Be careful what you look for,' Verderghast said from the darkness. 'You just might find it.'

CHAPTER EIGHTEEN

The gloom of Briardark coiled around the two men like a great serpent, cold and crushing. Samuel could feel his lungs compressed by the oppressive atmosphere, the stifling chill of the fog he drew into himself with each breath. Even for the beast-hunter, who'd braved the forest many times, fear pulsed through his veins. He could only imagine how much more pronounced the effect was on Aaric.

'She went this way,' Samuel stated when they reached a split in the path. 'Cicely must've been in a panic. Her tracks are easy to follow.' Agony brewed inside his heart when he reflected the terror his daughter must be in. 'She knows enough of woodcraft to do better than this,' he added, pointing at an almost perfectly defined footprint. 'I'm not saying she could throw me off the trail, but she could make me work to keep up.'

Aaric frowned and gave Samuel a warning look. 'If she is careless, it also means she's desperate. Capable of anything to defend herself.'

'I'll not believe that,' Samuel retorted. He pushed his way through the bushes, pursuing the trail left by his daughter. 'She wouldn't do anything to knowingly hurt me.' He paused and brandished the talisman he wore. 'Besides, aren't we protected from her spell?'

'From *that* spell,' Aaric emphasised. 'The dark magic that sustains her and draws off the essence of her victims. But she may have learned other spells, powers against which the talismans will offer no protection. I say again, we must be careful.'

Samuel offered no reply, but stormed ahead. He almost hoped he would lose Aaric in Briardark's labyrinth. The scholar was speaking of Cicely as if she were just any witch to be hunted and destroyed without compunction. But she was still his daughter. Whatever she'd done, whatever had to be done, he couldn't resign himself to that end. She had to be stopped somehow, but certainly not like that. Not the way Aaric intended, to kill her the moment they found her lest she cast a spell against them.

The hunter knew almost every inch of Briardark, some places better than others. It was this vague familiarity with everything the men passed that numbed Samuel's mind to exactly where they were headed. When he spotted the rocky shelf, it came as something of a shock. This landscape was burned into his brain. It was the trail Cicely and Marden had taken when tracking the wolf.

Samuel froze as a cascade of memories rushed over him. He knew now where Cicely was going. She was headed back to the place where it had all started. The spot where Marden died and she was bitten. The site of the tragedy that destroyed Samuel's family.

'Is something wrong?' Aaric asked, catching up to the hunter. 'Have you lost the trail?'

The only reply Samuel made was a slow shake of his head. He was too preoccupied with his own thoughts to answer Aaric's questions. His eyes darted to the rocky shelf, following it into the fog. Some two hundred yards ahead would be the clearing where the wolf had set upon his children. The place where he'd found the body of his son. The place where he now expected to find his daughter.

It was wrong! All of it! Samuel clenched his fists in silent rage. Sigmar, Nagash, whatever capricious gods were looking down on him, there had to be a limit to the misery he was expected to endure.

Samuel glanced aside at Aaric. The man was a scholar, erudite and bookish. He wasn't a woodsman. A tracker. He was dependent on Samuel finding Cicely's trail and following it. He'd certainly seen some of the more obvious signs, but that could work in Samuel's favour now. Because he'd shown the trail to the scholar, Aaric would suspect nothing now when he turned away from it.

'She took to the rocks,' Samuel said. 'The signs will be harder to spot now.'

'But you can still follow them?' Aaric asked, worried.

For an instant, Samuel hesitated. 'I can follow them,' he said, his decision made. He started Aaric across the rocky shelf, away from the clearing.

Away from Cicely.

'Where are you?' Cicely's voice echoed through the trees. She heard Verderghast reply from the darkness and hurried towards the sound. Just as each time before, when she reached the spot, he wasn't there.

'I need your help,' Cicely called to the shadows.

'Help,' Verderghast's voice called back to her. Doubt seized her in its talons. Was the voice merely an echo? Was she simply imagining it sounded like the physician? In her desperation, was she just hearing what she wanted to hear?

Crazy or not, Cicely plunged ahead. There was nothing else to do. She couldn't go back to Felstein. She *had* to find Verderghast.

Cicely cried his name again. This time, however, the response that reached her ears was from behind rather than ahead. Not the phantom voice of the physician but the sound of something moving through the brambles.

Instantly she crouched beside the gnarled trunk of an old oak. Cicely had learned enough woodcraft from her father to know that the noise wasn't that of some animal. It was something on two feet. Perhaps more than one individual. She almost wished she was hearing ghouls creeping after her. At least then the ordeal of trying to preserve her life would be lifted.

The bleak reassurance evaporated when Cicely considered a far more likely solution for the footsteps – someone from Felstein was pursuing her. Uncle Aaric with his protective talisman and his unwavering conviction. Or perhaps it was the ghastly templars Thayer had summoned, undead avengers stalking her through Briardark.

The futility of trying to elude pursuit sapped Cicely's stamina. She stumbled through the forest, her gait awkward and uneven. What sense was there in trying to hide her tracks? Her enemies would find her. Then the needle wouldn't matter. She'd be executed before she could replenish herself by magic. Perhaps that would be an end to it. Perhaps then she wouldn't fade until she was naught but a fleshless wraith.

'Come to me,' Verderghast's voice beckoned, inspiring just enough hope in Cicely's flagging spirit to push her onwards. The physician was close by. Relief might be just a few steps away. How bitter it would be to give up when salvation might be so near.

Cicely pushed her way through the brambles. To her horror she found that the branches were scratching her skin but she couldn't feel them. Her affliction was asserting itself again, exhausting the vitality she'd stolen from Rukh. Aaric's talismans had disrupted the enchantment, consuming the gains she'd made. Soon enough it would all be too late.

'This way,' Verderghast called.

Cicely forced her way through the bushes and found herself in a clearing. To one side was a rocky shelf she remembered only too well. Her path had brought her in a wide circle, doubling back to the clearing where they'd fought the wolf.

The familiarity of the scene was made complete by the lupine shape that trotted out from the fog. The dire wolf was more decayed than when she'd last seen it, its head denuded so that it was entirely skeletal. The hide along its sides hung from its exposed ribs in loose strips. The tail had fallen away entirely. Without fur to cover them, the claws on the creature's toes looked like an eagle's talons. The fangs in the lipless jaws gleamed like daggers.

At first it seemed to Cicely that the sockets in the wolf's skull were entirely devoid of awareness, for the menacing glow was absent now. She could feel the undead thing watching her, but she couldn't see it. Not until she appreciated the unnatural depth of the darkness where its eyes should have been. It was the reverse of light, a darkness that flared and rippled like a black flame. An un-light of indescribable malevolence.

Cicely held her breath, eyes riveted on the dire wolf. 'Why didn't you bring a weapon?' she groaned, though she wondered what good any weapon would do against a beast that couldn't die. Her body tensed as the undead creature stepped further into the clearing, every instinct alive with the urge to flee. She knew that to run now would only provoke the monster into pursuit. The longer she kept still, the longer it would delay its attack.

Yet the wolf paid her no attention. She could sense its horrible animosity, but as it had once before, it ignored her now. It kept itself angled towards the rocky shelf, its dark eyes alert as it stared into the forest. The sounds she'd heard had come from that direction. It was that realisation that made her understand. The wolf wasn't here for her, but rather her pursuers.

Slowly, each step more cautious than the last, Cicely moved past the dire wolf. It barely turned its head as she walked away from it. Once she was past the beast, she heard Verderghast's voice once more.

'No, it will not harm you,' the assuring words rasped from the shadows. 'But you must hurry, for there are others in Briardark who would.'

A flicker of doubt tugged at Cicely. Why didn't Verderghast reveal himself? Why this game of leading her by his voice? She sensed a sinister purpose in the physician's actions. She glanced back at the dire wolf. Its presence was too convenient. She'd thought it ignored her because of her affliction, but what if it did so because it had been told to leave her alone? What if Verderghast had gained some kind of control over the beast?

What if it had always been under his control?

The questions plagued Cicely, but so too did the horror of her situation. What choice did she have?

'*My life is yours,*' the phantom hissed in her ear. Strange yet familiar, she almost felt she could grasp who it was, but its identity once again slipped away.

Goaded on by the spectral presence, Cicely followed Verderghast's voice into the shadows once more.

Samuel led Aaric further away from Cicely's trail. If he could delay the scholar long enough, maybe his daughter would get away. He'd thought long and hard about what he was going to do, weighing the consequences. There was only one choice that offered Cicely a chance to survive. For him, it was the only choice he could make.

'I know how difficult this must be for you,' Aaric told him. 'Hunting your own daughter. But it has to be done.'

'This is the only way,' came the hunter's curt reply. Samuel made a show of searching for signs of a trail that didn't exist.

Aaric, it seemed, was growing anxious. It made him loquacious. 'It's what's best for her. She can't be saved, but we can extend her mercy. Make her passing quick.'

Samuel grimaced and shook his head. 'I need to concentrate on finding her trail.' He was relieved when Aaric stopped talking. He didn't need the scholar's words adding to his guilt... or his fear.

In the silence that followed, Samuel caught the distant sounds of someone moving through the forest. For an instant he feared it was Cicely, that she'd turned in this direction rather than deeper into the forest. Then he noted that there were two sets of footsteps, and his fear was magnified tenfold. The templars! It could only be the undead sent by the temple of Nagash. By what occult means they'd been drawn to the forest he couldn't say. All he knew was that they were heading away from Samuel and Aaric, towards the clearing where Marden had died. They were on Cicely's trail, and they didn't have him there to lead them astray.

Aaric's face was alert when Samuel turned towards him. The scholar might not be a woodsman, but he'd heard the sounds too. 'You tried to lead me on a false track,' he accused. 'Don't you understand, if she's left alone, Cicely will kill again. She has to be stopped.'

The scholar started towards the distant footsteps. Samuel at once realised the mistake Aaric had made. He thought the sounds belonged to Cicely. He caught Aaric by the shoulder and spun him around.

'That isn't her,' Samuel insisted, desperation in his tone. He didn't know what the templars would do to Aaric if he stumbled on them in the dark, but he couldn't imagine it would be anything good. 'Those are the principatuum. Listen. There are two sets of steps.'

Aaric did listen, and when he spoke again, he was contrite.

'Those must be the templars,' he agreed. 'Now it's even more important that we find Cicely.' He gave Samuel a reassuring smile. 'I was wrong to accuse you. At least the undead are looking in the wrong direction.'

Samuel felt as though a hot knife were probing his gut. 'You weren't wrong,' he said, dashing back the way they'd come. 'The templars are following her tracks. If they should find her first...'

The two men rushed back through the forest. Samuel was thankful he'd made such a show of looking for the false trail. The tactic had retarded their progress, leaving them with less ground to cover now that they had to backtrack. But would it still be too great a distance? That fear hammered at his mind. He thought of the one hope Aaric had tried to console him with. A quick and merciful death. Something Cicely wouldn't receive if the templars reached her first.

'Please, Lord Nagash, hold your hounds back just a little while,' Samuel prayed as they hurried through the fog-shrouded forest. The templars were certain to hear the two men crashing through the undergrowth. The noise might make them divert from the trail they were following. He didn't bother himself over how they would fare against the undead hunters – all that mattered was keeping them away from Cicely.

Samuel couldn't hear the templars over the clamour the two men were making, so when they were near the rocky shelf at a point that would intersect with Cicely's tracks, he motioned for Aaric to wait. It took only a moment of silence to ascertain that the undead hadn't diverted. They were still keeping to the trail.

'This way,' Samuel told the scholar. 'I know where Cicely's gone.' He didn't tarry to see if Aaric accepted him at his word but ran off along the slope. He stumbled several times in his haste, for the ground was uneven and would fragment under his boot, yet he maintained his frantic pace.

At last he saw the spot that was burned into his brain. Samuel's heart turned cold when the image of Marden's torn and mangled body came to him. The clearing was mostly obscured by fog, but he recognised the edge that abutted the slope. Steeling himself, he dropped down from the height. 'Cicely!' he called out into the grey mist.

A low growl answered him. From behind the veil, a decayed shape loped into view. The dire wolf, the fell beast that had escaped him before to wreak such havoc upon his family. Samuel drew the axe from his belt, cursing himself for leaving his spear behind. The brute glared at him with eyes of darkness. A dry snarl rattled through its skull.

Where was Cicely? The thought was torture. Samuel was certain her trail led here. What had become of her? Had she fled the wolf, or joined her brother as one of its victims?

'I'm going to cut out your heart and spit on it,' Samuel snarled back at the beast. He started to rush the brute, no thought in his mind except vengeful rage. The wolf leapt at him and the two adversaries collided. Samuel cried out as the long claws tore into his flesh. He felt his axe chop into the beast's shoulder only to glance off the bone. It was like striking sigmarite. The jarring impact caused him to lose his grip and send the weapon clattering off into the fog.

The combatants tumbled across the ground. Samuel sprang to his feet and smacked the wolf with his bronze hand as it started to rise. The skeletal head snapped to one side with such force that it would have broken the neck of a living animal. The undead beast, however, simply spun about and lunged for him. Samuel dove aside, landing in a sprawl.

The wolf twisted around with speed and agility Samuel had never expected from an undead thing. Its fangs gnashed together in anticipation, and such muscles as remained attached to its necrotic frame tensed for another leap.

Samuel thought death was upon him when the wolf sprang at

him. He expected to die under the fangs that had taken his son
and possibly his daughter. Instead, his eyes were dazzled by a
hundred bright, silvery flashes of light. The beast's body crackled
with dozens of tiny explosions and it jerked in mid-air, flung
back before it could complete its leap. The wolf rolled away, a
pained yelp rising from it.

'You should have waited for me,' Aaric said. One of his hands
was covered in silvery powder, no doubt the residue of whatever
he'd thrown at the dire wolf. He dropped down from the slope
and drew his sword from its scabbard. The silvered blade seemed
to glow in the fog. 'Unfortunately, that was all the tomb-bane I
had with me,' he added as he took up a defensive stance.

Before Samuel could reply, the wolf was back on its feet.
Smoke rose from its charred flesh and its exposed bones were
peppered with little scorch marks where the powder had burned
it. The beast threw its head back and uttered a chilling howl.
The sound was so deep and intense that Samuel could feel his
body quiver. Aaric, however, stood his ground, his sword held
in a guarding position.

'Foul beast! You'll not–'

Before Aaric could finish, the wolf charged at him. Just as
Samuel had been, the scholar was shocked by the brute's speed.
Bony claws slashed at him as the wolf sprang up from the ground.
The silvered sword slashed across its side, gouging the wormy
flesh and breaking several ribs. Aaric, however, was borne down
by the ferocity of the attack. By the narrowest margin, he was able
to intercept the wolf's jaws with the blade of his sword. Fangs
bubbled and blackened as they champed down on the silvered
edge, but the beast refused to relent. Its paws continued to rake
Aaric's body even as he strove to fend it off.

'Hang on!' Samuel shouted to Aaric. He scrambled across the
clearing and dove at the wolf. He wrapped his arms around its
head, pulling the denuded skull back. The force of both men

overcame the ferocious strength of the undead, but when it finally relented, it was with a suddenness that caught them by surprise. The dire wolf disengaged from Aaric's blade and spun about to snap at Samuel. Its fangs ripped into his tunic and belt, tearing his raiment to shreds but missing the man inside it.

'Nagash's black bones!' Samuel cried as he reeled away. The wolf was not to be denied. Shaking its head, it flung away the tatters caught in its fangs and lunged for the beasthunter.

Samuel resorted to a desperate ploy. Instead of trying to dodge the attack, he drove himself at the wolf. His shoulder slammed into its leaping frame and sent both of them pitching backwards. Man and beast struck the ground hard, but it was the wolf that recovered first. With a twisting roll, it regained its feet and made ready to resume the assault.

Before the dire wolf could rush Samuel, greenish light flared from its side. The beast was knocked back, snarling in pain. It snapped its head around to glare at the cause of its hurt.

Samuel expected to see Aaric with some different weapon from his strange arsenal. Instead, he saw the scholar giving ground to two skeletal figures that came stalking out from the fog. The undead templars. One of them carried a strangely curved sword in its fleshless fingers, while its companion gripped what looked like an over-sized crossbow with a boxy device mounted at the top of its frame. The principatuum advanced in menacing silence, the only sound rising from them the clatter of the equipment hooked to their bones.

The crossbowman aimed and shot at the wolf. Again there erupted a burst of green fire as the bolt struck home. The beast pitched and fell onto its side with an anguished yelp. Samuel didn't know what enchantments were bound into the templars' arsenal, but he was grateful for their efficacy.

At least, he was until the wolf suddenly rolled back onto its feet and rushed the skeleton warriors. If it was possible for a face devoid of flesh to show surprise, he knew that expression would have appeared on the templars' skulls in that moment. The crossbowman tried to loose another dart, but before it could, the beast was upon it. The skeleton was thrown to the ground. The wolf clamped its jaws tight about the crossbow, ripping it from the warrior and reducing it to ivory fragments with a side-wise shake of its head.

The other templar swung at the wolf with its crooked sword. The blade crashed against the brute's body but bounced away as if the blow had landed against solid stone. The wolf spun away from the prostrate warrior and pounced on the swordsman, bearing it to the earth. Claws scratched at the armoured bones while the fangs champed down on the helmeted skull, grating across its surface.

'Help them or we're doomed!' Aaric shouted. He came at the wolf from one side, slashing with his sword. The silvered blade sizzled against the brute's flank. The beast whipped away from the templar and snapped at Aaric, forcing the scholar to jump back. Before it could take advantage of his retreat, the cross-bowman was after it again. The skeleton warrior drove at the wolf, a pair of bolts clenched in its fists. It stabbed the missiles into the brute as though they were spikes. Ghostly fire flared from the impact as each bolt dug into the necrotic creature.

The wolf forgot Aaric and returned its attention to the cross-bowman. The skeleton sought to block the beast's attack with its arm and the lupine jaws clamped down on the armoured bone. The wolf snarled as it worried at the limb.

Samuel noted the action even as he searched the clearing for his axe. He caught glimpses of the fray through the swirling fog. He saw the crossbowman unhook a club-like weapon from its bones even as the wolf tore away its other arm. He saw Aaric bowled over after he hacked into the beast's leg with his sword, sprawled on the ground, helpless before the brute's fury. He saw the swordsman intercede, its crooked blade smashing into the lupine skull without effect.

The beasthunter abandoned his search for the axe and hurried instead to take up the sword Aaric had dropped. The scholar, battered by the wolf's assault, merely nodded when Samuel picked up the silvered blade. Armed again, the father turned towards the killer of his children. The wolf was ripping at the templar swordsman, trying to overbear the warrior and throw it to the ground.

'Forget about me, you murdering cur?' Samuel roared as he charged the beast.

The templar let go of its curved sword and instead grabbed hold of the wolf with both hands. The beast's fangs crunched down into its shoulder bones, but the skeleton maintained its grip.

Upright against the templar, the wolf was unable to twist away when Samuel struck it from behind. The silvered blade slashed through the mangy hide along its back. The wolf tried to tear itself free, but it was unaccustomed to fighting an undead opponent who didn't feel pain. The templar maintained its hold and Samuel struck again.

'For Marden!' he raged as the silvered blade crunched into the beast's spine. 'For Cicely!' he roared as he brought the sword cleaving through the wolf's backbone.

Cleft in twain by Samuel's repeated blows, the wolf fell away from the templar's grip. The hindquarters flopped and thrashed on the ground. Malignance persisted in the fore portion, however, and the mangled beast snapped at the templar swordsman until the other undead warrior marched over and brought its spiked mace crashing down. It took five hits to shatter the lupine skull. When the wolf's head finally crumpled, a black mass rose from it, a foul miasma that seemed to disgust even the templars. The undead drew away from it as the ghastly vapour gradually dissipated.

'I have seen something like this before.' Aaric shuddered as he watched the miasma disperse. There was a haunted expression in his eyes. Samuel wondered what could have shaken the scholar to such a degree.

'It's dead now,' Samuel said. His bronze hand tightened around the sword and he watched the injured templars warily. The undead, however, appeared intent only on recovering their weapons, uninclined to address their recent allies.

Aaric shook his head. 'It was far too strong to be simply a dire wolf,' he stated. 'A horrible vitality motivated it. Lent it both speed and strength.' He gestured at the templars as they recovered their gear from where it had been scattered during the melee. 'The weapons they use are crafted from nadirite. They would have destroyed something that was merely undead.' He held out his hand and took his sword back from Samuel. 'This blade was employed by vampire hunters of the Order of Azyr, yet even it was scarce able to hurt the beast.'

'What are you saying?' Samuel asked. The scholar's mounting uneasiness was beginning to infect him.

'I'm afraid to even say it aloud,' Aaric said, 'and I pray to Sigmar that I'm wrong.' He pointed at the wolf's corpse. 'This much I will say. The same power that vitalised that animal could be the same magic Cicely has been using.'

Samuel started to wonder what that could mean. Some sort of arcane infection that had been passed on to Cicely by the wolf? Before he could think too deeply on the subject, he noted that the templars were moving off into the fog. It took him only a moment to realise why.

'The principatuum are taking up Cicely's trail now that the wolf is dead,' he said with a gasp. For a desperate moment he considered confronting them. Only the appreciation of how reckless such an effort would be held him back. The undead had been battered by the wolf, but he was certain they'd be able to withstand anything the two men could hope to do to them.

'The templars of Nagash are unwavering and unrelenting,' Aaric said. 'Once they're set upon a task, they will see it to the very end.'

Samuel scowled at the undead as they vanished into the grey mist. 'We can't let them find Cicely first,' he told Aaric. 'They might be unrelenting, but they're slowed by the wounds the wolf inflicted. We can outpace them. Get ahead of them and find her first.'

Aaric gave him a stony look. 'She can't be saved,' he declared.

'Please!' Samuel implored. 'Think if it was your own daughter. You couldn't stand by and do nothing.'

With a sigh, the scholar nodded. When Samuel started off through the fog on a course parallel to that taken by the templars, Aaric was only a few steps behind him.

CHAPTER NINETEEN

Briardark's gloom wound itself around Cicely like a shroud. There was only the grey fog now, the trees reduced to indistinct shadows barely perceptible through the veil. Her adjusted perceptions, attuned to shadows and murk, were confounded by the preternatural miasma around her. She could feel it seeping into her, thousands of phantom fingers trying to pull her apart.

Verderghast's voice beckoned her through the night. 'This way.' Cicely thought she could hear sounds of conflict somewhere in the distance, but the impression faded as the fog grew thicker. A flush of terror raced through her as she wondered if it truly *was* fog. Perhaps the energies she'd taken from Rukh had vanished quicker than she'd expected. Cicely pinched the flesh of her arm and savagely twisted it. She could still feel skin between her fingers, but there was no sensation of pain.

'Come to me.' The distant voice fanned the embers of Cicely's dying hope. Fending off the exhaustion that dragged at her, she hurried on. Though the landscape around her remained obscured, she could tell she'd left the grim vastness of Briardark. She was crossing a cultivated field. Somehow, in a manner she couldn't understand, she'd turned around and circled back to Felstein.

'Only a little farther.' Verderghast's words were more distinct now. For the first time, Cicely felt that she was indeed getting closer to the physician.

'*My life is yours.*' The spectral whisper spurred her on. She now felt a kinship with whatever it was that dominated the chorus, a connection greater than what she'd shared with Marden or her mother. What *was* this phantom?

Abruptly, the fog lessened, receding as though burned back by the breath of Dracothion. Cicely could see a multitude of dark objects rise up from the ground all around her. As the mist became still thinner, a shudder swept down her spine. She was surrounded by gravestones. She'd been drawn out of Briardark only to step into a cemetery. A particular marker reared up before her, one that she knew too well. It was Marden's tombstone.

'In a way, this is where it all began,' came a voice. What had seemed to Cicely to be the shadow cast by her brother's gravestone suddenly moved towards her. The dark shape became more distinct... and familiar. Verderghast gave her a wan smile and a brief nod by way of greeting.

Desperation overwhelmed all other concerns, and Cicely rushed to the renegade physician. 'You have to help me,' she pleaded, dropping to her knees and taking one of his hands between her own. 'The magic isn't sustaining me.'

Verderghast patted her head. 'No, it isn't, is it? The meddler from Gothghul Hollow is to blame. He's disrupted the enchantment.'

Cicely looked up at him, flinching when she saw the stern disapproval in his expression. 'I tried to stop him. I did try.'

Verderghast pulled away from her grip. 'I know you did.' Though the words were consoling, the tone was acidic. 'There wasn't anything you'd hesitate to do to save yourself. You'd killed to keep yourself alive long before we met. From the very first, your soul has been stained with murder.'

The caustic speech caused Cicely to recoil. 'I used the needle you gave me to keep from dying.' She held her hands up to Verderghast, displaying their ethereal pallor. 'I was fading, diminishing. Worse than death, I'd have become a wraith, a nighthaunt, my spirit cursed to wander and wail–'

'You've brought the needle with you?' Verderghast interjected. Cicely nodded and withdrew the onyx needle from where it was concealed among the laces of her bodice. The physician gingerly plucked it from her fingers. He held it up to his face and peered at it for a moment. There was a strange look of both admiration and disgust as he studied it.

'So much evil,' Verderghast remarked. 'It has become filthy with it.' He offered Cicely a nod of approval. 'You've exceeded yourself. I didn't imagine you'd endow this vessel with half so much wretchedness.'

Cicely's soul railed at the physician's mocking disdain. Her mind was beginning to understand that she'd been used somehow, exploited for some occult purpose. Her heart, however, clung to her fast-fading hope. 'I did what I had to do to stay alive. To keep from becoming one of the undead!'

Verderghast waved the needle at her. 'Oh, you won't become a wraith. Was that what you feared? No, my murderous little pet, what's happening to you is far worse than that.'

'Help me!' Cicely reached for the physician, but he drew back, interposing Marden's gravestone between them.

'Why should I?' Verderghast scolded her. 'What, after all, have you ever done for anyone else? You take and take and take. That was why I chose you, because I could tell that there'd be no compunction. You'd do just what I needed, no matter how hard you tried to tell yourself you wouldn't.'

'*My life is yours.*' Cicely could hear the phantom tone all around her. Her eyes widened with horror when Verderghast's expression changed. A cruel smile played on his features.

'Ah, the call of the Neverborn!' Verderghast crowed. He gave Cicely a quizzical look. 'How long has it been calling to you? I wonder if it has grown stronger alongside yourself?'

Verderghast looked down at the needle again. 'You've empowered this device through all the murders you so wilfully executed. The dark power you've invoked will give me just what I need.' He carefully placed the needle into a pouch on his belt. 'Someone as selfish as you may take some comfort in knowing that multitudes will pay for what you've done.'

'It was all a lie,' Cicely moaned, unable to cling to any semblance of hope now. She doubled over as a wave of sickness assailed her, revolted by the crimes she'd committed. 'Everything I did was to save my life...'

'Indeed?' Verderghast chided her. 'When was the last time wine tasted right on your tongue? When was the last time the light didn't sting your eyes, or the darkness beckon to you with its sinister comfort? Does the sound of laughter torment you? Does the smell of a flower turn your stomach? When did you last sleep and find it restful? Can you say you are cheered by the company of the living, or do you retreat into seclusion? It is always lonely in the grave.'

'I've been sick,' Cicely protested. 'I've been sick, but I know I'm alive!'

Verderghast shook his head. 'You're wrong. The wolf killed you, not the boy.' The physician tapped the top of Marden's gravestone. 'There was still a flicker of life in him. But you? There wasn't any life for me to save. There *was* a body and spirit I could restore as one of the undead.' His expression became contemplative for a moment. 'I have some skill at necromancy. I can endow those I conjure from the tomb with such a semblance of life that they seem truly alive.' He focused again on Cicely and tilted his head. 'They could fool learned scholars. Even fool themselves. For a time.'

The necromancer gestured at Marden's grave. 'I had to get your permission, of course. You had to agree before I could take that last spark from your brother – your *younger* brother, I should say – before I could invest your corpse with a simulacrum of life.' Verderghast's eyes glimmered with malice. 'I knew you'd agree the moment I saw you.' He laughed and wagged his finger at her. 'You see, you'd done it all before. I don't suppose your parents ever told you about your *other* brother? The twin you strangled as you were born? His spirit has been chained to you by that strangler's noose, lingering beside you, watching a life you were too selfish to share.'

'The Neverborn,' Cicely shuddered. In her mind she heard again that phantom voice, strident, commanding, drowning out the rest of the chorus. *My life is yours.* It wasn't an expression of loving acceptance and understanding but a damning accusation. The voice of her sins.

Cicely collapsed to the ground, shock shivering through her frame. She couldn't deny the revelation. She *felt* its awful truth, felt it tightening around her in a crushing embrace. Dead. All this time, all she'd done, and it was to preserve something that was already lost. Her heart cracked as the monstrous guilt surged up inside her. A glottal sobbing was the only sound that rose from her throat when she tried to speak.

'Yes,' Verderghast nodded. 'Now you understand the folly of your crimes. What is best for you, as it is for all things, would be to have never been.' Pain filled the physician's eyes as he looked down at Cicely, but it was a suffering corrupted with a merciless hate. She could see that now, and she marvelled that such a magnitude of rage could be sustained by anyone. A fury too epic to be fixated upon any one person or people, or nation. It was a vengeful passion that marked all existence as its adversary.

'Why?' was all Cicely could say.

Verderghast waved his hand at the fog. 'I've been lost in mists more impenetrable than these. Lost longer than mortals can comprehend.' Bitterness dripped from his voice like venom. 'I prayed to every god I could name, but none delivered me from my torment.' He shifted his gaze back to Cicely. 'Now, through you, I'll repay my suffering a thousandfold. Mhurghast will come, and not even the gods will stop it.'

A rage of her own brewed up within Cicely, fanned by the treachery of the man she thought could help her. Her hand tightened about the knife on her belt. Her eyes glared coldly back at Verderghast.

Before she could stir for the rush that would bring her to grips with Verderghast, the necromancer's gaze shifted to Marden's grave. 'The Neverborn has waited for vengeance for such a very long time. I think we should indulge it, don't you? It has no shape of its own, but its hate is strong enough to give shape to others.'

Cicely could feel the power that Verderghast channelled into the morbid soil. A thin plume of greasy smoke wafted up from the ground. As it rose, the billowing darkness began to assume a vaporous shape. Cicely saw the suggestion of hunched shoulders and skeletal arms. A hooded robe, ragged and tattered, drooped about the apparition. The bony hands clutched at a shaft of blackness that condensed into the splintered haft and rusted head of a vicious glaive. From under the robe's hood, a fleshless head protruded. Not a human skull but the elongated muzzle of an animal. Yet despite the bestial nature of that visage, Cicely knew a hideous kinship. There was something about the phantasm that compelled her to give it a familiar name.

'Marden!' she gasped, horror blotting out all other thought. The knife fell from her grip, its blade stabbing into the earth at her feet.

'You, above all others, should know the dead don't rest easy in the graves here,' Verderghast stated. 'The Neverborn calls them back.' He waved his hand to encompass the cemetery around them. Cicely managed to tear her eyes away from the horrible spectre that was somehow also her brother. The terror of a moment before was eclipsed by the emotion that now thundered across her senses.

Felstein's graves were disgorging more apparitions, a cavalcade of gheists torn from the underworlds. A spectral chill wafted through Cicely's body as she observed the manifestations billowing up from their tombs, gradually taking on distinct shapes and forms.

'There are no strangers to you here,' Verderghast pronounced. He stepped away from Marden's grave and pointed an accusing finger down at Cicely. 'I merely provided the instrument. It was you who taught yourself how to use the needle. You who chose the deeds that would bind it with infamy.' He stalked past the stunned Cicely, contempt in his voice as he walked away from the graveyard. 'You know these people, and you put every one of them where they are now.'

The condemning words pierced Cicely like a sword. She watched Verderghast walk into the fog, forcing herself to do so until the instant he vanished completely. For she knew that as soon as he was gone, her attention would be compelled to the spirits rising up all around her.

When the moment came, Cicely gave vent to a scream that echoed across the whole of Felstein.

The nighthaunts were ghastly in their macabre shapes, yet, like the bestial spectre assumed by Marden, Cicely found it impossible to deny the essence cloaked within each apparition. There was a skull-faced being with heavy chains dripping from its wrists and neck that she immediately recognised as Alastair Greimhalt. A faceless entity wrapped in a long white shroud, its hands clasping an icy dagger, evoked the memory of Cousin Anya. Others rose, all of them identifiable with someone whose image Cicely had woven into the tapestry. A court of the dead, the dead slain by her own hand. Even Marden, for had she turned him back when she found him in Briardark, her brother would never have died.

Awful as all the rest were, Cicely's heart trembled in anticipation of a still greater dread. Slowly, she turned and looked back towards Marden's grave. Past the bestial apparition, she could see another grave, that of her mother. From this plot, too, a cadaverous phantom was forming. A grey, wispy cowl draped over a withered body. Like all the nighthaunts, the entity had no legs but simply hovered over the ground. There was no face peering out from the cowl, only a wasted skull. Funereal flowers were still pinned to the tresses of matted hair that billowed away from the spectre's head. Agony filled Cicely as she recognised in this fearsome, wretched vision the spirit of Emelda. The arms that had held her so often reached out to her, only there were no longer any hands attached to the wrists. Instead, there were long scythes of blackened bone.

'Mother.' Cicely's voice broke in a desperate appeal. The wraith tilted its head to one side, but there was no expression of forgiveness or understanding or love. Only the deathly stare of the malignant, pitiless and inexorable.

A low growl rose from the thing hovering over Marden's grave. The phantom lowered its glaive, pointing it at Cicely's heart. Uttering another predatory snarl, the spectre charged.

Samuel was stunned when he discovered that the path they were following was leading away from Briardark. 'She's circling back to Felstein,' he told Aaric, perplexed.

The scholar was equally puzzled. 'There's no reason for her to do that if she intends to escape.' Worry kneaded his brow as he considered the problem. 'Something isn't right,' he warned Samuel. 'There's something at work here that we don't understand.'

'Whatever it is, it doesn't matter,' Samuel declared. 'I'm going to find my daughter.' He cast a glance over his shoulder. They could faintly hear the sound of the skeletal templars moving in the distance. 'I won't leave her to *them*.'

Aaric nodded. 'In that we are agreed. Ciccly has to be stopped, but perhaps she can answer questions before the end.'

Samuel clenched his fist at the calculating way Aaric referred to his daughter. 'This is about helping Cicely now. I don't care about anything else.'

'Or anyone,' Aaric reproached him as they hurried through the fog-choked forest.

'She's all I have left,' the hunter said. He knew it wouldn't make a difference to Aaric. Perhaps he said it to bolster his own resolve. To give him the determination to keep going.

The rough floor of the forest gave way to open ground. Samuel knew they were entering the fringe of cleared terrain that skirted the edge of Briardark. Soon they were moving through a pasture, the smell of grass and sheep replacing the wild scent of woodland. Instead of the sense of brooding malice he always felt within Briardark lessening, Samuel found his anxiety only increasing the nearer they drew back to Felstein. Was it his fear for Cicely, his worry that she'd gone back because of some self-destructive impulse, or was it something more primal than that? He knew his agitation was provoked by an external cause when Aaric expressed his own misgivings.

'There's a wrongness to the air,' the scholar cautioned. His fingers curled and made the sign of Sigmar. 'The workings of dark magic are felt by the flesh even when their cause is unknown to the brain. Be on your guard.'

Unconsciously, Samuel's living hand closed about the talisman. If there was witchcraft at work, could it be Cicely's doing? Another murderous spell to sustain herself? Would they be in time to stop her? Did he even *want* to stop her?

The fog around them finally began to thin. Samuel realised
with a start that they'd emerged from Briardark only to find an
even more sinister setting. Files of dark tombstones spread before
them on every side. Generations of Felstein's dead, consigned
into Nagash's keeping. He could see the skull-headed images of
the god engraved upon the stones, grinning their fleshless smiles
as they guarded the graves.

'She's brought us to the cemetery,' Aaric said. His hand closed on
Samuel's shoulder and drew his notice to the shadows that drifted
among the graves. 'Nighthaunts,' he hissed in a shuddering voice.

Raw fear pulsed through Samuel when he saw those grim
apparitions. Shrouded phantoms with wretched skulls for faces,
when they deigned to have a face at all. Chainrasps dragged
their rattling shackles over the gravestones while the cowls of
banshees billowed in an ethereal wind. He saw a dark figure with
its countenance locked behind a rusted helm bearing a sword of
such size that it seemed to crush the spectre under its enormity.
There was a black and terrible thing that flew about the cemetery, a scythe clenched in its bony fists.

'Necromancy,' Aaric rasped. 'She's conjured a host of malignants to attack her hunters. To attack us!'

Samuel didn't know which was more monstrous, to believe
Cicely capable of such profane magic or that she'd evoke such
spells against her own father. A moment later, however, he saw
that Aaric was in error on at least one account. After the ini-
tial shock of seeing the nighthaunts, he noted that the entities
weren't coming for them. They were converging upon a different
part of the cemetery. Through the mist, he could see a figure
crouched down near Marden's grave.

'Cicely!' Samuel shouted to the cowering shape. Perhaps his
daughter had conjured up the nighthaunts, but if so, she had no
control over them. The malignants weren't fanning out to protect
her – they were instead converging to destroy her.

'No! They'll kill you!' Aaric caught at Samuel as he started to rush to help his daughter. 'They'd overwhelm us if we tried to fight them.'

'I won't let them murder my child before my eyes,' Samuel snarled, twisting free. He heard Aaric call after him, but the scholar's words were just meaningless noise that couldn't pierce the panic hammering through him. He had to save Cicely. There was no room in his mind for any other thought.

The hunter's blade chopped into the drifting form of a chain-rasp as it glided towards Cicely. Samuel felt the numbing chill of the blow crackle up his bronze arm, but it wasn't until it flowed into the flesh of his shoulder that he appreciated the pain that went with it. The bite of steel caused the apparition to dissipate, but only for a moment. As he rushed past the being, he could see its tatters already coalescing again.

'Cicely!' he shouted again. His daughter didn't react but remained slumped on the ground in an attitude of transfixed horror. A monstrous creature rushed at her, a hunched apparition shrouded in black with a long glaive and a bestial skull protruding from beneath its hood. Samuel spurred himself to greater effort, hurdling gravestones as he ran to intercept the charging wraith.

He won his desperate race but only just. Interposing himself between the bestial malignant and his daughter, Samuel should have been easy prey for the entity. Instead, the phantom recoiled, its fleshless visage somehow conveying an impression of shock. Samuel's eyes widened in terror as he focused on the creature. For just an instant he saw through its monstrous guise. The rusted glaive changed into a spear he himself had carved. The equine skull transformed into Marden's face.

Tears dimmed Samuel's eyes as he stared at the agonising vision. His axe hung limp in his hand, dragging his metal arm down to his side. 'Marden,' he whispered, the name cracking as it rose from his throat. He could feel the spectre's attention shift to him, though there were no eyes in the sockets of its skull to

exhibit the direction of its gaze. For a moment he felt the unsettling mixture of misery and hate that was the wraith's scrutiny.
Then the apparition turned towards Cicely again. It moved to
rush past Samuel and attack his daughter.

'Cicely! Run!' Samuel yelled as he swung his axe at the glaive-
wraith. His blade was turned by the rusted weapon, but because he
struck it from an angle, the blow was deflected back at the spectre.
There was a strange impact as it crashed into the bestial skull, as
though the being were at once both insubstantial and solid. He
saw the edge of his axe cleave through the hood and the roof of
the skull within it. He felt sick to see the spectral debris fly away
from the thing that had been his son. The glaivewraith froze in
place, transfixed as its broken essence slowly crept back to rejoin it.

'Run!' Samuel ordered Cicely, dragging her to her feet. She was
only dimly aware of him, her eyes staring away across the cemetery. He followed her gaze and gaped at the hideous entity that
came stalking towards them. It was a scythe-handed spectre, its
skeletal features snarling at them with insurmountable enmity.
Something withered inside him when he felt, as he had with
Marden, a woeful kinship. He knew he was looking at Emelda,
but unlike Hephzibah's visitation, there was nothing of love that
lingered in this fearsome spirit. He understood Cicely's paralysis
of horror, for he felt his own body freeze as the harridan glided
towards them.

'Over here!' Aaric's shout snapped Samuel from his daze.
Tightening his grip on Cicely, he spun her around and started
her running towards her uncle. The scholar stood between several gravestones with a pouch in his hand. He was pouring a
shimmering powder onto the earth, its grains twinkling like star-
light as they touched the ground. 'Get into the circle!'

The harridan sped after its former family. Samuel felt the edge
of a bony scythe slice down his tunic as he ran, biting just deep
enough to draw blood. An eerie wail rose from the pursuing

phantom. Samuel forced himself to greater effort, pushing Cicely ahead of him. Whatever it had been in life, the malignant would show them no mercy now.

Events transpired quickly when they reached Aaric's circle. Samuel saw a bright light flash when Cicely reached the spot. His daughter was flung back as though she'd run headfirst into a wall. There was no such obstruction to his own passage, and a lunge brought him across the barrier of shimmering powder. The harridan, chasing close behind him, was rebuffed by the schol-ar's ward. He saw it flung back much as Cicely had been, its spectral essence disrupted by the protective energies. Streams of ectoplasm spilled away from the spectre as it flew away. Much like the glaivewraith, it froze in position while its scattered ener-gies slowly drifted back to it.

'Cicely!' Samuel cried, turning to see his daughter sprawled on the ground. Her violent rebuff from Aaric's circle had jarred her back to full awareness. There was such a look of frantic appeal on her face that Samuel at once tried to go to her.

'Stay in the circle,' Aaric enjoined him. 'The celestial salts will repel the undead.' The scholar emphasised the last word.

Samuel refused to accept what Aaric was telling him. He jumped across the shimmering line and took Cicely in his arms. 'I've got you,' he assured her. He turned back to the circle. He'd carry her into its protection if that was what it took.

Cicely struggled in his arms, trying to pull away. She felt impos-sibly cold. Impossibly light. It was as if Samuel was carrying a wisp of icy fog. When he looked down at her, he could see the bones beneath her pale skin. Her hair was like a tangle of shadow spilling from a fleshless skull. Her eyes were hollow specks glim-mering at the bottom of deep pits. 'It's no good,' she protested, her breath rank with death. 'It's too late. Save yourself.'

The hunter shook his head. 'Without you, there's nothing worth saving,' he told his daughter. Around them, the other nighthaunts

were closing in. There was just a narrow gap between the apparitions and the circle. Tightening his hold on Cicely, Samuel tried to
dash between the spectres. A hideous revenant, a rusted mask under
its cowl and a massive sword in its hands, barred his path. It thrust
at him with its blade, and he felt the icy tip of the sword pierce his
breast. Crippling pain brought him to his knees. He dropped Cicely,
leaving her to roll across the ground. She screamed as she tumbled
towards the circle and was thrown back by the celestial salts.

'Get away from her!' Samuel snarled as the revenant turned
to Cicely and lifted its sword. He lunged at the spectre, passing
through its ethereal body. His axe, however, crashed against the
massive sword and pulled it away from its intended victim. Still
partly inside the phantom, Samuel could feel its frustrated rage.
A surge of ghoulish energy sizzled through him, and he was
expelled from the wraith to land beside Cicely on the ground.

The revenant loomed above them, its blade poised to strike.
'Get away!' Cicely shouted at her father. In a wild spring, she
threw herself towards the spectre and raked her hands against
its mask. Her savagery was such that she ripped the rusted metal
away. The revenant lost cohesion, drifting apart and spilling backwards. Then the mask Cicely held billowed away in a stream of
black smoke, snaking through the air to rejoin the greater part
of the disrupted malignant.

'Hurry!' Aaric called to Samuel.

'Yes, go!' Cicely implored her father. More of the nighthaunts
closed in upon her, brandishing the mouldering weapons they
bore in their bony hands.

Samuel only shook his head and raised his axe. He wouldn't
abandon his daughter. If that meant he would die, then he would
die. Looking at the phantoms surrounding them, he accepted
that there was no escape.

Suddenly, an anguished shriek rose from the spectral throng.
Samuel could see one of the chainrasps writhing in its fetters,

a black energy spreading outward from where a sword had pierced its chest from behind. The apparition rapidly dissipated, and this time its tatters didn't come streaming back to reform its shape. When the chainrasp vanished, he could see its killer standing where it had been. One of Nagash's templars wielding a nadirite sword. The fleshless warrior swept its merciless gaze across the graveyard, then slowly marched forwards. The other templar limped after it, guarding its flank with its spiked mace.

Exhibiting an uncanny unity of purpose, the nighthaunts shifted to confront the skeletal templars. A scythe-wielding wraith descended upon the swordsman, slashing its armoured arm so that it hung brokenly at the warrior's side. A sweep of the nadirite blade cleft the phantom from crown to collar and its shadowy form rapidly evaporated. The maceman met the rush of a shrieking chainrasp, crushing it to the ground with a brutal blow of its weapon. The templar was in turn attacked by the harridan, one bony sickle shearing through the side of its skull and exposing the hollow cavity within.

Given a respite, Samuel tried to get Cicely into the circle. 'Quickly,' he urged her. She shook her head and resisted. Before she could speak, Samuel felt a stabbing pain in his side. He looked down to see the edge of a glaive biting into his flesh. The bestial skull of Marden's vengeful spirit snapped its teeth at him and dug the blade deeper. Not all of the malignants, it seemed, had forgotten their original prey.

'It's me you want! Not father!' Cicely screamed at the glaive-wraith. She seized the weapon's haft and struggled to pull it free. The apparition twisted about and gnashed its teeth at her.

'Marden,' Samuel groaned. There was still that echo of his son's presence about the ghoulish entity. Enough to turn his insides cold as he swung the axe at the spectre but not enough to stay the attack. His axe crunched through the bestial skull, smashing through its jaw to pulverise the eye sockets.

Samuel didn't know if the cleaving stroke dealt the glaive-wraith any permanent harm, but as it recoiled from the assault, Cicely succeeded in wresting the weapon away from the stunned phantom. She reversed her grip and impaled the spirit on the bladed head. The apparition writhed for a moment, a mournful baying echoing from its jaws, then it lost cohesion, rags of its dark shape drifting off into the night.

The glaivewraith's dying shriek brought several of the malignants spinning away from their fray with the templars. The masked revenant, reformed after Cicely's attack, led a wailing pack of nighthaunts rushing towards Samuel and his daughter. Against the spectral mob, an axe and a phantasmal glaive wouldn't accomplish much.

'Bring them this way!' Aaric shouted. The scholar's voice descended into a litany of words in a language unknown to Samuel, but there was something about the sound that provoked hope. Without questioning Aaric's intentions, the hunter shoved his daughter towards the circle.

Aaric had the pouch of celestial salts in his hand. As the fugitives ran towards him, he opened the bag's mouth wide and made a sweeping throw. The shimmering powder struck the spectres in a billowing cloud. What happened next amazed Samuel.

The revenant at the fore of the pack began to dissolve, its ectoplasm spilling away from it in molten streams. The spectral substance sizzled as it splashed to the ground. The rusted mask, the dark shroud, even the massive sword, all dripped away like wax from a burning candle. In a matter of a few heartbeats, the apparition was utterly consumed. The wraiths and chainrasps behind it were likewise destroyed, the speed of their banishment dependent on the amount of celestial salt that had lighted upon them. None, however, could defy the powder's potency.

Aaric sagged down within the middle of the circle, his face drawn and his breathing laboured. Whatever rite he'd performed to evoke the enchantment had clearly exhausted him. 'A practice intended to be performed by one of Sigmar's Stormcast Sacrosanct isn't so easy for a mere mortal,' he muttered, all but collapsing to the ground. 'It is only by divine grace that I wasn't annihilated along with the malignants.'

Samuel started towards the scholar to render him such feeble aid as he might, but then he heard Cicely's horrified gasp. 'Mother,' she shuddered. Once again, he followed the direction of her gaze. The scythe-handed phantom was speeding towards them, the skull of the templar it had been fighting impaled upon one of its blades. The other bony blade was clear, however, and the spectre was eager to stain it with mortal blood instead of undead bone.

The hunter dove between the harridan and Cicely. 'Forgive me,' he pleaded as he swung his axe at the macabre remnant of his wife. Samuel's distraught mind made for a sloppy attack. He struck too wide and missed the skull-like face. The harridan had no such sentimental baggage, all its kinder feelings purged by the transformation into a nighthaunt. The arm encumbered by the templar's head lashed out and smashed into Samuel. He felt the detached skull shatter against his ribs, then the cruel bite of the scythe as it raked across his flesh.

'Emelda,' Samuel groaned as he struggled to remain standing. He tried to raise his axe to block the sweep of the harridan's other blade, but he knew he wouldn't be quick enough to save himself.

'Mother!' Cicely shrieked as she sprang at the spectre. The glaive punched through the middle of the harridan's cowled shape. By main effort, Cicely swung the impaled phantom around, then slammed it into the earth. The entity screamed as it collided with the edge of Aaric's protective circle. The ring of celestial salts blazed with blue light as it flared across the grim manifestation. Like cinders crackling in a strong draft, the harridan's shape fragmented and was scattered into the wind.

'Mother.' Cicely cast aside the glaive, hurling it as though it were a venomous serpent. She stared down at her hands, hands that had twice committed matricide. Samuel could see the misery that twisted her visage, but no tears would flow.

His daughter was beyond tears. Samuel realised just how mightily the draining affliction had consumed her. She was so pale that he could see the veins under her skin, so drawn that she seemed a mere skeleton herself.

It was the thought of skeletons that alerted Samuel to a change that had come upon the cemetery. The crash of blades and the wailing of malignants had fallen away. He knew the harridan had settled one of Nagash's templars, but what of the other?

Turning, the hunter found his answer. The skeletal swordsman stood amid the fading essence of the nighthaunts it had vanquished. The armoured bones of its unnatural construction were splintered and chipped, but there was enough left of its body to retain hold of the black sword it held. Enough animation left in its legs to set it marching towards Cicely.

Samuel could feel the blood trickling from his wounds. When he moved, a broken rib tore at his flesh. His battered and abused body urged him to desist, but his heart commanded otherwise. Perversely, only his metal arm remained strong. Firming his hold on his axe, he stumbled forwards to meet the undead templar. 'You'll not have her,' he vowed, glaring defiantly at the remorseless skull.

A voice so deep it seemed to stir from below the cemetery rattled through the templar's frame. 'All that is mortal comes to Nagash. Today he demands the corrupt.' The embers in the warrior's eye sockets blazed angrily. 'Do not be eager to speed your own dissolution.'

'You'll have to take her from me,' Samuel spat. His eyes roved across the templar's battered frame. The skeleton was damaged, but so was he. Any advantage its injuries might have afforded him were lost by his own weakness.

'Relent and desist,' Aaric commanded the templar. The skeleton turned its head to regard the scholar as he stepped out from the protective circle. 'The evil you were sent here to stop has been stopped. Return to your tomb-temple.'

'You have no command over me. The corrupt flesh must be rendered to Nagash,' the sepulchral voice intoned. The templar pointed its sword at Aaric. 'Those who would interfere are also forfeit.'

The skeleton warrior took a step towards Aaric. As it raised its blade, the scholar brandished his silvered sword. 'I warn you again to relent.'

The words were wasted on the templar. Its nadirite sword clashed against Aaric's silver. Mortal and undead strained against one another's strength. Both had been weakened during the battle, but neither seemed able to overwhelm the other.

Suddenly, Aaric broke free. He dove to one side and let the templar stumble forwards. The skeleton shifted about with eerie agility and stabbed its blade at the scholar. The nadirite weapon narrowly missed Aaric's shoulder, sinking into the ground instead. Before the templar could recover from its thrust, the silver sword flashed upwards. There was a flash of light as the blade slashed across the skeleton's neck and sent its skull spinning away among the graves. The headless body remained standing for a moment, then shattered when it collapsed to the ground.

'I'd hoped to avoid that,' Aaric stated as he inspected the edge of his sword. 'It's not to be taken lightly, destroying a templar of Nagash. There may be repercussions, even for a man who was once one of Nagash's generals.' There was dread in the scholar's eyes as he thought of the consequences that might be visited on him.

Samuel nodded. 'You have our gratitude,' he said, glancing back at Cicely.

Aaric fixed him with a stern look. 'I meant what I told the templar. This evil ends here. Tonight.'

Samuel growled at the imperious tone. He hefted his axe once
more, but his arm was dragged back down to his side by a cold,
firm grip. He looked aside to see Cicely beside him, her face
more wan than ever.

'It's too late,' she said. 'I know you want to help me, but it's
too late. You have to let me go.'

Samuel shook his head, panic overwhelming his mind. 'You
don't know what you're saying,' he insisted. 'Use your magic
to save yourself.' He snapped the cord of the talisman he wore
and threw it away. 'Take me. Use my energy to sustain yourself!'

Cicely gave him a sad smile. 'Even if I could, I'd never do that.
I've done so many terrible things, some unwittingly, some deliberately. But I couldn't do that.' She held up her arm and showed
him where her flesh had been pitted and scorched. Samuel could
see shimmering flecks of celestial salt still burning their way
through her body.

'I'm already dead,' Cicely said. 'One of the undead.' Samuel
winced as his daughter's appearance continued to decay before
his eyes, becoming steadily more spectral. 'For longer than I
knew. It wasn't only Marden the wolf killed. I died too that night.'

'What happened?' Aaric asked her. Though he was keen to hear
her answer, Samuel saw his hand tighten about his silvered sword.

'A man,' Cicely said. 'Verderghast, he called himself. I thought
him an outcast physician, but he was in truth a necromancer. He
couldn't restore life, only usurp death.' A shiver swept through
her, and she stared down at her fading hands. 'For a time, at
least.'

'Then we have to find him!' Samuel snapped. 'Force him to
use more of his magic.'

Cicely frowned and stepped away from her father. 'He's gone.
He got what he wanted from me, an enchanted needle black
with my sins. He's gone to spread more evil elsewhere. To conjure Mhurghast.'

Samuel felt a repugnance in the word, hearing it as he did now. Its effect on Aaric was even more pronounced. He paled and began to tremble. 'Mhurghast? What did this man tell you about Mhurghast?'

'Only that it is an evil even the gods cannot oppose,' Cicely said, her breath fading into a hollow rasp. Her eyes darted to the talisman Samuel had thrown away. 'I know what awaits me. To prolong it is more than I can endure.'

Too late, Samuel realised her intention. Cicely seized the talisman before he could move to stop her. Clutching it in both hands, she clasped it to her breast above her heart. The awful, gradual decline he'd noted, the withered pallor, now intensified. He saw the bones beneath her flesh as her skin became completely transparent. Then the bones themselves took on an ethereal quality. Cicely's eyes lingered on Samuel before they too evaporated like mist before the sun.

'Forgive me.' His daughter's voice rang in his ears. A last appeal for her father's love. Then she was gone, vanished as though she'd never been. Aaric walked over and prodded the abandoned talisman with his toe. It crumbled into ash at his touch.

Samuel fell to his knees, the axe tumbling out of his nerveless fingers. The pain of his slashed and battered body was as nothing compared to the torment that filled his heart. 'I should have let her do whatever she needed to. Helped her whatever way I could to keep her alive.'

Aaric set a consoling hand on the hunter's shoulder. 'She was already lost to you. You could have done nothing. She knew that at the end.'

'Go back to Gothghul Hollow,' Samuel snarled at the scholar. 'If I'd never brought you to Felstein, my daughter would still be here.'

'No, she wouldn't,' Aaric said. 'She was marked, cursed to be consumed by Mhurghast.'

Samuel brushed his hand away. It didn't matter how much truth there was in Aaric's words; he didn't want to hear them now. 'Leave,' he ordered. 'You've done what you came here to do.'

'Your wounds need tending,' Aaric said, trying to pull Samuel to his feet. 'And we must try to find this Verderghast.'

Samuel glowered at the scholar. 'Whether I live or die, I want no more help from you.' His voice dropped to a shallow cough. 'As for Verderghast, if I did find him, there's only one thing I'd want of him. I'd ask to go where my daughter's gone.'

The hunter's eyes brimmed with tears as he looked across the desolate graveyard. 'I'd ask him to show me the way to Mhurghast.'

There was no terror for Samuel in that dread name now, only a desperate sense of longing. To join his daughter, to go where he wasn't allowed to follow.

To embrace the torments of Mhurghast.

ABOUT THE AUTHOR

C L Werner's Black Library credits include the
Age of Sigmar novels *Overlords of the Iron Dragon*,
Profit's Ruin, *The Tainted Heart* and *Beastgrave*, the
novella *Scion of the Storm* in *Hammers of Sigmar*, and
the Warhammer Horror novel *Castle of Blood*. For
Warhammer he has written the novels *Deathblade*,
Mathias Thulmann: Witch Hunter, *Runefang*
and *Brunner the Bounty Hunter*, the Thanquol and
Boneripper series and Warhammer Chronicles: The
Black Plague series. For Warhammer 40,000 he has
written the Space Marine Battles novel *The Siege of
Castellax*. Currently living in the American south-
west, he continues to write stories of mayhem and
madness set in the Warhammer worlds.

CASTLE OF BLOOD
by C L Werner

Seven families arrive at an ancient castle, expecting a grand feast – but each guest brings the weight of their own expectations as well, not to mention hidden agendas and a thirst for revenge that will push them into darkness as evil approaches.

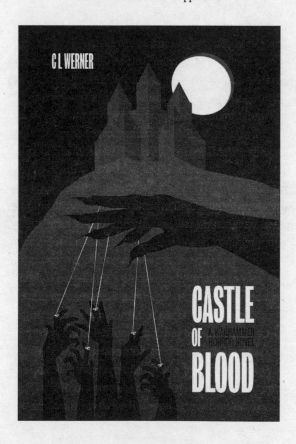

An extract from
Castle of Blood
by C L Werner

Magda brought the slim, rakish blade whipping around. The sword slashed across its target, ripping deep into the bloated paunch. Innards spilled out and streamed across the copper-sheeted floor. A smirk of satisfaction teased at the young woman's lips. She quickly tried to correct herself and adopt a more sombre pose, but she already knew it was too late. She had exposed herself and would now suffer the price.

'A lack of focus will get you killed.' The scolding words rang across the room.

Magda turned around and sheathed her sword. She set her hands on her hips and threw back her head in an effort to look defiant. Inside, though, she felt as if a bunch of mice were running around her guts. However hard she worked, however independent she thought herself, the displeasure of her father made her feel like a guilty little girl caught swiping fruit from the larder.

Ottokar Hausler stamped his way across his shop, each step

a little heavier than the last. He used his left hand to brush away the belts and scabbards that hung from the beams. The right did not so much as sway as he walked, locked in place at his side. A dark glove covered the right hand, and the sleeve of his doublet covered almost all of the rest. There was only a little patch behind the wrist that was uncovered, revealing a flash of silver.

'You have to concentrate,' Ottokar said. His face was full, just on the verge of becoming flabby. The sharp nose was tinged red and the cheeks were flushed. There was still a keenness in his eyes, but it was dulled by the sheen of liquor. The sound of swordplay could still rouse him from his cups.

Magda swept a stray lock of night-black hair from her face and matched her father's judgemental stare. She pointed to the stuffed target dummy she had disembowelled, sand still running from it onto the floor. Unlike her father's, the glove she wore was to better her grip on a sword, not hide an infirmity. 'My technique improves every day,' she proclaimed. 'I'm faster and more accurate–'

Ottokar waved aside her boast. 'Skill is not enough,' he said. 'Discipline! Discipline is the key. You can be fast as lightning, precise as a viper, but still be an amateur with the sword.' He came a few steps closer and then stamped his foot down on the pedal that controlled the target dummy.

Magda whipped around, and the blade leapt from its scabbard and ripped across the throat of the sackcloth dummy. More sand rained down on the floor. She started to turn back to her father. Only then did she realise he had stamped on the pedal a second time. The dummy was swinging around, a wooden sword in each of its eight arms. There was no time for her to dart in and strike, and no chance to parry all of the enemy swords. She jumped back and crashed to the floor.

'Never let down your guard,' Ottokar warned.

'My blade crossed its throat,' Magda countered. 'If it had been a man, he would be dead.' She rose to her feet and started brushing dust from her breeches.

Ottokar shook his head. 'Some men take more killing than others, and the dead do not stay as dead as they should be.' He sighed and gave her a studious look. 'I would think that your paramour would have told you something about those kinds of things.'

It was one barb too many for Magda. Perhaps he was justified in criticising her ability with the sword, but he had no authority to speak about anything else she did. Ottokar had forfeited that right a long time ago.

'You surprise me, father. You condescended to take an interest in me.' Magda recovered her sword from the floor and swept it through the empty air. 'Aside from what I can do with this.'

The sharp words caused Ottokar to look away. He glanced across his workshop, at the swords hanging on the walls and resting in barrels. The forge and the anvil, the ingots of bronze and iron and steel that he would shape into weapons. In one corner, each perched on its own stand, were elegant blades crafted in another time, weapons Ottokar would not allow anyone to buy. They had to be earned, bestowed on those the sword-smith felt were worthy of them. Guilt gnawed at Magda when she reflected that she was one of the few to have been given one of those swords.

'This is my world,' Ottokar said. 'This is the only place where I am any good to anyone.' He reached over with his left hand and gripped the lifeless hulk that had replaced his right. The motion caused anger to swell within his daughter.

'Spare me the melancholy,' Magda snapped. 'You lost your arm in a duel, not your life.'

Ottokar looked at her, his eyes glittering with emotion. 'Were they not the same thing?'

'Only for someone who cares only about swords,' Magda retorted.

'You were too young to remember…'

'Yes, I was too young to know who you were before you lost your arm. That's an excuse I have heard many times, father. I weary of hearing it.' Magda slammed the sword back into its sheath and marched towards the shop's exit. 'Do one thing for me,' she said as she passed Ottokar. 'Wait until I've left before you crawl back into the bottle.'

Magda could hear her father stamping his way across the workshop while she climbed the stairs that led up to the family's home above the business. Briefly she thought about going back and apologising for her harsh words. She discarded the idea. She didn't have anything to apologise for.